Hunted

An erotic retelling of

Beauty and the Beast

Cerys du Lys

ISBN: 1492213772
ISBN-13: 978-1492213772

Book design by Cerys du Lys
Cover design by Cerys du Lys
Cover Image © Depositphotos.com | Sergey Mironov | Szefei

The author published an earlier, serialized version of this story online.

CerysduLys.com

DEDICATION

To Jessie, Shandre, and Kevin:

You're all a bit strange, and that's why I like you.

CONTENTS

ACKNOWLEDGMENTS

First off, I'd like to thank you for reading this!
Fairy tales are known to most people, and I think
they're close to many people's hearts, so I hope that
you enjoy my retelling of a classic. I took a lot of
liberties with the storyline, but I tried to keep a lot
of what makes a fairy tale a fairy tale.

Second! I want to thank every one of my writing
and author friends who helped me get this far. I
don't think I could have done half of what I've
done without you all, and I appreciate everything
you've done for me. There's far too many people to
list here, but I'm grateful for everyone's help.

Thanks so much! I hope you enjoy the story!

HUNTED BY THE BEAST

MICHAEL PULLED DANYA through the woods behind his family's estate. "Come on, Danya! Hurry, hurry up."

She rolled her eyes and laughed while they rushed through the forest in the dark of night. "Where are we going?"

"It's a place. It's back here. You'll love it."

She had no doubt in her mind that he meant to seduce her. Not only was he drunk from his family's party, but whenever he looked at her he had a hard time staring at anything but her breasts.

He stopped now and did just that, his head teetering on his neck as the stink of alcohol from his breath washed over her. He leered at her chest, smirking.

"This can't be it," she said. "This isn't anywhere! It's the middle of the woods."

"Danya," he said, releasing her hand and turning to face her. "Is it true?"

"Is what true?" she asked, acting coy.

"There's rumors, you know, in town? Your father always says it, too. When he's away and your sisters are busy, the days you watch his shop are always the ones he makes the most money."

"I'm good at sales?" she offered.

"Good at sales, or good at fucking in the backroom?"

She slapped him across the face, but not hard, nowhere near enough to hurt. He didn't move away from her. In fact, he moved closer, his eyes looking into hers and his lips inching towards her own. It was, perhaps, the first time he'd looked at her face all night.

"Come on," he said. "I won't tell anyone. Just give me a sample or something? Maybe I'll come by the shop one day when you're watching it and pay for your full services. What do you think?"

She sighed. So, perhaps she'd fucked one of the errand boys in the back of her father's shop. What was she supposed to do? The man needed money or he wouldn't deliver the goods her father had ordered, and her father hadn't left her anything to pay him with. Her father was like that now, ever since he'd lost a majority of his fortune because of a mishap with cargo ships a long time ago; always promising to repay people and pay his bills and this and that, but he never had the money.

And she'd given one man a blowjob when he said he needed extra incentive to purchase one of their exquisite lamps. But he tipped really well and paid at least double what it was worth. Danya pocketed some of the coin and paid their landlady discretely so she would give them a little more time before throwing them out on the street. Her father was perpetually behind on the rent.

Everything else was her own doing, though! Or, more like she didn't do anything sexual to make the money. Maybe she flirted, flaunted her body, gave some of the women tips on how to heat up their sex lives, but that was it. Mostly that was it. She couldn't remember everything now, but she didn't sleep with the customers too often. And when she did she rarely enjoyed it much. It was business, another aspect of it, and if her father couldn't keep their finances in check then she didn't want to suffer for it. This was as good a way to solidify her stability as any, right?

Michael loomed over her, pressing her against the rough bark of a tall pine tree. He put a clumsy hand on one of her breasts, squeezing it through the sheer fabric of her sundress. Pressing close to her, he rubbed his crotch against hers.

All in all, it wasn't very exciting, but what was she going to do? She was a little drunk herself, though not too much, and was stuck in the middle of the woods with him. She'd hoped he wanted to talk to her about something, maybe dreams and how his family could help hers with their troubles. Something nice, possibly romantic, or at least pleasant. Michael did have one of the richest families in Belfast, and his father was known as a considerate gentleman.

Michael, as far as this was going right now, was not as proper as that. He fondled her breast while he searched deeper and lower for something else to occupy his other hand. Right now he had a grasp on the tree behind him, but when he focused through his drunken state she had no doubts he'd find her dress and pull it up and go searching beneath her panties. His mouth latched onto her neck, sucking.

"Michael," she said, trying to sound soft and seductive. "Michael, stop for a moment."

He stopped with his mouth, but not with his hands. "I want to fuck you so bad, Danya."

"I know, I know, but--"

He grew tired of groping her through her dress and wrenched the top of it down so he could see her bare skin. Her firm, large breasts wobbled and swayed in the open air.

"Fuck, you've got a nice pair," he said. To add to his comment, he pinched one of her nipples.

"Michael, look. I'll give you a handjob,

alright? How about that?"

Before she could say more, he had his pants unbuckled and lowered past his knees. His throbbing erection bounced to attention in front of her. Drunk, she thought, but not too drunk to stay hard or want to get laid.

She knelt in front of him and cupped his balls in her hand. He glanced down at her and bent over, grabbing for one of her breasts. If she wanted to stop this she needed to go fast. And, anyways, maybe he'd talk to her afterwards about her family's issues? Maybe this was like negotiations? Not the kind she really wanted, but whatever worked, right?

She spit on her hand, foregoing ladylike etiquette, and grabbed the base of his cock. With one hand she squeezed his balls and with the other she stroked him. Slow at first, to spread her makeshift lubrication, but then she went faster. Michael groaned, barely able to stand. If it weren't for the tree at her back and his hands braced against it for balance, she thought he would have fallen as soon as she first grabbed him.

...

THAT SMELL! THE SMELL OF RUTTING BEASTS! Of animals fucking on the ground with wild abandon without a care in the world. Oh, he knew that smell. He knew it so well it hurt. It always made him... what was the word? He hardly spoke to others now, so sometimes the more difficult words eluded him. Not sick, no. Angry? Not that, either. Upset. Yes, a little. Something more, too, though.

He looked up and saw a sliver of the moon. A guttural howl escaped from his throat and echoed through the thick forest air.

He wanted to find the source of the smell. One part of it, the male's musk, he was indifferent to, but the female had a sweet, undeniably delicate aroma. His cock, long past the point of arousal and now blazingly hard and exuding strong heat, bobbed in the air as he ran fast through the woods to find the mating pair.

...

MICHAEL WAS A TOUGH SELL. LIKE SOME customers she knew, he wanted more and more. Not satisfied with her handjob, he grabbed her ponytail, yanked her off the ground, spun her around, and pressed her against the pine tree. She yelped in surprise, confused at first and unable to see anything in the darkness of night. Her breasts spread outwards, wrapping around the tree as if she were embracing it with her chest, and the rough bark grated against her skin.

Michael kept a tight hold on her ponytail while he grabbed blindly for the skirt of her sundress, managing to catch the hem in his fingers. Pulling it up hard so her rear was exposed, he then searched for her panties. It didn't take long before he shoved them aside. Lumbering around like some massive beast, he stomped towards her and pressed his cockhead against her ass. He pushed forward, intent on entering her, but went for the wrong entrance.

"Michael, that's my butt!" she shrieked.

Before he could understand what she said (because she expected he wouldn't care where he stuck his cock, as long as he got it in her), she reached back and guided him towards her pussy. Maybe she hadn't expected the night to go like this, but it was happening now so she figured she'd make the best of it.

Michael pushed into her, separating her folds and spreading her wide with his cock. The spit-lube from her failed handjob assisted him in stuffing himself deep inside of her, where he immediately leaned against her as if he were dreadfully tired.

"Fuck me," she whispered, turning her head to look over her shoulder at him. "Come on, Michael. Fuck me."

She tried to sound seductive, but she wasn't much into it. He was quickly showing the effects of alcohol, and she thought if he didn't cum soon he wasn't going to. Better to finish this fast than to deal a blow to his manhood that would make him keep trying to get off all through the night. She didn't want to deal with him continually poking her in an attempt to prove his masculinity.

And, anyways, it was kind of hot if she thought about it differently. Not that hot, but she imagined a scenario playing in her mind. She thought of some man behind her, a rugged, faceless huntsman, who happened upon her in the middle of the woods after a long day's work. She was lost, of course, after having had a quiet picnic in the woods, and now it was evening. But, oh, how would she find her way home? The huntsman wouldn't know any of that, but he'd see the tantalizing curves of her body, her round, heavy breasts and tight, pert ass and the faint "V" as her tight dress pressed against her thighs and crotch.

Michael wasn't a huntsman, far from it, but when he thrust into her she pictured her imaginary man, alone in the woods for years at a time with no woman to sate his carnal desires, pouncing upon her and taking her right then and there. She'd be surprised, like she'd been surprised when Michael yanked her off the ground by her hair, but the absolute lust dripping from his passionate actions would convert her. This was her fantasy, at least, and the huntsman would pound his cock into her in sharp, jerky movements, then release his desire inside her.

And afterwards he'd introduce himself to her and apologize for his actions. Oh, she'd say, flustered, it's no problem, just, perhaps could you help me out of these woods? And he would say yes, except why didn't she spend the night at his log cabin? It'd be very late by then, so she would agree, and after a dinner filled with sexual tension the huntsman would do his best to act proper and she would pounce him and they would make love all through the night.

Her fantasy got as far as the thrusting, and her arousal grew frantic and wet from the images in her mind, but Michael failed at playing the part of her huntsman. Instead, just as Danya was about to orgasm, he thrust himself into her one last time and let loose. His first jet of cum was strong, and she thought he might be able to finish her off if he kept it up. The second barely shot anything, and then she felt his cock squirming inside of her with a few final dribbles of white cream before Michael shuddered and pulled out.

He collapsed on the ground in a heap. In a few seconds, pants bunched around his ankles, he was snoring.

Danya stood against the tree, completely and utterly dissatisfied, with cum leaking out of her and dripping down her thigh. At least if she'd done this at her father's shop, like Michael insinuated, she'd be able to clean up afterwards. Ugh, this was disgusting.

She heard a howl in the woods and looked up. The moon wasn't full, but she didn't know if wolves only howled during full moons? Apparently not, since this one had howled while the moon was just a sliver. She fixed her panties and her dress, pulling it up over her breasts and down to cover her ass, then quickly knelt beside

Michael.

"Michael," she said softly, tapping his shoulder.

Nothing.

"Michael!" she said more urgently. This time she grabbed his shoulder and shook him.

Nothing.

"If you get eaten by wolves, it's not my fault. I'm not going to stay here and be a meal for an animal."

With that, she ran through the forest, heading back to his family's home. She could see fireworks coming from that direction; the night spectacle they'd planned for all their party guests.

...

THE MALE WAS SPENT, HAVING MATED WITH THE female. The male didn't interest him, so he left him slumbering on the forest floor.

The female was running, though. Teasing him, making him chase her. Her scent mixed with the male's seed as it slid down her tender legs, leaving a trail through the woods for him to follow. He sprinted after her, spotting faint traces of her long, tied-up, raven-black hair vanishing behind trees up ahead.

She wore a dress, a pretty thing. How long had it been since he'd seen a dress like that? An eternity, or more, and this saddened him for a moment, but the constant thrum of his arousal, pounding through his hardened cock, soon brought him back to the task at hand.

The other male was weak. She deserved a strong man, one who could breed with her until her stomach bulged, filled with offspring from their fierce mating.

He would chase her and show her he was strong.

...

DANYA RAN FASTER THROUGH THE WOODS. Michael's parent's land was just up ahead, and the fireworks were shooting up faster and faster. They boomed through the air, the lights illuminating bits and pieces of the darkened woods.

She ran fast because something was chasing her. Or she thought it was. It briefly struck her that maybe she was imagining it. Perhaps it wasn't real. Except, no, she could hear the pounding of footfalls behind her, the crunch of leaves, and the snarling of a beast.

It was the wolf, she thought. The one that howled earlier. It had eaten Michael and now it wanted her for dessert. She wasn't going to be a meal for a wolf, though. At least not without a fight.

She broke through the outskirts of the forest and sprinted through the fields towards the revelers at the fireworks. Someone saw her and pointed and she ran towards them. Would the wolf come and eat all of them? Was she luring it towards everyone for a massive meal? She hoped not.

She blacked out just as someone ran towards her and put their arms out to catch her.

...

THE PARTY WAS A WEEK PAST. NO ONE HAD noticed the cum on her legs, thankfully. Sweating while running through the woods, with her thighs pressing against one another, had eliminated most of the evidence of her and Michael's illicit romp. She'd been saved from having to explain where he was after falling unconscious, too. The local physician said it was the effects of too much alcohol combined with heavy exertion. Everyone said there was no wolf, either. Hallucinations, and again that was blamed on the alcohol.

Michael used the same excuse when he came to talk to her at her father's shop a few days later. "Sorry about that, Danya," he said. "I was drunk. I don't want you to get the wrong idea. It was a one time thing. I don't want to marry you or anything."

She nodded. "It's alright, Michael. I understand. I was a little drunk myself."

"Unless--" he started to say. "If you want to make some extra money, we could...?" He jerked his head towards the back room.

Danya might have said yes. It was a slow

day, and while they didn't need the money right away, she knew they'd need it eventually. Except she was pissed at Michael, and he hadn't given her any satisfaction the previous time. Maybe he'd be better when he wasn't drunk, or maybe he'd be worse. There was a certain amount of pleasure to be gained from reckless fumbling, and if he couldn't even hold off cumming until he brought her to climax when he was drunk and she was excited by her fantasies, she doubted he could do it when he wasn't drunk and she was annoyed with him.

Also, her father walked in just then, carrying a bag of useless trinkets. He set them down on the shop counter, greeting her and Michael with a friendly hello, then began rummaging through his worthless crap.

"What did you get today, daddy?" she asked, feigning interest. By the looks of it, nothing good. She hoped he hadn't spent a lot on it, because they'd be hard-pressed to sell any of this.

Michael left quickly after that.

...

LATER THAT NIGHT, AFTER THEY SAT DOWN TO A family dinner, Danya heard a crash in the alleyway beside their home. Her father looked up, then shrugged.

"A cat," he said.

"Is it a cat?" her youngest sister, Felice,

asked.

"I bet it's an elephant," Alena said. "A big, yellow elephant."

Danya rolled her eyes at her little sisters. They were sixteen and eighteen respectively, and a little daft. She thought they took after her father more than their mother (whereas Danya always imagined herself being like her mother), except-- well, she was still here, taking care of her father so perhaps she was a little daft, too. Her mother had left years ago, leaving the three sisters to mostly fend for themselves. It hurt at first, but she could hardly blame her; if Danya could leave right now, she thought she would.

"I don't think it's a cat," Danya said, and with a silly glare towards Alena she added, "or an elephant."

"It could be!" Alena squeaked.

"I do so wish it were a cat," Felice said, wistful. "I'd like a cat."

"I'm going to check." Danya scooted her chair out from the table and stood. "Whatever it is, I think it's rummaging through our trash. I don't want to have to explain to anyone why we have garbage lining the side of our house."

Her father grunted, then shrugged and went back to dinner. Both of her sisters began discussing whether it would be a cat or an elephant, if it were either, if Danya hadn't said it was neither. Danya sighed and left them to their silly argument.

She left the house through the back entrance where they grew a small garden, instead of the front through the shop and to the streets. Rumors already made their way through the small city and she didn't want to cater to more by having people see her head into the alleyway alongside their house in a flimsy nightgown for no apparent reason. The garden was nice this time of year, too. The light from her neighbor's windows shone dimly on the flowers, leaving a sort of ghostly feel to the area, as if it both existed and didn't exist all at once.

Danya snuck through the gardens towards the little fence door leading to the alley. Unlatching it, she quietly stepped through and shut it behind her. The alley was dark this time of night, but she could see faint impressions of images through the shadows. All their trash was scattered on the ground, with the trash baskets knocked over amidst the junk. More odd than that, someone had moved them from their usual place to a spot right below her window. Her window--which she distinctly remembered closing--was open, the drapes fluttering in the slight evening breeze.

There was someone in the house. They'd come in through her window and were going to rob them. Perhaps murder her whole family, or wait until they slept and torture them until morning, and, and...!

Danya scrambled back to the garden. She tried to fling open the fence door, but she forgot she'd re-latched it and it wouldn't budge at first. Her fingernails dug into the wood, pulling with all her might, before she calmed enough to carefully undo the latch and gain entrance to the yard. Running in her silken nightgown through the small garden, she dashed past the back door and into her house.

Her family was fine, her father and Alena and Felice still eating dinner and chatting amongst themselves. She wanted to scream and yell at them to get out of the house, but maybe that would alert the intruder and he'd catch them before they could escape, then kill them in a minute's notice. With screaming out of the question, at least for now, she had only one other option in her mind.

She would go upstairs and confront the intruder by herself, and if it came to it she would scream and her family would hopefully run from the building while she distracted the burglar.

The stairs by the backdoor creaked beneath her feet and seemed loud beyond belief. Danya crept up them as quietly as she could, but each creak sounded louder than the first and then she could hear the thumping of her heart, pounding in her chest. The man who'd broken in must be able to hear her, could hear everything. Even her thoughts seemed too loud and she feared he might know her intentions and thwart them by going back out the window and running into the house through the back door to attack her father and sisters.

Frantic, wild thoughts roamed through her mind. She had no lantern up here, but they kept spare candles in holders at the top of the stares for emergencies. Grabbing one, she lit it with a match from a matchbox next to the candles and held it aloft. The flames danced, sending shadows through the sleeping quarters of the house.

All of the doors were closed, so she hoped the infiltrator was still in her room. If only she had a lock on her door she could lock him in and then run away, but she didn't. Cautious, scared, and witless, she touched the doorknob to her room and turned it. The door opened without a sound, hinges oiled, but it was a small concession compared to the cacophony of her trek upstairs.

Her room was a mess, and not at all like she left it. The window was open, drapes waving about. The linens on her bed were a mess and scattered this way and that, some thrown to the floor and others twisted into knots. The intruder had thrown open her dresser drawers and tossed all of her neatly folded laundry to the floor. Or, she noted, not all of it, but mainly the lingerie and undergarments.

Most of which, she now noticed, were laying in a trail towards her closet door. The thief, who apparently had a penchant for woman's delicates, must have sought refuge in her closet when he heard her on the steps. She walked closer, scared, unsure why she would continue moving towards imminent demise but unable to stop herself. Her hand reached for the doorknob on the closet and her mind screamed for her to pull her arm back and run away, but her body didn't listen.

The door swung open. An animal hulk of a man was sitting on her closet floor, his form shrouded in the darkness. The candlelight from her candle illuminated him slightly and she saw a heavy beard growing on his rugged jaw. Except beards only covered parts of a man's face, and this one seemed to engulf all of his. A flash of yellow lit up his eyes as the candle's light found them, and he bared his teeth and snarled. He looked for all the world like a wolf trapped in a man's body. Clutched in clawed hands, he held bunches of her panties and a few flimsy negligees, sniffing at them.

Danya screamed bloody murder. The wolf-man leaped into the room and clasped a hand to her mouth. He jumped so hard and fast that the next thing she knew she was laying on the bed with him atop her. His eyes contained something akin to curiosity and he stared at her intently.

Still holding his hand over her mouth, keeping her pinned to the bed, he moved his head lower. He sniffed at her nightgown, down to her stomach, then to her crotch. She felt a heady rush of self-awareness when his moist, hot breath blew across her cloth-covered core. The beastman sniffed long and hard, but never touched her except to hold her down and keep her quiet.

Her father shouted something upstairs. "I

heard you scream. Danya? Are you alright?"

The beastman jolted up, surprised. He stopped sniffing at her and jumped away and off the bed. She watched him flee out the window, entranced by his grace as he leaped, landing in the alleyway without a sound.

"I'm fine, daddy!" she yelled downstairs. Her heart pounded hard and heavy still, but she managed to talk without giving her fear away, or so she hoped. "I'll be down in a moment."

"Alright, darling. Just checking."

Danya ran to the door and shut it tight. She took the chair from her desk and propped it up against the door so no one could enter. The window remained open, a light breeze fluttering the curtains around like before. Scrambling to her bed, she jumped onto it and yanked her nightgown above her waist.

She imagined the beast breathing on her again, his almost-human nose sniffing at her crotch. She imagined him thrusting it against her, smelling her up close and personally. Jamming her fingers against her clit, she rubbed it hard and pretended it was the beastman and his nose.

His other hand, in her mind, left her mouth, and she gasped out loud. He traced his claws against the nightgown, teasing her skin beneath the thin fabric, then clutched her breast. To imitate this, she grabbed her breast hard and pinched her nipple between her nails. It hurt, but he would be rough with her, wouldn't he?

Her hips gyrated, needing something to grind against, except her imagination provided a much better possibility than what actually existed. To make up for this, she snatched a pillow from behind her and flung it between her legs, then flipped over fast and ground the center of her body against it, hard. She pretended the wolfman was pressing her against the bed, watching her squirm in delight as he toyed with her.

She came hard then, her orgasm bursting through her body and arousal soaking the pillow beneath her. Flailing, grinding against the pillow with everything she had, she rode her pleasure, wanting to extend it, until she lay exhausted on her bed.

What was that? She didn't know. She tried to figure it out, but couldn't. Some strange, primal lust had overcome her. She was so scared at first, but then what? For some reason she didn't think the beastman would hurt her. She didn't know why, but she didn't think he would.

Before heading back to dinner, she fixed the sheets and blankets on her bed and refolded her undergarments. She briefly considered keeping the window open, but it was getting colder so she closed it, but not before looking outside for a moment to see if anyone was there.

The alley below her, the small backyard garden to the left, and the streets to the right, were all empty. Only piles of upturned trash remained.

...

DURING THE NEXT WEEK DANYA RECEIVED multiple strange notes. They all appeared at random spots in her house, though mainly the areas she frequented often, with no rhyme or reason as to how they got there. The first contained handwriting she couldn't read and was signed with an "E." The next was slightly more legible and came with a flower. Not a normal flower from a florist, though. It was a wildflower that only grew in the mountains nearby and wouldn't take well in the soft soil that the city florist preferred using. Also, said the florist when she asked him about it, it was a crude flower and nothing like the wonderful roses or tulips he carried.

Danya thought it was a beautiful flower. Petite, and she could fit it easily in the palm of her hand. Only one, so she couldn't put it in a vase, but for the rest of that day she wore it in her hair behind her ear.

Then another note arrived, and she made out a few words of it. Lake, it said somewhere, and come. The person wanted her to go to the lake.

By the time another week passed, and she'd received notes on each day, she managed to understand the gist of them. Many of the words were misspelled, but this was what it said:

"I need to see you again. I have an urge. You are the only one to fix it. Come to the mansion in the woods by the lake. I will see you. I watch you always. Go tomorrow. E."

Danya didn't now what to make of that.
Alena snatched the letter out of her hands and read
it aloud while running around the shop to escape
Danya's wrath.

"Well, you can't go there," Alena said,
matter-of-factly. "That's where the beast lives."

"What beast are you talking about?" Danya
asked, snatching the note from her sister.

"The *Beast*! The one in the story. A man
who angered a witch and she cursed him to look
like a beast. I think the story's not true, though.
I've been by there once with school friends and it's
all just wrecked and ruined looking. We were
going to go inside but there's a tall iron fence with
spikes at the top and the gate is locked. The lake is
nice to swim in, though, but I wouldn't go at night.
Cre~ee~py!"

"I doubt it's the same place," Danya said.

"Probably not." Then Alena grinned. "Or it
is and you've got a date with the beast!"

"It's not the beast, you twit." Danya stuck
out her tongue. "If it were, he'd have signed the
note with a 'B' and not an 'E,' don't you think?"

"He can't spell half the other words, so I
don't expect he knows how to spell 'beast,' either."
Alena laughed and ran out of the shop, presumably
to tell her friends that her sister had a date with the
beast.

...

DANYA DIDN'T GO TO THE MANSION BY THE LAKE the next day like the letter asked. First off, she couldn't because she needed to tend to her father's shop by herself that day, and second, she doubted the authenticity of the note in the first place. Could it be the beast? The beast was a story and didn't exist.

Except what was that wolf-like man she saw in her closet? A daydream, probably. Some rabid fantasy she'd dreamed up in a strange fit of whimsy. A bit of imagery to suit her aroused state, and she'd made it all up.

And, yes, maybe she imagined it, but that didn't stop her from becoming further aroused by the notion.

The delivery boy arrived and she had money to pay him, but she coaxed him into the backroom instead. He shuddered under her ministrations as she knelt in front of him and took the entirety of his cock in her mouth. When he came, his cockhead throbbing between her lips, she swallowed all his cum and licked her lips afterwards.

He delivered the items for free.

That wasn't enough for her, though. A customer came in next, an older man near to her father's age, though maybe a little younger. She told him she had some wonderful items in the back, and would he like to go look at them? Unwittingly, he followed her. When she showed him a piece of trash that her father thought they could sell and asked him if he would like to purchase it for a few coins, he scoffed at her.

He stopped scoffing when she lifted the skirt of her dress and moved aside her panties to show him her glistening cunt. Stuttering, stumbling, he worked at his pants and barely managed to undo them before she pushed him to the ground and skewered herself on his rising cock. She ground against him, pressing her clit against his fat stomach, imagining she'd caught the beast and was taming him with her wiles. The man screwed up her desires by cumming faster than she thought possible, but he did buy the piece of junk she'd showed him for twice what she'd asked, so it wasn't all for naught.

Next, a couple entered the store. The woman drifted apart from the man, eying random baubles and trinkets. The man, more practical, asked Danya what the best item in the store was.

"I need it," he said in a whisper, "for an anniversary present for my wife."

Danya nodded knowingly to him and crooked a finger, inviting him to the back room to see the best wares.

That's what he thought, at least. Before he knew it, and with few objections, he had her bent over a crate and was pounding into her pussy. He had a nice cock, though too smooth for her to fully pretend it was the beast's. Better prepared, lasting longer than the other man, he inched Danya closer and closer to her orgasm. Best yet, he was frantic and wild, wanting to finish with her before his wife caught on that he was gone, and this suited Danya wonderfully.

Her firm breasts pressed against the sanded wood of the crate beneath her and she pretended the man's leather gloved hands were that of the beast. Her mouth opened into an "O" and she looked up, eyes practically rolling into the back of her head. Staring at her through the window of the storeroom was an angry looking man with hair covering the entirety of his face and his eyes gleaming a sharp yellow.

Danya's inner depths clenched in orgasm as the beast watched the man's cock drive into her. He slammed into her one final time before filling her quivering, sucking pussy with his cum.

"Honey?" his wife called from the storefront. "Where are you? Have you found anything? Are you back there?"

The man panicked. He wiped his cock clean on the skirt of Danya's dress and lifted up his pants, buttoning them fast. Running out of the backroom, he returned to his wife.

"Oh, no, there's nothing there," he said. "That shop girl had to run an errand, so she won't return for awhile. I'm not sure there's anything we want here, anyways. Did you find something nice?"

"I liked this." she said. "I think we should get it." Danya didn't know what it was, but apparently she showed it to her husband.

"Oh. Yes. Actually, I've seen a nicer one down the street. Shall I show you?"

"Alright."

Danya remained on the crate, listening to the tinkle of the bell above the front door as the couple left. The man's cum soaked into the wood below her crotch. She stared out the backroom window while the wolfish man watched her. He bared his teeth and snarled, then ran away.

Danya closed the shop early. Later, she told her father she was feeling ill.

...

THE NEXT DAY, STATING SHE NEEDED MEDICINE from the local doctors, Danya instead went to Michael's family's estate. Not to see Michael, because she still disliked him, but because his place was the closest to the woods. And the woods were where the mansion by the lake was.

Danya wore a plain brown dress so as not to attract attention. Beneath that, though, she had on an expensive matching set of panties and a bra. Both were dyed with small spots and made to look like the fur of some wild animal, a fierce leopard. It seemed fitting, if she were indeed about to meet the so-called beast.

She didn't know what she expected by going to the mansion, though. She didn't know if she actually believed the beast existed, either. Perhaps she'd dreamed everything. Some odd state of mind. Supposedly woman became more aroused at certain times of the month, and while she'd never noticed it as desperately as this before, she was starting to believe it was true.

And how would the beast feel if he did find her? The letter he sent, if he sent it, said he had an urge. She assumed this was sexual in nature, but maybe not? He could want to eat her, she supposed. But, if he had a sexual urge, and he'd watched her fucking another man in the backroom of her father's shop, maybe he'd be angry. Would he want to devour her instead of fucking her, if that's what he even wanted in the first place? Would his rage at seeing her with another man overcome his lustful intentions and force him to end her life right then and there?

She didn't really know how that would work. She didn't know much beyond the fact that as she walked through the woods she felt dreadfully afraid. Afraid of everything. The smallest chirp from a cricket caused her to jump and made the hair on her arms stand on end. When a squirrel skittered in the branches above her, she hid behind a tree.

Yet she continued on. Enthralled, like a trance, she needed to go and she did. She must have walked for hours, but it seemed more like ten minutes. The lake presented itself at her feet, the waters lapping up to lick at her revealed toes above her sandals. She bent down and touched the water with her fingers then rubbed the cold liquid over her chest and arms to cool her down and calm her nerves.

The ramshackle mansion in the woods was at the other side of the lake.

The beast was standing right behind her.

She turned to look around and saw him, and then she screamed but it was too late. He ran forward and grabbed her by the waist, picking her up. Her screams went unanswered in the middle of the woods. The beast carried her, kicking and screaming, towards the entrance of his mansion. The gated fence unlocked and opened as if by magic when he approached, and shut after he carried her through. They ran down the winding path to the front doors of the mansion, and those too opened and closed on their own.

When he had her inside, she'd screamed so much that her throat was dry and parched. He put her down on a lush, red carpet in the foyer just inside the doors and stared at her.

His nostrils flared, sniffing, but he held his composure and stayed away from her crotch even if his eyes kept darting downwards every few seconds.

She looked at him then, all of him. He stood on two legs like a human, and appeared mostly human except for the hair covering the entirety of his body. His legs were strong and muscular and long and he looked like he ran ten miles a day or more. Up further, his cock stood at attention, the head glistening with precum. He had less hair here and on his legs and chest, more like a thin layer of fur than anything else. Actually, now that she saw him up close, the top of his head and his jaw had the most hair, thick and shined. When she thought on it, he looked almost like a very tanned person with a full beard and thick head of hair; the kind of hair she wanted to run her fingers through and grab and pull him towards her into a passionate kiss.

The beast stood there, letting her inspect him, and then he spoke. "Sorry," he said.

She looked at him, confused. "Why are you sorry?"

"I need," he started to say, but his voice cracked. "I need you. I have need since I saw you in trees with man."

"Who?" she asked, then answered her own question. "Oh, Michael."

"He is not good enough," the beast said.

Danya laughed. Boy, was he right. Michael definitely wasn't good for much. "Do you have a name?" she asked. Becoming bold, she stepped forward and put her hand on his jaw, caressing his face up to his cheek. "Are you here all alone?"

"Everett," he said. "Yes. Alone."

"You need me," she said, slowly. "What do you need of me?" She moved closer to him, gently exploring his face with her hand.

"I need." He stumbled for words, looking unsure of himself. "I'm sorry," he said before moving his hand to cup her sex. "I need."

Danya smiled at him. He was so strong and masculine, the epitome of manliness in her eyes, but so fragile and delicate at the same time, confused and unsure. "I'm very thirsty," she said. "Do you have wine?"

"Wine," he said, practically running to fetch it. "Yes, wine. I have."

He disappeared from her sights, vanishing down a long corridor and through a doorway. When he returned, he carried a bottle of wine and two glasses. The wineglasses looked miniscule in his massive hands and she laughed when she saw them.

"What?" he asked, frowning.

"I don't think we need glasses," she said.

Taking the glasses from him carefully, she set them aside on a small table by the doors. He'd uncorked the wine from wherever he'd gotten it, so she lifted the bottle to her mouth and drank deeply. It tasted rich and luscious, with a hint of a floral scent to it. Danya swished it around in her mouth, savoring it, then swallowed. She offered the bottle to Everett and he drank as well, grinning.

"Good?" he asked with that same goofy grin on his face.

"I want you," she said.

The beast transformed. Wanting to please her before, wanting to gain her acceptance, once he had it he no longer intended to play awkward flirtatious games. He grabbed her around the waist and lifted her into the air. Before she knew it, they were in a sumptuous dining hall, her sitting on the end of a table while his pulsing cock prodded against her dress-covered stomach.

"I need," he said.

"Yes," she said. "You need."

He tried to enter her, but she still had her dress on. Acting gentlemanly for a second, he struggled to lift off her dress without ripping it with his claw-like fingernails. She laughed and he looked at her oddly.

"Rip it," she said. "Tear it all off. Take me."

He snarled and pulled on her plain brown dress. His claws sunk into the fabric, never touching her skin, and he shredded it down the sides before tearing it from her. Now she sat before him in only her leopard-looking bra and panties, ripe and fit for the taking by any true beast.

He stared at her long and hard, taking in all of her, waiting. He seemed to like just looking at her. She liked it, too; the mounting tension, palpable between them. His prodding cock throbbing, pressing against her stomach, but doing no more. She saw his nostrils flare slightly and got an idea.

Inching away from him for a second, she kicked off her sandals and let them fall to the floor. He watched her as she slid out of her panties and held onto them. Grinning at the undergarment, she rubbed it against her slick folds and then lifted it towards him. He strained to control himself, but finally gave into his urges and drove his nose into her hand and the arousal-scented panties.

Everett went wild, truly a beast. He rocked against her, his cock sliding up and down her stomach. She inched forwards again until she was on the edge of the table, and at this angle his cock found the folds of her pussy and slid between them, up and down alongside them. His cockhead moved between rubbing against her clit to poking at her belly button, and back again, grinding against her, while he sniffed frantically at the panties in her hand.

She tossed them away, across the dining table. Everett looked at her, frowning, but she remedied this by moving his cock downwards until it barely entered her wet slit. Danya wrapped her legs around him and pulled him in by the waist, feeling every inch of his shaft as he pressed into her. Everett, unsure from the loss of the panties, soon found his way again.

He pulled her close to him and filled her with his cock. Danya winced and screamed out at the size of it, but wanted more and more. The beast inside of her pulled out fast, then slammed back into her, faster than any man had ever fucked her. He left her slowly next time, every throbbing vein and twitch from his cock exciting her in tantalizing ecstasy, then he filled her up in the same slow, agonizing fashion.

"I need," she said. Her hands wrapped around him and her fingernails dug into his back. "I need!"

Everett teased her, pretending to thrust into her, but stopping halfway. He repeated this a couple times, smiling at her urgent tugs, until finally he gave in and sheathed his entire cock inside of her. Danya screamed, yelling out her pleasure, and urging Everett on. He thrust and pounded into her, the soft fur on his stomach pressing against her clit every time he slammed in, building her up and up to much needed release.

Just as she was about to orgasm, he stopped. Her mind blanked, confused, frustrated. When she opened her eyes he was gone and she wanted to shriek in anger, but before she could he had his face buried between her sopping folds. He sniffed hard, devouring the scent of her arousal with his nostrils. His tongue moved out to lick at her slit while his nose tormented her clit, rubbing back and forth, digging into her pleasure pearl.

Danya climaxed, fierce and slick. Everett lapped up her juices and covered his nose with her orgasm's scent. He kept going, pushing her on and on, until she lay exhausted on the table.

"My fucking god," she said. "Fuck."

Everett wasn't done with her, though. He jumped atop the table and gently, but urgently, dragged her to the center of it. Flipping her so her stomach touched the smooth wood, he hurried behind her and then drove his cock into her sore, abused cunt. She yelped and squeaked, but grinned at his imperative lust.

The table rocked beneath them. Bent at his

knees with his cock delving into her at an angle, he lowered his arms to her waist and roughly grabbed her hips, fucking her faster, using his entire body to forward his motions. More crude and crass than any of her previous lovers, she wasn't sure if she could handle him, but she desperately wanted to. Every time he entered her, he grinded himself inside of her so her crotch and clit rubbed against the smooth wooden table. Her breasts heaved, squished beneath her, wanting to flatten but too large and pert to do anything but act as cushions for her upper body.

Her whole body ached now, her long walk through the woods and his rough handling of her taking its toll. He pounded into her and her pleasure rose, but she felt like she needed to rest, too. She clenched her thighs together, her whole body tensing, and squeezed her orgasm forth, needing it despite her fatigue. When her pussy tightened, begging for his cock, he bucked into her and howled.

Orgasm wracked her entire being and she tightened every muscle in her body as much as she could. Who cared about being sore later? This was the most exquisite thrill she'd ever experienced. Everett's cock jerked inside of her, pouncing like its own miniature beast, and erupted. The first jolt of cum splattered her insides hard and she expected the second to come just as fast. Surprising her, he moved back, half-pulling his cock out of her, then slammed back in just as the second jet of cream claimed a place inside her. Again and again he did this, a third, fourth, and fifth time. By the tenth, his strength was wavering, but his cum seemed nearly as strong and thick as the first batch. She felt his warmth inside of her and his seed seeping out of her and onto the table.

Her orgasm calmed, slowing to a quiet thrum, and his stopped, as well. He buried himself inside of her one last time, laying atop her, breathing on her neck. She turned her head to look at him and lifted her hand feebly to touch the side of his cheek. Sniffing at her hair, he lifted her torso up slightly so he could cup her breast in one hand.

This, she thought, was amazing.

As they spooned in their odd position on the table, something strange happened. A large grandfather clock against the wall chimed the time with four loud peals. In the center of the clock face a light sparked, appearing into existence out of nowhere, then clambered from out of its timely prison. It floated nearly six feet off the floor and dripped sparkles like confetti downwards. The little bits of light spread out and coalesced into the shape of a man, then shimmered bright and blinding.

Danya blinked, but was too caught up in the afterglow of her orgasm and the safe, warm feel of Everett's arm around her and his body pressed against her to do more than watch.

When she finished blinking, the figure of an elderly gentleman wearing a butler's uniform took

the place of the shining light. The gentleman
gasped, startled, then looked at the pair in front of
him on the table. He smiled and bowed
courteously.

"I see the master has found a mistress. Has
it been a long time, sir?" the butler asked.

"Yes," Everett said. "Long. I need." He
squeezed Danya's breast and pressed against her,
his half-hard cock teasing her aching body.

Danya wriggled beneath him, feigning
discomfort, but if he wanted to take her again right
then and there she would have let him in a
heartbeat.

"I believe I am the first to return," the
gentleman butler said. "If that is the case, please
allow me to fetch you and the lady a meal from the
kitchens. It will take some time, so I do hope you
both have a means of keeping occupied?" He
waggled his eyebrows at them, smirking.

"Yes," Everett and Danya said rather
quickly.

The butler left, laughing as he went.

"I need," Everett said to her when they were
alone again, "but... we wait. You rest. Then more?
Good?"

He moved to her side and she nuzzled
against his chest. "Yes. I want, too. Is it the curse
from the story? Will me staying and doing this
bring everyone back? Will you change?"

"Yes," Everett said. His brow scrunched up,
thinking. "I need... for more, though. You under-

stand? Not curse. Curse is bad, but I... want? I like. I need."

"I understand," Danya said. She curled her body against his, as cozy as if she had a warm blanket covering her and was laying by the fire. "Let's rest. I'm tired."

"Yes," Everett said. "Sleep."

CLAIMED BY THE BEAST

 LENA SCRAMBLED THROUGH THE gates of the private mansion hidden in the woods just as they shut behind her. A close call, but she made it, except... her dress was now stuck in the gate. When she tried to run straight through, to chase after her sister, the hem of her skirt caught between the closed metal entryway and pulled her backwards and to the ground. She faltered, skidding to a stop, and toppled onto the dirt pathway leading towards the mysterious mansion.

"Dammit," she whispered to herself,

watching her sister, Danya, being carried off.

And, she knew Danya wasn't sick! Her older sister didn't even sound sick, and those letters she'd received all throughout the preceding week, the ones signed by some man naming himself "E," were suspicious. No doubt this adventure her sister was on had something to do with that, Alena thought. She knew the story as well as anyone; a man cursed by a witch to look like a beast was living in the abandoned mansion in the woods. Besides that main detail, the stories varied on the specifics. Some said he'd eaten all of his mansion attendants after taking the form of a beastly man, while others said the witch cursed them, too, entombing their souls in various artifacts around the house. One man might be stuck in a clock, while another was a fork, and... well, they could be anything, really.

Alena didn't expect the beast to actually exist, but here he was. She'd followed Danya into the forest, wondering what her sister was up to, and all of a sudden the man appeared, the beast, and he'd picked up Danya as if she were a trinket for the taking.

Alena thought she should be distressed about the kidnapping of her sister, but it was exciting! The beast, here, and he was after Danya. For what? The letters said he had a need, an urge, and Alena thought she knew exactly what that was about. All men had needs and urges, and most of the time they involved their cocks. Which, Alena

noted, was a rather fun and interesting urge to
have. She was no stranger to this. In fact, she
loved it.

Despite her older sister treating her like a
child, Alena was an adult. Almost nineteen now,
and fully prepared to set out on her own, or so she
liked to think. Her family had little money to spare
since her father was a crackpot merchant and her
mother had left them a long time ago. Danya did
her best to help out and keep them from living a
life of poverty on the streets, though. Alena
appreciated her older sister for that, but still, she
wanted more, too. Not from Danya, but from life.
From everything.

She tugged at her dress. Maybe she could
pull it through the closed gates and get free.
Bracing her feet against the bottom of the iron-
barred enclosure, she pulled as hard as she could.
An inch came loose, then a little more, and...

Her dress ripped, causing her to fly
backwards and land hard on her rear. The shock of
the fall sent her tumbling to the ground in a heap.
Her eyes went wide, then she laughed at the
ridiculousness of it. She was free, though, wasn't
she? That was good. Getting up off the ground,
she went to brush her dress down and continue on
her way, except there was quite a bit of cloth
missing.

She glanced back towards the gates. Most
of the lower half of her dress was now stuck
between the metal, having ripped when she tried to

pull it loose. Or, only a small part was actually in the gates, with the rest of it trailing down to the ground like a banner. This left Alena wearing little more than a blouse--the upper remnants of her dress--with only a thin strip of fabric covering the waistband of her panties and the very upper tops of her thighs.

This was not at all how she wanted to approach a mysterious mansion in the woods to confront her sister and the beast and see what they were up to, but as it was she had little choice in the matter, didn't she?

She frowned and headed down the dirt path.

...

EVERETT FUCKED DANYA. HE FUCKED HER hard and fast and with a primal urgency, like the beast he now was. He remembered an earlier time when he would have catered to the every need of one of his potential mates, charmed them completely be-fore breeding with them. Did he call them mates then? Was that breeding? He remembered other words, recalled some other definition and meaning, courting and seduction and coupling.

No, those others before weren't mates, were they? They could have been, though. He had sex with women, but they despised other terms. And the privacy! Argh! They needed to perform their sexual acts discretely so others wouldn't discover their--their what? There was a word for all of this, for everything, but it had been so long since he'd talked with another person, had a conversation with someone, that he couldn't remember them.

None of it mattered. He took Danya on the table. She begged him for it, removed her panties and stuffed them into her crotch before shoving them at his nose. That incited a lustful rage within him. The scents! Before, when he was human, he remembered the pleasant scents of flowers and food, but now, as a beast, he knew more. Perhaps he was still a little human; he could see some resemblance beneath his fur-covered body if he peered into a mirror, but that was it. He thought of himself as a beast, like the witch who cursed him wanted. That witch, that curse, was it bad? He knew it was, but the smell of lust dripping from Danya's luscious cunt and the sweet scent of it drenching her panties was nothing less than sublime.

He liked that word: sublime. It was one that he would always remember.

There was another woman, too. Perhaps another potential mate? She followed him into the gates. He let the gates remain open for just a moment longer than necessary to allow the girl in, calling on his family's inherent magic used to control various facets of the mansion, but no more. She was caught now, his, trapped. She smelled like Danya, but different, too; her sister, he assumed.

He would find her later and free her and let her into his house and offer her his hospitality.

The idea intrigued him. He flipped Danya over onto her stomach and crammed his heavy shaft into her. She was so tight! The witch thought she cursed him, but as a beast he was more. So much more. His savage cock, larger than he remembered it ever being when he was a mere human, thrashed into Danya as if they were both wild wolves rutting in a ditch in the middle of the woods. Every sensation, each clench and squeeze from her gluttonous depths, assailed his cock.

He loved it. He would breed with her, release his seed deep inside of her, and bring his mansion back to life. The witch said it would never happen, that no woman would willfully fuck a beastman, but the witch was a spiteful creature who underestimated him.

The witch was wrong, but Everett knew he was a little wrong, too. It was wonderful, slamming his cock into Danya's tight body, watching her glistening lower lips pulse and suck and consume his shaft as he pounded into her, but it was more, too. He liked her. He wanted her to stay, and he wanted her to like him.

She did, too. He knew. She spoke with him, talked in small sentences so he could understand. He appreciated it, but he would impress her later, too. He was no idiot, but years and years of isolation had muddled his com-prehension of regular, everyday life. He would rediscover everything he had lost, though. He would revive the servants of his household through the act of sex and restart his tutoring. He would invite Danya to stay with him forever, too. Eventually, once he dispelled the witch's curse, he would be handsome again. Someone truly worthy of her.

And if doing all this involved giving in to his primal lust and rutting with her atop the dining hall table while she moaned in ecstasy beneath him? Well, there were worse ways to remove a curse.

When he came Everett pushed back the urge to howl; to claim her as his so soon. His seed shot deep into her. Focusing, intent on fulfilling his need, he slammed into her again. Again. More. Each time, no matter how much cum he'd already filled her with, it seemed endless, as if he'd always have more to give her. He couldn't stop, didn't want to, and he indulged in the exquisite feeling of her own erratic orgasm pulling at his cock while he mated with her.

...

ALENA PANICKED. SHE COULDN'T GET INTO THE mansion. The door was locked, first off, and the windows were too high up for her to even consider sneaking inside. She could see through some of them, but to get to the handles in the middle where she might try and see if they were unlatched involved climbing smooth stones and maneuvering her feet onto a ledge about three inches wide. Alena was no acrobat, so this was out of the question.

What she needed to do, she decided, was find what room her sister and the beast were in, and then rap on the window. Perhaps they wouldn't like it, but what else should they expect from her? She was trapped within the mansion grounds now with no way out. If they wanted to send her home, she needed someone to open the gates for her, anyways.

Not that she intended to go home. Or, not if Danya wasn't leaving, also. Alena fully planned on staying, on experiencing the excitement of the beast and hearing his story. Oh, he was a prince at one time, they said! Though people said a lot of things. She wondered which of the rumors were true? It never hurt to wonder, but sometimes it could lead to disappointment. She knew this firsthand. Sometimes she wondered at her father's transactions, his going off and finding curious goods for the family store. He always said he had found a rare heirloom, something wondrous that no one else had seen or heard of before, but all he did was bring back some lamp or other with nothing interesting about it.

The beast, though, he would have good stories. A witch wouldn't curse a man for nothing, would she? And banish his servants to who knew where? Or was the rumor that he'd eaten them the true one? If so, Alena thought she wouldn't learn much about it; he'd probably eat her as soon as he caught her on his land. A rather morbid thought, but she preferred being practical in the face of danger. If she was eaten, she very well wouldn't be worrying much about anything, now would she?

Movement, in a window nearby. Just a faint bit, some reflection on the glass, but it must be them. Alena went towards it, creeping along close to the outer wall of the mansion. Grabbing the ledge of the window, she stood on tiptoes and looked inside.

She saw her sister on her stomach on a dining hall table, with the beast crouching behind and over her. Neither of them wore clothes. Actually, Danya had her bra on, some fancy bit of leopard-patterned fabric, but that was it. The beast was rock hard and massive, his throbbing cock slamming into her older sister's slick folds.

Alena opened her mouth wide. She didn't want to see this! Not her sister. Fuck. That was... fuck! She staggered backwards and her foot caught on the raised root of a nearby tree. She fell to the ground. Again. How many times was this going to happen? Today was not her lucky day.

Still, a tree, that was good. She crawled over to it, sitting on the ground with her back to the trunk, hiding behind it. She'd wanted to tap on the window and get the attention of her sister and the beast, except it seemed they were otherwise preoccupied. Her sister! Gods, Alena wasn't really worried in the first place, at least not too much, but she'd never expected Danya to be *fucking* him. At least not this soon. And not right out in the open like that.

They looked so into it, too. At least from what she could see. She preferred not to remember the look of ecstasy on Danya's face (what little of it she saw), but the beast definitely seemed blissfully unaware of anything except slamming his massive shaft into a pussy. Just a pussy, Alena thought, not anyone's in particular.

It could've been her own, even? Right. Possibly. And...

A dangerous thought to let loose, but she did it anyways. She imagined herself on the table instead of Danya, with her stomach pressed against the smooth wood while the beast held her down and ravaged her. His thick cock swelled with passion as he filled her to the brim with his primal cream. Alena sighed, daydreaming, wondering at it.

Wondering was, perhaps, her downfall.

Without realizing it, her hand found a nest inside her panties. She slipped her fingers beneath the waistband of her underwear and imagined all sorts of naughty things. The beast pounding his cock into her, the force of it sliding her ever so slightly across the table until they reached the edge, and in a fit of madness he snatched her up and leaped to the ground. All while still fucking her, of course. She didn't know the logistics of how that would work, but it sounded wonderfully erotic in her mind.

She grew more and more aroused. Her fingers idly stroked her labia, gathering her wetness and spreading it over the sensitive folds. Oh, how would it be when he came? She was curious about that. She'd toyed with boys before, led them into private areas or let them lead her, where she succumbed to their charms and let them let down their pants. She was somewhat skilled at handling their cocks by now, either with her hands or her mouth or a bit of both, but she remained reticent about letting them have sex with her.

Except, oh, she was so dreadfully curious. Honestly, how did it feel? When she had a man in her mouth, she could tell when he was about to explode, his climax overcoming him. She could feel his cock begin to expand the slightest amount, his pulse quickening and beating through his engorged shaft, and then the frantic spasms as he shot his cum into her throat. It was always so fast, so interesting!

Her hand moved of its own accord now, slick between her glistening folds while she imagined what it was like to feel a man's climax inside her. Not with any man, though, but with the beast. The boys she knew, or the few, far older men she'd managed to seduce as a random game, were nothing compared to the size of the beast's cock. She couldn't even see all of it, what with half of it sheathed inside of Danya's pussy, but it was big. If the tremors preceding and happening at the point of orgasm for a regular man were exciting, she could only imagine how the beast would feel.

Deep inside her and--oh! Her hand found the top of her slit, teasing at the hood of her clit and then rubbing it back and forth. That felt nice, she thought. This wasn't about nice, though, it was about the sensation of a throbbing cock unloading into her with all it was worth. She rubbed her clit more, imagining it. Something big, yes. To match the size of his erection. The scene playing in her head involved so much cum that it overflowed out of her and splattered onto the table. Enough cum, she thought, to fill a goblet and drink from. Not with a goblet, no, but she did that sometimes if she felt like it, just swallowed a man's cum when he released inside of her mouth and splashed the back of her throat. Men liked it, it seemed. Sometimes she would open her mouth and show them their sticky cream, her eyes twinkling with mischief, before pursing her lips, swallowing, and opening her mouth again to show them it was gone. That was a trick one of her friends told her about, and while it wasn't that exciting for her, the look of intense excitement from the man after she swallowed his seed was exhilarating.

Except there was no swallowing when it came to having your sex filled with cum, was there? Not exactly, anyways. Alena stroked her clit faster, now in a frenzy of need. She imagined the beast finishing with her, drenching her insides, while her needy body sucked all of it up. Was that exciting for a man, too? Did he enjoy it? Did men find the idea of fucking a girl and filling her up exciting, possibly impregnating her with their potent seed?

Fuck, who cared about them? She loved it! She didn't want children, at least not yet, but the naughtiness of it, the thrill and risk and idea of it, sent her over the edge. In a panic, urgent to satisfy her lust, she grabbed at her panties and pulled them lower. Not too far, but far enough, and when she was through they lay bunched by her knees, giving her completely free access to the core of her body. She rubbed at her clit with one hand while she thrust two fingers from the other hand inside of her, hoping to somewhat replicate the sensation of a cock. Two fingers didn't do the beast justice, but it worked well enough for Alena. In a matter of moments, she was grinding her hips against empty air, imagining the roughness of the beast as he made her a vessel for his climax, an orgasm blazing through her.

It felt--it felt good. It was good. Perhaps she had never let a man fuck her, but she'd let them get her off before. And she'd played with herself, too. It was always good, but she wondered if maybe it would be better with a man? Inside her, that was. With the beast, with...

Alena heard a cough, heard someone clearing their throat. Startled, caught with her panties around her knees and her dress ripped so she couldn't hide her exposed body, she tried to back away. Unfortunately the tree was still behind her and she went nowhere.

Looming above her, naked, with a glossy shine on his erect cock from the remnants of his last sexual encounter, was the beast.

"Hello," Alena squeaked.

"Danya's sister, you?" he said, some awkwardly phrased question.

"Yes," Alena said. "Um, I'm sorry about this but I seem to have, uh..."

Honestly, she didn't know how she was supposed to explain the panties. The dress, perhaps, but panties didn't just lower themselves. Also, the fact that the lips of her pussy were a glorious, puffy red and obviously moist from recent exertion was not a point in her favor.

"I need," the beast said to her. "I need a lot."

...

DANYA AWOKE AFTER NOT REALIZING SHE'D fallen asleep. Gods, of course she'd fallen asleep, though. Everett, the beast, was amazing. He'd taken her hard on the table and showed her just how amazing he could be. He was some primal, lusty man, and despite the fact that he had hair covering the entirety of his body, he was a wonderful lover. Perhaps he was better because of it, she thought. If he needed to make up for the shortcoming of looking like some beast of a man, doing it through sexual prowess was definitely a fine way to go about it.

Except where was he now? They would sleep, he said, and wait for the older man to return with food before presumably fucking like animals once again. Twice again... three times again... Would they do it on the table, right in front of the man? Give him a show? Danya wasn't entirely displeased with the idea. In fact...

No, better not to think of that now. It would only arouse her, and with no one to sate her needs she didn't need something like that. Though she wondered if that worked as a way to summon Everett back to her? Would he smell the scent of her arousal if she lay on the table and blatantly masturbated? Would he find her splayed out, playing with her pussy, legs spread wide for the entire mansion to see?

She was exciting herself, and was of a mind to try it and see what happened, except her stomach growled. Eating nothing since breakfast this morning was taking its toll, and she needed to find food before enacting her plan. Perhaps a reminder to the butler about the meal would remedy that, or better yet going to help him. Afterall, she cooked most of the meals at home, so it couldn't hurt to offer him assistance. Maybe she could get a snack in the process.

Not knowing exactly where the kitchens were, and having no clothes besides her leopard-patterned bra, she wandered the halls of the mansion while mostly nude and lost. The butler had gone this way, she knew, but where exactly after that? It didn't take long to figure it out; the smell of food wafted through a large double doorway and led her right there. Bright light shone through the cracks around the edges of the doors, like some illuminating beacon. A gateway to culinary riches unknown.

From the smell of it, the riches were delicious.

Caring little if the butler saw her naked (since he'd seen her like this already, hadn't he?), she reached for the handles of the kitchen doors and opened them. Once she had sight of the inside of the room, she gasped.

Everything was moving on its own! Every little piece of equipment in the room, all the knives cutting and spoons stirring pots, dishes being washed by invisibly held rags, everything. How handy! Really, who wouldn't like that? If she could have items prepare themselves for a meal, she'd definitely love it. In the middle of the automation was the butler, sorting through food goods and tossing them into a boiling pot or preparing them to go into an oven, piling them on platters and racks.

Danya walked towards him and smiled and said, "Hello."

The butler smiled back, eyes twinkling with glee, and looked up. When he saw Danya standing next to him with only one scant article of clothing covering her nubile body his eyes widened. "Oh. Hello, Mistress. Is there something I can do for you or Master Everett?"

"No," Danya said. "I'm a little hungry, though. I thought I'd help if you want?"

The butler shrugged. "You need not worry. Dinner arrangements are coming along fine. There's very little left to do that isn't already being done."

Danya nodded. She watched a knife slicing through a thick slab of meat and organizing it into tiny chunks. The butler walked over once it was done and shuffled the meat onto a roasting pan before setting the pan into a brick oven.

"I'm Horatio, by the way," the butler said conversationally. "If you need me for anything around the mansion, feel free to summon me." With that said, he went back to work.

Danya was entranced. He moved so efficiently. It intrigued her. She watched him work tirelessly, preparing a meal, and seeming to care so little about having just come back to life after having his soul imprisoned within a grandfather clock. Was that what happened, anyways? She didn't know for sure, but she'd seen the spark of him leave the clock and when she blinked he was there. No matter what it was, he'd been gone for a long time, at least according to Everett.

How long? It didn't matter to the butler, it seemed. Now that he was back, he needed to attend to the mansion's duties, which currently involved making a meal. Oddly, this aroused her.

Not for any of those thoughts. Meals were nice and she liked them, but she hardly found them arousing. Nor the fact that he was old, though that didn't take many points away from him. He looked fine and handsome, with fancy servant's attire and fine, white hair.

What aroused her was the idea that he was back and couldn't have had sex with a woman in so long. And still, seeing her in front of him, practically ready for the taking, prepared for sex much like the carrots he was collecting were prepared to be boiled, he did nothing. He worked, and not a single thing more.

Would he enjoy it if she gave him a show? If she convinced Everett to let him watch them fucking, have the man hide in a closet with a slatted door so he could peer through the openings and spy on them?

Or, why do all that? Why shouldn't she reward him herself? Everett had left her without a word or a note, so she hardly thought he deserved an explanation for her leaving him, and it wasn't as if they were married. He needed, he said. Yes, well, she needed, too.

Danya removed her bra and tossed it onto an empty table. Horatio didn't seem to notice, or if he did he acted like he didn't care. Oh, she would change his mind, and very quickly. Walking towards him with a seductive sway of her bare hips, she sidled next to him and put her chin on his shoulder, watching him work. Her breasts pressed against his back, her supple flesh finding a home against the cloth of his suit.

Horatio gulped. "Mistress?" When he turned around he got an eyeful; all of her, nude, her tight body, presented and prepared for him, waiting to see what he could do with it.

"You were gone for a long time, weren't you?" she asked.

He backed away from her, trying not to look at her gently swaying breasts. Trying, she noted, but failing. "Yes, yes I was. It's no trouble, though. Not the Master's fault, but the witch's curse. I know this."

"Mhm." She nodded and walked towards him like a predator stalking her prey, almost as if she were the beast now. Horatio continued backing away until he found himself pressed up against the kitchen wall with nowhere left to go.

"I only want to reward you," she said. "Everett is nice, but you look like you could use a treat for good service."

"Yes, well, it's reward enough working here," Horatio said. "It's a wonderful place. You'll see how nice and lively it is once the others return. Which, speaking of, where is Master Everett now? Shouldn't you two be...? Not to be crass, but you both seemed to enjoy yourselves, and..."

"Later," Danya said. "I want to enjoy you now."

Horatio gave her a confused look, which

gave Danya just enough time to crouch on her knees in front of him and undo his pants. She unbuckled his belt and unbuttoned his pants and pulled them down to his ankles along with his underwear.

Maybe he was an older gentleman, but from her current vantage point she wouldn't have guessed it. Not entirely up to speed with her advances, his cock looked ready and willing to catch up at any moment. She grinned as it twitched upwards, almost like a nod of approval, freed from its confines.

"Mistress, really, you don't have to..." Horatio started to say.

"I know," she interrupted. Before he could say anymore, she cut him off by licking the head of his cock.

Horatio braced himself against the wall, knees trembling. "Oh, gods," he said.

He didn't become instantly erect, but he was close to it. His cock sprung up, slapping against her nose and making her laugh. "How long has it been since you've been with a woman?" she asked.

"Mistress," he said. She made it hard for him to speak by stroking his shaft in her hands and teasing the tiny slit at the end of his cockhead with her tongue. "I--it's been a very long time. Before the curse, I dallied with one of the maids, but we had a fight and after that it was over a year--"

"That's no good," Danya said.

She wrapped her lips around his cock and

leaned forward, taking him into her mouth. Thankfully he wasn't as big as Everett, or she didn't think this would work. He was big enough, though. Plenty big to make it a pleasure to suck his cock. She could feel his size, his twitching, his cock squirming in her mouth. She bobbed her head up and down along his shaft before easing him out of her mouth and licking at the curves between his cockhead and shaft.

Horatio grunted and grabbed her hair, but quickly let go after realizing who he had a hold of.

Letting his cock fully out of her mouth, she stroked him in long, steady beats. "You can pull my hair," she said. "I want you to talk dirty to me. Treat me like that maid. Tell me how angry you are with me, as if we're arguing all over again."

Horatio nodded, gulping. When Danya took him into her mouth again, he grabbed her hair. Tentatively at first, careful, but when she didn't object he took in fistfuls and guided her along his cock. Faster, he wanted, and she went faster.

"Darcy," he said.

She looked up at him, watching him. His eyes were closed, remembering the image of his lover. The idea of it, her playing the role of some lowly maid, excited her. It wasn't far from the truth, really, except somehow after fucking Everett she'd been elevated to the role of mistress. She decided to be a very benevolent mistress, though. Why shouldn't she reward the servants for good behavior?

"Darcy," Horatio repeated. "It's--it's--"

Danya stopped for a moment. "Go on. You may say anything."

He nodded, pursing his lips. "Darcy, I know the Master had sex with you, and I despise it, but I still..."

Fuck! This was delicious. Everett had seduced the maid, stolen Darcy away from Horatio for the night? Better still, the woman had a name somewhat similar to her own, at least the beginning of it. And... how must this be for the butler? Everett had taken his Darcy, and here she was, Everett's mistress, worshipping Horatio's cock?

"You're a dirty fucking whore!" Horatio screamed.

In his fantasy, this re-enactment, he lost himself. He clenched at Danya's hair and shoved her forcefully onto his cock. Danya choked, gasping and gagging and shocked, but not for long. This was wonderful! He was no Everett, but he was better in some regards. Angry, truly angry, and taking her, his passion and emotion showing through. He held her on his cock, forcing himself deep into her throat, while he screamed obscenities at her.

Then he pulled her away and shoved her back down. This time Danya was ready for it. She let his cock slide into her mouth, his cockhead hitting against the back of her throat. She grabbed at his hips, gripping his ass so she could try and force more of him into her mouth. She had every last inch of his manhood inside her, and Horatio seemed to want her to know it.

When she swallowed, the sensation sent his cock twitching in her mouth. Breathing through her nose, staring at his crotch up close, she felt horribly aroused. This was... fuck! He bucked his hips against her face, fucking her mouth, and she desperately wanted him to use the rest of her body but didn't want to ruin his fantasy.

"And what--" he said in between thrust, "--will you do--" His cock banged against the back of her throat. "—if you become pregnant?"

Danya squeezed his ass with one hand, then snaked the other around to his thigh. She coaxed him to spread his legs a bit, then snuck her hand towards his seed-heavy balls. Grasping them in her hand, she squeezed, rolling them between her fingers and urging him further.

"He can't recognize the child as his own! He's too important to marry a common servant! Everyone will think you're a hussy! Some lady of the night! A cheap trick!"

Horatio went on a rampage. He fucked her throat for all he was worth, pounding his cock into her mouth. Danya tried to keep some semblance of a regular blowjob, like the ones she'd given to numerous men before, but this was something else entirely. Horatio didn't seem like he even wanted anything resembling normal, which was fine by her. She praised his shaft with her lips, lubricating the way with her tongue as she rolled it around every curve and crevice she could find while he stuffed himself into her mouth.

His balls tightened and she squeezed them harder. Horatio grimaced, on the precipice of pleasure, but she wouldn't let him fully relent and release. He slowed his thrusts, trying to push past the agonizing pleasure of her squeezing, the pressure making it difficult for him to climax, she knew. Still, he was about to cum and there was little more she could do about it.

In a last ditch effort to prolong him, she moved her other hand to the base of his cock and wrapped her thumb and index finger around it, cutting off his orgasm's point of escape. Horatio screamed, enraged.

In his fantasy, whatever was going on in his mind, it wasn't very happy. He pulled Danya hard onto his cock, broke through her squeezes, and forced a massive jet of sticky cream into her throat. Again, then once more, thick, gooey cum shot into her mouth, and then he finished. She grinned, drooling on his cock and swallowing his load as he came down from climax.

His cock softened in her mouth and she licked and cleaned it with her tongue. Post-climax, Horatio softened as a person, too. His hands let go of her hair and he acted less tense now, more relaxed. He opened his eyes and looked down at her with a smile before realizing who exactly was on her knees in front of him.

"Mistress!" he said with a gasp. He helped her up from the ground and wiped a stray bit of his cum from her lips with the cuff of his suit coat. "I'm so dreadfully sorry."

"Oh, it's fine," she said. "Did you enjoy it?"

"It was..." He searched for a word. "It was very cathartic. I'm sorry you had to learn of Master Everett's indiscretions that way, though. He's a fine man, mind, but his inclinations tend towards a philanderer's nature. I am sure with the passing of time he has calmed his passions, though."

Danya desperately hoped this wasn't the case. If their rabid coupling on the dining hall table was a one time thing she would be disappointed.

...

How HAD SHE GOTTEN HERSELF INTO THIS mess? Alena had no idea.

The beast (his name was Everett, she learned) held her up against a tree. He'd introduced himself at least, and she'd done the same, except then he'd just went right to the point. He needed.

What did he need? A bad question to ask, apparently. He didn't know how to explain it, so instead he showed her. Kneeling beside her, he touched her wet pussy with the palm of his hand and said it again. "I need."

Alena lost her sense of self. She needed, too! She needed a lot. Hell, she needed most everything, she thought. Everyone needed some-thing at some time, and it all changed, and...

That wasn't this, but it might as well be. When he touched her crotch, spread her folds with his fingers, she couldn't think and didn't answer. Instead, she leaned into him, excited as he caressed her slick folds with his hand, and then...

Before she knew it he picked her up high. So high that she could grab the lower branches of the tree above her, which she did. The beast sought her smell, her dripping arousal, and he dug his nose into her sex. Alena shrieked, caught off guard.

"Yessssss," she hissed. She had a feeling that it wouldn't matter what she said or did, as long as her body reacted to the beast's min-istrations. And, oh yes, she definitely did that.

He didn't spend much time sniffing and rubbing his nose against her clit, though. Alena didn't mind. She wanted to see his erection up close, to feel it in her hands, and when he lowered her a little she expected to do just that.

Except, no. When he lowered her so that she could no longer hold onto the branches, he was far closer to her than before. So close that her legs were on either side of his body, with her panties still near her knees and wrapped tight around his back. The fabric of her underwear stretched to accommodate his presence. He lowered her more, a little more. She looked down to see exactly what he was doing.

His massive erection twitched upwards, straining high, and slowly he continued lowering her onto it. The way things were going, in only a few more seconds he would have her skewered on his thick and throbbing cock.

He stopped when the head of his cock bounced against the folds of her pussy.

"I need," he said. "You need?"

Alena bit her lower lip and nodded, afraid that if she said anything she would change her mind. This was it, though! No more playing with men, teasing them with her hands and her mouth. This was a real man, a beast of one, who was going to fuck her properly. He was going to fill her up like she dreamed of before and...

And then he did it. Alena cried out in shock at the feeling of him inside her. He wasn't even all the way in! Fuck... it hurt, but...

Everett smiled at her. "Slow," he said.

Alena nodded, but couldn't think much more. She closed her eyes and let herself feel everything, not worrying about seeing it. He slid her down his shaft a little more, further, pushing past any resistance and grinding himself into her. Alena whimpered. It was painful, but it felt so good, too. Was this how it always felt?

No, she learned. Or at least, the pain wasn't constant. Everett held her against the tree while she kept her legs wrapped around his waist and pulled his throbbing shaft out of her. Slowly still, but faster than before, he filled her back up. Out, then in again, and faster still. Alena bit her lip and let out a moan.

"More," she said. "I want it faster."

Everett grinned. He leaned in and nipped at the side of her neck with his teeth, then licked her throat. Alena shuddered, feeling weak in the knees and helpless. Because, what could she do, anyways? Here was this beast, his cock digging deep inside of her, doing what he wished with her body, licking her like some piece of meat. Gods, that idea aroused something primal in her. It helped that the beast wasn't actually too beastly. He was... caring? Caring but forceful. Urgent and needy, but patient.

This time when he thrust into her, he pushed her up. She gasped, feeling him slamming into her sex. He grinned and she felt his warm breath on her face. Instinctively, not even sure why she did it, she craned her neck forward and sought out his lips. She found them with her own and kissed them, kissed him over and over.

The beast hesitated for a second, unsure. Had she done something wrong? Oh, gods, she didn't want to ruin this. But, no, he kissed her back after. The bristles of hair covering his face tickled, felt nice, soft, as he kissed her back. She pressed her lips hard against his own, letting her tongue lick him, too. The beast thrust into her harder now, treating her less like a gentle doll and more like a fuck toy. She squeaked every time he slammed into her, but she kept kissing him.

Her tongue snaked into his mouth, playing with his. He let her, and they swirled together in a mix of unexplainable sensation. There was something about him, his mouth, his everything, that was more animalistic and raw. She'd kissed before, but not like this. It was like his mouth wanted to dominate her, but she was fighting against it in a wild game of control. She wasn't sure if she was winning or losing, and didn't really care because it felt so good, so exciting.

Alena didn't quite know what she was supposed to do, but her body understood the gist of it. She squeezed against his intrusion, the pressure of his cock pressing against her sexual tunnel and coaxing her into doing it unbidden, and the beast let out a growl. Oh, so he liked that? Well, fuck, she liked it, too. She squeezed again, clenching hard onto him. It was like a game of tug of war, almost; a power struggle. Could he force his cock past her sexual defenses? The better question was: did she even have a chance of stopping him from pounding his cock into her?

Why the hell would she want to do that in the first place?

It didn't matter, she soon figured out. His rhythm echoed through her and she was powerless to stop it. More, again, pounding, further. It had started happening awhile ago, but she couldn't quite explain it yet, though she knew it now. All of a sudden, like some abrupt fire, she realized an orgasm was upon her. It felt entirely like, and

Hunted

unlike, every one of her previous orgasms. When it happened, she knew it immediately, but before it had just seemed like a pleasant, building tingle. Odd, strange, but what the heck, of course sex would feel good. That was the whole point! And obviously it would feel differently now. Being brought to orgasm with a massive cock stuffed into her tight slit wouldn't feel the same as a climax without one.

Still, she wasn't fully prepared for this. She screamed out her lust, praising the beast's prowess. "Fucking, yessss... fuck!" Verbal eloquence was something she currently lacked.

Her body thrashed, wanting to explode, but the beast kept her in check. He held her so she didn't fall, and kept pounding into her, prolonging her orgasm. She held onto him, wrapped her arms around his back as best she could and pulled herself towards him. He removed her from the back of the tree and held her ass in his hands, bucking his hips up to stuff her full with his cock. Alena screamed out loud again, forgetting they were ever kissing. Her mouth sucked at his neck and for some reason, like he had, she licked frantically at his throat.

When she came down from her climax, she felt wonderful. He thrust into her still, but a little slower now, letting her relax. Her breathing grew hard and heavy, fast, and she wondered if he wanted to do it again. Could he? He didn't seem ready to stop, so she thought maybe.

Cerys du Lys

"I need," he said in her ear.

She nodded fast. "You can. You can cum in me, alright? It's alright. I want you."

The beast walked with her, holding her on his cock as he did. He brought her towards a patch of grass nearby. Thrusting hard into her a few more times while holding her aloft, he then crouched down and lowered her to the grass. Once her back touched the ground, he loomed over her and kissed her hard on the mouth. Needy, desperate for more, she kissed him back.

This time there was no slowness, no consideration, only fucking. That was fine by Alena, though. She wrapped her legs around him, pulling him towards her as he pushed deep into her. One, two, a hundred times, she didn't know and lost count after ten thrusts. More, pleasure, yes, a constant singing trill, but not enough for another orgasm. She didn't know if she could again, after having already cum twice--once from him and once from herself--but she didn't care. He felt so wonderful inside of her, so perfect and right.

And then he howled. He slammed hard into her and stopped, stuffing her completely. The noise boomed out of him, just like that. Alena shivered at the sound of it, basking in his warmth and dominance.

It felt nothing like how she imagined. There was no way to understand how this would feel without feeling it, and she felt a little silly for trying to understand it before. Feeling it now, though... it amazed her. Everett's cock twitched, pulsed, and shifted, squirming to move farther into her. His seed erupted out of his cockhead and flooded into her. Warm, so warm, and wonderfully satisfying. She wanted more, and the beast was happy to oblige.

As he came, his cream spreading inside her, he ground his hips against her and shoved his cock as far into her as he could. His feet dug into the ground, pushing, and he inadvertently sent them both sliding across the grass. Only an inch or so every few seconds, but it was a curious feeling. Alena watched him, felt him inside of her, filling her, sliding her on the grass and... and breeding with her, mating, impregnating her? Could he, could they? She didn't know, but she found the idea horrifying and erotic. She wanted him so badly.

Her pussy clenched around him, squeezing the cum from his cock. Harder, pressing him, and then something more. It was completely unlike the first time she'd orgasmed with him, but amazing nonetheless. Her inner depths convulsed around his cock, an orgasm streaking through her, but a steady, constant thing instead of the frantic, urgent spasms from before. It felt stronger, more reliable, and the beast seemed to feel this, too. His cock twitched with the same rhythm as her steady climax, pressing against her inner walls as her pussy clutched against him.

Alena wanted to shout out some litany, to

tell the world how much she loved this, but no words came to her. Instead, she smiled at him, held him inside her, kissed at his face, his lips, his cheeks, and reveled in the feeling of his cock flooding her womb with his needy cream.

Everett collapsed on top of her, spent. He rolled over onto his back, his cock popping out of her and his seed leaking from her ravaged folds. Alena wasted no time in crawling atop him, laying on his fur-covered body, and kissing his chest and nipples and stomach. The beast sighed, watching her with a happy look on his face.

She curled up close to him, her dress-covered torso pressed against his bare chest. She laughed at that. All this time and she still had her ripped dress on. Oh well, she'd lost her panties, at least. They were somewhere around here, but she didn't really care enough to find them at the moment.

"I really liked that," she said, kissing his nose.

"Yes," Everett said. "I, too."

"I know you're very tired, and I am, too, but do you think we can do that again sometime?" she asked.

He answered with a grin.

...

"WHAT EXACTLY...?" DANYA ASKED.

Horatio smiled at her. "Darcy enjoyed this

if we were in the kitchens alone late at night. I would set it up and then go about my work. I'm sure you will enjoy it, too, Mistress."

Danya wasn't positive about that. Mostly, she had no idea what he was doing. The butler had grabbed an old-fashioned tapered rolling pin, a jug of olive oil, and two clean and dry terry cloth dish rags from a cupboard, brought them over, then told her to lay down on top of one of the food prep-aration tables. Honestly it made no sense. If he wanted to fuck her, she was fine with that, but as an older man he probably wasn't up to the task of becoming erect so soon after she'd brought him to climax.

"The kitchens are magic," he said. "Actually, the entire mansion is magic, but it's all of a different kind. In the kitchens you can make any of the tools perform as you wish, in a repetitive motion. Darcy and I discovered this particular use after a night of heavy drinking."

"Which is...?" Danya asked.

Horatio didn't bother to explain anything to her. Instead, he took one of the terry cloth rags and placed it on her stomach. Rubbing it across her skin as if she were a dish in need of washing, he wiped it up towards her breast and then gently scrubbed. Danya arched her back in surprise when the soft roughness of the cloth sent a pleasant sensation through her skin. It tingled, tiny thrilling pricks of intimacy tracing little lines across her breast and teasing at her nipple.

The man cupped her breast in his hand, holding the rag over it, then moved it in a circular motion. Danya wriggled, enjoying the attention to her breasts, and wondering why she'd never thought of this before? Granted, it probably wasn't at all the same if she did it to herself, and none of her other lovers had cared to experiment on her body with dish rags, but... she really wondered why they hadn't? This felt strangely amazing.

The next thing she knew, there was another cloth circling her other breast, attending to that one with its gentle rubbing. Horatio wasn't holding the first, either. She stared at it in awe, trying to deduce what was going on. The arousing sat-isfaction she gained from the cloth was clouding her ability to think rationally, though.

Before she knew it, both rags were moving on their own, perfectly cupping her breasts and gently scrubbing across her smooth, sensitive flesh. This man, Horatio, was a genius.

"They're supposed to be for cleaning," he said. "Of course, they'll do whatever you have them do, but the initial intent was for cleaning. Or, this rolling pin was for dough, but..."

He picked up the rolling pin, an old tapered sort; thicker in the center, becoming thinner at the handles. Opening the jug of olive oil, he liberally slathered it onto the rolling pin, rubbing the oil into it much like a man might stroke his cock. Maybe that was just Danya's sex-addled mind thinking devious thoughts, but she dreadfully wanted a cock right about now. Was Horatio possibly ready for more?

He smiled at her before pressing his oiled palm against her slit. He rubbed the oil across her folds, eliciting a sharp gasp from her. She thrust her hips upwards, lifting herself from the table with her legs. Horatio teased her slit, rubbing the oil in and toying with her plump labia. He tweaked her sensitive pearl and rolled it around lightly between his thumb and forefinger, then patted it with his palm.

"More," she said. Just one word. No time for anything else.

"Oh, yes, of course, Mistress."

More was--she didn't know what more was, but it felt a bit odd. Not a bad odd, but definitely not a cock thrusting into her. Still good, though. When she looked down, managing to keep her eyes from rolling into the back of her head from the heavy sensation of mounting pleasure, she saw the rolling pin pressing inside her. Horatio pushed it farther, the girthy center stretching her folds as the thinner handle pressed in deep. The rolling pin stretched her even wider than Everett's cock had, and she found herself clutching at the table, trying to grab it in her fingers. Her nails dug into the smooth wood, scratching. Too full, too much--but it felt so good.

And then it came out. Danya didn't realize she'd been holding her breath. She breathed fast and heavy, frantic to catch her breath so she could concentrate on this feeling again.

The rolling pin pushed into her. "Is that a good speed?" Horatio asked.

"Faster," she said through pursed lips.

The pin picked up its pace. "Now?"

"Faster!" she said.

By the time he got it right, the rolling pin was pounding hard into her. The wood had no give, unlike a cock, and when her inner depths squeezed against it the feeling was so strange. The oil, too, letting the wood slide in and out as if this were the simplest thing in the world. Horatio stood at her side, admiring his handiwork.

"Are you pleased, Mistress?"

"Fuck," she said. "Yes."

"Alright. I'll leave you as you are now. I'm going to finish dinner. Whenever you're fully satisfied, please let me know." As an addendum, he said, "Oh, Darcy enjoyed pleasuring herself with her fingers while she lay like this, too. If it helps, feel free to try it."

Danya immediately scrambled to do so. Her hand made a beeline for her clit and she rubbed at it furiously. It helped that she absolutely loved Horatio's fantasy, and her vicarious ful-fillment of it. Gods, she was so aroused during that session before, but she couldn't very well seek out her own pleasure while satisfying him. Besides the fact that he was so forceful with her, she just didn't have a free hand at the time. It wouldn't have been the same as this, anyways. Now she was playing a similar role as Darcy again, but this time it was for her own benefit.

The rolling pin slammed in and out of her sex, stretching her to gaping and then giving her some minor relief before cramming back in all over again. The rags massaging her breasts were slower, but constant, never ceasing their work. Her nipples hardened with each passing second, almost painfully so now, intensifying the effect of the cloth as it stretched to encompass the nubs and the soft, rough fabric rubbed against her sensitive skin.

This couldn't continue like this, or at least she couldn't. In another few moments she would be thrashing in orgasm, completely undone, with no control. Through glazed, half-lidded eyes, she saw Horatio humming to himself while he pulled a pan of succulent meat from the oven. He acted completely oblivious to her writhing in ecstasy on a table only a few feet away from him.

That was it. She squeezed hard, her pussy grabbing at the rolling pin to no avail, and her orgasm crashed into her. The rolling pin didn't care, though. She couldn't rub at her clit any more because the pleasure was too intense, but the rolling pin never stopped. The cloth rubbing her breasts just made the whole situation worse, too. Worse in the sense that--dammit--she hadn't felt anything like this before. Usually when she came, with herself or a man in her, there was some relenting. Maybe not intentionally, but when she squeezed against a cock it couldn't go into her as fast as it previously had, nor as deeply, and so she could let her orgasm ride through and subside before hoping to lift it back up.

The rolling pin was having none of that. It wouldn't let her down from her orgasmic high. The ecstasy pushed into her, pouring through the pin, pounding, stretching all of her. Horatio dutifully came over and lifted the jug of oil above her pussy, letting the slick liquid drip out and onto her folds, oiling up the pin some more. Before he left, he patted her pubic mound, laughing heartily as she arched her back and let out a moan.

This rolling pin was ridiculous. Danya gave in to it, letting it keep her in a heightened state of pleasure, while she tried rubbing at her clit again. Too sensitive! Except, oh gods. How the hell had that happened? She'd only rubbed her clit a tiny bit, such a small amount, but from the constant, insatiable pleasure pounded into her by the rolling pin she felt another orgasm burst through her immediately after she touched herself.

Sharp, quick pulses, echoing through her body, reverberating and extending the blissful sensation that was already there. She screamed loud, then covered her mouth for fear of Everett hearing her. Would he care? She didn't know, but it just felt odd knowing he might walk in on her being fucked by magically moving inanimate objects, and with Horatio traipsing around in the background, preparing their meal. In fact, she'd rather Everett walked in on Horatio fucking her than him seeing this. That would be easier to explain.

The rolling pin didn't really care about any of that. Danya tried to touch her clit again, dared an attempt, and managed a second of it before spasming uncontrollably. Then another. Oh gods. More. Touching, softly, convulsing, thrashing, squirming, touching, wriggling, forever, constant, insatiable and unstoppable.

She wasn't sure when, but Horatio returned and stopped everything. Danya lay on the preparation table, drenched in sweat and oil and arousal. She opened her eyes and watched him set aside the rolling pin. Placing one of the towels in a bowl of soapy water, he washed her body, rubbing away the glimmering slickness. Once finished, he helped her off the table, assisting her while she wobbled on uneasy legs.

"Is the Mistress satisfied?" he asked with a grin.

"Mhm," she said.

"Dinner will be ready shortly. Shall I escort you to the dining hall? Would you like me to find a dress you can wear, or shall you and Master Everett eschew clothing for the evening?"

"Maybe find one and let me know?" she asked. "I'm not sure."

"As you wish."

He helped her back to the dining hall, giving her a shoulder to lean on. Her feet, if they really were feet, didn't work very well, but she managed to hobble along the lushly carpeted hall-way and back to the massive table. Horatio helped her sit, pulling out a chair and lowering her into it. He poured her a glass of water from a pitcher on the table.

"It seems that another servant has arrived," he said, gesturing towards the water. "This wasn't here before. I shall have to find out who. This shall be a boon for when I bring out the dinner platters. If you'll excuse me, I'll attend to the evening meal immediately."

Danya nodded. "Yes, of course."

Left alone and to her own devices, she looked over her shoulder and out the large bay-styled windows. Turning her chair around, she chanced to get a better view. Far off, she could see the gardens, with an overgrown hedge maze even further in the distance. A lovely tree that looked like it might be perfect with the addition of a pleasure swing hanging from its branches grew alongside the mansion, too. And nearby the tree, laying on his back, was Everett.

Danya thought to knock on the window, to catch his attention, but then she noticed something quite odd. Laying atop Everett, naked from the waist down, was a girl. Everett, of course, was naked, too, and...

Wait a moment. Danya jumped out of the chair and rushed to the window, stumbling. Was that--yes, it was. The couple had clearly just had sex, which annoyed her, but besides that the woman was her younger sister, Alena. Why was Alena here, and why was Everett fucking her? Why? Why? She didn't understand any of this.

Neither of them noticed Danya watching them. Alena curled onto Everett like a lovesick puppy, kissing his face and his cheeks and...

Danya couldn't watch anymore. Spinning away from the window, she stomped back to her chair at the table and sat in it, almost knocking it over with the force of her anger. The chair teetered, but kept its balance. Danya stared at the water Horatio had poured for her, then picked it up and took a hefty swig. And another. Why did she have water? She wanted alcohol.

Horatio returned, frowning slightly. "I couldn't find anyone else, but I'm sure they'll show themselves soon. They must have gone off to attend matters elsewhere. It's a large domicile and--is everything alright, Mistress?"

"Yes," she said through clenched teeth. "Everything's fine."

"Are you sure?"

"Yes!"

"Alright. I'll return in a moment with the first course. I do hope Master Everett arrives shortly. I'll chime the dinner bell just in case." Horatio left her to her anger.

Oh, Danya could summon him, she thought. Oh, yes, she could very well do that. Maybe she would, too? Just go to the window, bang against it, catch his attention. Yes, that's what she would do. She stomped over, ready to alert him to her knowledge of his transgression, except when she arrived at the window neither he nor her younger sister were anywhere in sight.

Had she imagined it? Had she...?

"Hello," Everett said. He walked into the dining hall as if nothing had happened.

Danya scrunched up her brow, staring at him. "Hello."

"Are good?" he asked. "You?"

Danya frowned. Hallucinations? Yes, of course. Alena wouldn't be here, couldn't be here. Why would she be? Danya ran towards him, burying her face in his chest. The fur, his warmth; it comforted her. "Oh, I missed you," she said. "You weren't here when I woke up."

"Is alright," he said, patting her hair. "It is alright."

Horatio returned pushing a cart carrying a tureen of soup and a pile of bowls. "Oh, Master Everett, good. I was just about to chime the dinner bell for you, but I see there's no need."

Strange hallucinations, Danya thought. Soup would help. She was so hungry. She was so hungry before, and then Horatio, and...

Everett only smiled at her, helping her sit, oblivious to the fact that she'd just given his butler a blowjob and let him set her up on a table to be fucked over and over again by a magical rolling pin. Perhaps she had no right to be upset over him sleeping with another woman, but--well, she wasn't about to tell him about any of what she did, either. So...

"Soup, Mistress?" Horatio asked, offering her a bowl. "It's minestrone."

TAKEN BY THE BEAST

LENA WAS IN LOVE. SHE THOUGHT she might be in love. She knew it was too soon to say, supposedly, but then what were these feelings? The fluttering in her stomach and the giddy sensation she felt whenever she looked at him.

Everett was a beast, literally. From right out of the stories, too! Rumors and tall tales, everyone said, but then here he was. Alena found him after following her sister, Danya, through the woods. Everett had taken Danya, just hefted her older sister up on his shoulder and carried her through the gates to his hidden mansion in the forest. Through quick thinking and fast action, Alena had slipped through the magical gates before they closed.

And now here she was.

She caught them, Danya and Everett, having sex on the dining room table. Peering through one of the mansion windows, wanting to find the pair so she could shyly tap on the glass and ask that they let her in, she'd instead discovered them in quite an uncomfortable position. Uncomfortable for Alena, at least, who didn't want to see her sister, naked, with another man. Everett, though, his passion and need, the way he thrust his hips and used his cock with reckless abandon...

Gods! Alena wanted him. She had wanted him, but she couldn't watch what was going on, not when it involved her sister. Instead, she'd hidden by a tree and fantasized about it happening to her. The beast, Everett, discovered her and came to make her dreams come true, though.

She loved him! She loved him so much. It was silly, childish, but no, it was none of those things. It was true and she knew he must love her, too. If not, she didn't know what she would do.

Being no stranger to men, she was a stranger to the actual act of sex, but Everett had been so caring and sweet. He went slow, listened to her, did as she asked but not too much. He knew everything; her limits, her needs, her desires.

He'd lifted her high up and pressed her against a tree, shoving his face into her wanton pussy, then lowered her onto his cock to fuck her gently, finally ending the act with a needy rutting session on the cool grass just outside his mansion's dining hall window...

And they cuddled afterwards. She lay on his chest, glowing and brilliant, wanting to kiss and caress him all over. His seed leaked out of her slit and onto his stomach and the ground, but that was one of the best parts. She felt wanted and needed, so very much desired. He hadn't just had sex with her and tossed her aside; he made love to her, careful and beautifully, came inside her like a husband to a wife, and now he was making sure she would remain safe.

Everett lifted her off his stomach and pulled her to her feet. They stood, just the two of them, in his mansion courtyard. Secretly right in front of Danya! Alena loved that idea. She liked her sister and wouldn't really want anything bad to happen to her, but apparently Danya wasn't enough for a man like Everett. Alena was, though. He wanted her, wanted to be with her, and even now he was showing how much he cared for her.

"Come," Everett said. "We go."

He took her hand. The soft, fur coat covering his entire body felt smooth and warm to the touch, and she twined her fingers with his. Everett glanced over and smiled at her and then he ran.

He was fast; too fast. Alena tried to keep up with him, running as best she could, but without shoes (or clothes for that matter) she couldn't keep pace. They sped through the neatly trimmed grass, slipping past a simple garden with trees and benches, heading to the side of the manse where Everett's household kept a more elaborate garden with every vegetable imaginable, then to a tiny guest house in the rear. Alena moved by her own two feet for half of this run, but when Everett began pulling her forward because she couldn't keep up, he soon opted for lifting her off the ground and carrying her over his shoulder instead.

Alena laughed at this. It was so fun! Playful and exciting like love should be, she thought. Everett ran with her and she watched the passing landscape drifting away behind them. Looking down, devious, she ogled his bare backside. He wasn't too hairy, at least not like a real animal. Beastly, of course, but more like a man with a short coat of fur than anything else. He looked fearsome from afar, and dreadful up close if she didn't know any better, but otherwise she rather enjoyed his appearance. Teasing him, reaching as far as she could, she slapped at his rear. A loud smack sounded in the yard when her hand hit his ass. She grinned.

In reply, Everett groped her backside. She only meant to tease him, but this was so much more! Gods, she couldn't even believe it. He ran with her, his strides perfect, while his hand squeezed one of her rear cheeks. Alena gasped, shocked, her body twisting. The beast held her tight, though, never letting her fall.

And then his hand delved deeper. He snuck it between her legs, his longer, slightly sharpened fingernails grazing along the inside of her thigh until he reached her slippery slit. Wet and ready from their previous session on the grassy ground, he toyed with the remains of their mixed climax, coating her slick folds with it. His fingers massaged her pussy lips, urgent and daring, and then he thrust a finger inside her. Alena jolted, surprised, but she loved it. She let out a moan and reached down once more to grab Everett's ass with her hands. While he pleasured her with his finger, she squeezed his butt, growing more and more frantic as her excitement rose.

But then they arrived. He stopped suddenly and put her down on the doormat in front of his guest home. She squeaked, then whimpered, and looked at him with pouty lips.

"Everett," she said, whining but not meaning to. "Will you come inside, too? I want to cuddle with you. Please?"

Everett grinned, but shook his head. "No, Danya sister, Alena. You go. Make home for you. I return..." He furrowed his brow, contemplating his options. "I come later. This is good?"

Alena's lips curled into a sly smirk. "I want you to cum now!" Her hands darted out, snatching his half-hard cock in her fingers. If only he let her, she knew she could make his stay worth it. If only, if...

Everett laughed and pried her fingers away from his shaft. "Later, Alena-sister. I go now."

Before she could complain and whine and look at him with demure, upset eyes and pout and convince him to stay with her forever, and... he left. Sprinting across the grassy field in front of the guest house, he abandoned her to her own devices.

Oh well, Alena thought. He *was* the *beast*— the one from the stories—and he did have a whole mansion to attend to. He hadn't eaten her alive, which was definitely a point in her favor, so she thought he must like her. Or, he had liked her, but now he obviously loved her. He'd left her here for the time being, like any other man leaving his lover in the mornings when he needed to go to work. That was it. Nothing more or less. He said he would return and she knew he would.

In the meantime, she decided she would explore this house of his. Tiny in comparison to the mansion, but it was still a rather good size. At least as large as the apartment she shared with Danya, their younger sister, and their father. *At least*, she thought, but from the outside she couldn't quite tell how big it really was.

Only one way to find out, right? She wrapped her dainty fingers around the brass doorknob and twisted it, then pushed the door open.

...

EVERETT LEFT ALENA AT HIS MANSION'S GUEST house. She would be safe there, he knew. She could make a home for herself and remain for as long as she wanted. He liked Alena. She was good.

She had a scent like Danya's, but different. Younger and more fragile, like a faint whiff of delicate flowers. Danya was stronger and a better mate because of that, but he liked Alena, too. They would both help him in ending the curse placed upon him and his household by the witch, Beatrix. For every time he mated with a woman who truly wanted him, more of his servants would return to life. The witch had trapped their souls in different belongings in and around his home; in the large grandfather clock in the dining hall, in the chandelier high above the table, in the pieces of the tea set he kept in a glass-doored viewing case, in everything.

After he'd mated with Danya on the dining hall table, his butler, Horatio, escaped from inside the grandfather clock. Who had he rescued after taking his pleasure from Alena's body in the mansion yard? He didn't know yet, but he looked forward to finding out.

Or, he had looked forward to it, but when he arrived in the dining hall to take his dinner with Danya, something distracted him. His nostrils flared, sniffing, trying to discern the scents assailing his senses. In his beast-cursed form he could smell everything, anything, but different. With Horatio back, his sense of smell had dulled somewhat, though. And with this other, unknown person returning, it dulled a little more.

Still, he figured it out. Danya's arousal helped him. The smells were from her at first, but when Horatio entered the dining hall, pushing a cart filled with a tureen of minestrone soup, all the pieces snapped into place.

Danya, he knew, had fucked his butler. Not exactly though, no. With her mouth. Everett smelled remnants of Horatio's seed, hidden within his pants, and the same scent came, though very diluted, from Danya's sweet breath. He sniffed hard once more to make sure he had it right. Yes, that was it.

It angered him! It did at first, but then he calmed. There were no signs of Horatio having mated with her in a true way, which was good. Danya was Everett's and he did not intend to share her. If the only thing that happened was something involving her mouth, Everett was fine with that. No more, though.

But he knew what this meant. Danya was not satisfied. Everett thought he had mated her well, and he knew that she was sated after they'd coupled atop his dining hall table, but he hadn't expected her to need his cock again so soon afterwards. He thought he could escape for a few moments and go to Alena and sate her, too, but no.

Danya needed a lot.

This, Everett thought, was good.

...

DANYA SIPPED AT THE BOWL OF MINESTRONE soup in front of her. She was still concerned and more than a bit upset at what she'd seen while glancing out of the dining hall window, but she tried to let it slip away from her mind. Was it a hallucination? The more she thought on it, the less she believed this. Somehow, some way, she knew Alena was here. Her younger sister had tempted Everett away, but Danya wouldn't allow it. She loved Alena, she really did, but she couldn't let the eighteen year old hussy take Everett from her.

But, it wasn't just Alena's fault. Everett needed to learn, too. Michael, one of the richer boys in town, had tried to act similarly towards Danya but she refused to accept that. In the woods, drunk, they fooled around, and then later he came to her father's shop when she was alone and told her they couldn't be together? Oh, but he'd fuck her again, he said, if she *wanted*. Right then and there, too, in the backroom of the store, like some item ready to be purchased and wrapped. Except Michael didn't want to take her home; he just wanted to window shop.

Danya gritted her teeth as she filled her spoon with soup. Why would anyone treat her that way? She enjoyed sex and she knew it was a bargaining chip sometimes. She had used it in the past in order to make sure her family stayed comfortable. Her father was forever lax on bills, and made horrible business decisions. Was it so bad if Danya needed to sleep with someone in order to make a sale on a big ticket item? It wasn't as if she wanted to do it (at least not most of the time), but elsewise she and her younger sisters would end up living on the streets. With their father, too, but that's what he deserved in a lot of ways. She loved him, and yet... he made everything so difficult.

This soup was delicious. Fresh vegetables, steamed and tossed into a hearty broth at the last minute, with perfectly cooked pasta mixed in, too. When she made soup, she couldn't worry herself over the exact textures of everything involved. She favored stews for this reason, where it mattered less, or sometimes simple soups like chicken noodle. This one, though, was exceptional. If the soup was this good, she wondered what the main meal would be like?

A spot of broth slipped from her mouth and down her lips, trailing a liquid path to her chin, and then dropping onto her bare breasts. After their rough coupling on the dining hall table, neither Danya nor Everett had bothered putting clothes back on. Horatio, the butler, didn't seem to care, and then why should she? It was warm enough in the mansion.

Prim and proper, she picked up the napkin

from beside her soup bowl and dabbed at the soup on her chest and chin and lips. Belatedly, she noticed Everett watching her.

Seated beside her, Everett licked his lips. He had bits of soup matted into the fur-like beard that covered his entire face. Grinning, looking aggressive and predatory, he scooted his chair closer to hers and then leaned to the side. His face dipped low, aiming straight for her breasts. Sticking out his tongue, he lapped up the remnants of dribbled soup from her naked body.

It wasn't erotic, not at first. But he didn't stop. She shivered, sighing, when his tongue traced from the center of her chest and up to her collarbone, then back down to the tops of one of her breasts. He tickled his tongue lower, teasing, lower still, until he barely brushed past her (now) stiff nipple. Suddenly he stopped, moved his head away from her chest, laughing.

"You eat, Danya," he said. "Eat, good."

She picked up her spoon again and placed it into her bowl of soup. Everett resumed his previous position, circling her nipple with his tongue. The spoon dropped from her hand and fell into the bowl, the silver handle clattering against white porcelain.

His rough tongue raked against her sensitive skin, leaving a lingering trail of saliva in its wake. Danya arched her back and parted her lips, letting out a silent cry. But, again, Everett stopped.

"Eat," he said.

Eat, yes, that was all well and good and-- fuck! He was on her again, his tongue, his lips. Wherever he went, sliding his tongue across the skin of her breasts, he left a cool, wet line. She shivered, half from the feel of his moist kisses as they cooled on her skin and half from a desire for pleasure. Her hand wavered, unsure how she should do this, and she picked up the spoon.

Watching the soup, holding the spoon carefully and moving it slowly so she didn't drop any, Danya brought it to her mouth. As soon as the spoon slipped past her lips, Everett popped her nipple into his mouth and rolled it with his tongue. Danya gasped, harsh, almost spitting out her soup, but she managed to control herself. When she swallowed, letting the warm, delicious food slither down her throat, Everett toyed with her nipple once again.

She went in for another spoonful of soup, a little faster this time. Then another, and one more, and...

Everett practically devoured her breasts. As she ate the first course, he lapped at her chest. His tongue flicked her nipple up and down and to the sides, and when he satisfied himself with the one on that breast he moved on to the next. Danya wriggled, her ass sliding across the velvet seat cushion of the dining hall chair, unable to control herself while he tormented her. She managed to keep the soup in the spoon for the most part until some devilish idea took her.

Nearly finished, almost done with the soup, she brought one more spoonful to her mouth. But, at the last moment, she spilled it down her chest and towards Everett's waiting lips. He saw her out of the corner of his eye, must have known it wasn't an accident, and yet he remained there, lips tightly latched around her right nipple. When the soup dribbled towards his lips, a bit of it slipping onto his cheek, Danya sprang into action.

She took his face in her hands and pulled him up to her. His slightly sharpened teeth scratched across her skin as she lifted him away, but she didn't even care. Moving to meet him, she pressed her mouth against his cheek by his lips, sucking at the soup on his fur-covered face, and then kissed him hard. On the cheek, the side of his lips, towards the center, until her tongue snaked out and met with his inside his mouth.

She wanted him--needed him--so very badly. The memories of seeing him with her sister slipped out of her mind, replaced by a thrashing desire within her. She pulled at him, wanting him to come closer somehow, but she already had all of his face and there was no way he could move any closer with his lips. Instead, swiftly, Everett slid forward, kicked away his chair, scooped her out of hers, and then took her place. She sat in his bare lap, facing him, kissing him, her tongue wrestling hard with his.

His erection throbbed between them. When

he'd placed her in his lap, he pulled her forward sharply, not giving her any time to object to the rough treatment. Now, pulsing and twitching and ready to take her, his cock wasn't in the right spot to do it. She frowned, looking down, wanting to fix this mistake, but Everett pulled her closer still and put his hands on her face, twisting her chin up so that she looked him right in the eyes.

She rubbed against him, whimpering. Eyes half-lidded, wanting so badly to be taken by this beast, but the only thing she could manage was to grind her crotch against the side of his shaft. His thick erection pressed against her stomach and her clit and her lower lips. She squirmed and moved so that she had him just right, his shaft parting her pussy lips and pressing alongside her slit, and then she bounced on his thighs in some heavily erotic dance.

All thoughts of soup left her mind, replaced by hunger for a different sort of meal.

Everett bent her backwards so that the middle of her back pressed against the silken tablecloth and the edge of the table. She leaned away further, arching her back until her head touched the top of the table. Riding him, grinding against him, she sat like that, content. Everett squashed her breasts in his hands, groping and squeezing them. The tips of his nails pressed hard into her flesh, but she was too caught up in gaining her pleasure to notice.

Someone coughed behind them. "Excuse

me, Master and Mistress?"

Danya's eyes snapped open and she stared at the intruder. Horatio stood there with another cart of food, this time carrying a honey-glazed ham on a large platter. Everett looked over his shoulder, spied the ham, and nodded.

"Yes, food. Danya eat," he said.

Horatio coughed again, clearing his throat. "As you wish."

The ham looked delicious, no doubt, but Danya wasn't in the mood to eat right now. She wanted something else, something more, and she tried to ride Everett's beast like she'd been doing, but he grabbed onto her hips and kept her rooted in place on his lap. She frowned and pressed harder, hoping to overcome him. Whether his curse gave him strength or he was strong to begin with, it didn't matter; she had no hopes of fighting against him.

Horatio cut slivers of ham, slicing cleanly around the bone and delivering the pieces onto the plate nearest his Master and Danya. One, then another, three, and a fourth, all slathered with thick, sweet glaze. "I shall bring the rest shortly," he said once he finished.

And, he left. The worst part about this was Everett removing Danya from his lap and standing at the side of the table.

She eyed the ham a moment longer, then scrambled to get to her knees and take care of Everett's throbbing erection. With her mouth?

With her hands? She didn't even care, just as long as she riled him up enough so that he took her body right then and there. But, he stopped her before she started.

Putting his hands under her arms, he picked her up off the ground and spun her around. He pressed her against the table, towards the plate, so that her face was nearly on the food. She shrieked, caught off guard, and dug her fingers into the tablecloth. The silken cloth bunched up in her hands.

"Danya eat," Everett said. "Eat, good."

Before she could protest and tell him exactly what was on her mind, which was quite unladylike and improper, he pressed his huge cock against her slit. She--yes, yes!--she wanted this, exactly this, and her mind drew a blank on every word she'd thought to say. Everett slid his cock up and down her folds, letting her arousal glaze his erection much like the sweet honey on the ham, and then he thrust himself inside her.

Her body bucked against the sudden intrusion. Biting her lower lip and slamming her fist onto the table, she refrained from crying out like some cheap whore. But, oh, she wanted to. She wanted to so very badly.

Everett pushed into her, rough and forceful, but so tantalizingly slow, too. Slower, further, as far as he could, until his balls slapped lightly against her arousal-engorged clit. Then he stayed there, not moving, not fucking her, not doing anything... she couldn't stand it.

"Eat," he said.

Dammit! Danya knew what she needed to do, but how could he expect this from her? She snatched the fork and knife from the napkin and stabbed one of the pieces of ham on the plate. Delirious with desire, angry at the fact he wouldn't just ruthlessly couple with her and be done with it, she sliced through the meat. Angry, but careful not to stab herself with her fork, she thrust the morsel into her mouth and chewed.

Everett watched her, and as soon as she started eating, he pulled out of her slightly. When she dragged the serrated edge of the knife across the ham again and pushed another bit of meat into her mouth, Everett slammed his cock into her once more.

This time he didn't stop.

Her body rocked against him and the table, caught between the two. He kicked at her legs and spread them apart so he had a better vantage point for shoving his cock into her. When next she went to stab at the ham and rip it into shreds with the knife, Everett put one foot onto the chair and positioned himself so that the head of his cock drove into her at a new angle. He entered her to the hilt, his thick, throbbing shaft grazing against a new, more pleasurable point inside her. She closed her eyes, wanting to scream aloud, but incoherent thoughts refused to put action to her desires.

When he pulled out of her and she opened

her eyes, she noticed she'd stabbed the table instead of the meat. The prongs of her fork poked through the fabric of the tablecloth and dug into the wood of the tabletop.

The beast thrust into her, crushing her body against the table. Her breasts mashed against the plate and onto the ham, becoming covered in glaze and juice. She wrenched the fork loose and managed to stab it into a part of the ham before Everett pounded into her again. And then she cut halfway through the meat. Then fully. Slammed the food into her mouth right before he slammed into her again, and...

No food. No more. Danya grabbed the edge of the plate while Everett fucked her from behind. She flung the annoying thing at the wall, meal and all, and it shattered into a million little pieces. Unperturbed, Everett didn't stop. He fucked her; wild and reckless, thorough and complete.

She shrieked, pushing back against him, wanting more, more. His fur-covered body scratched against her ass and the backs of her thighs, goading her on. Everett grabbed her hips and pulled her back onto his cock at the same time as he thrust into her, slamming her hard against his muscled thighs and crotch.

And then he picked her up, all while continuing to thrust into her, and tossed her on the carpeted floor. Shocked at him handling her like this, and so easily at that, she opened her eyes wide and her mouth wider. Landing on her back on the ground--thud!--not hurt but having the breath knocked out of her, she stared up at Everett. He grabbed her thighs, pulled her across the carpet until she was close enough for him to skewer with his cock, and then took his pleasure from her once more.

This was too much--so animalistic and aggressive!--and she couldn't control herself anymore. Her orgasm built up, higher and higher, and she closed her eyes, concentrating. Every inch of him, entering her, the veins of his cock sending shivers through her body. His fur-covered hands and nails holding onto her thighs, easily able to pierce through her skin if he got carried away, but he knew how to keep that part of himself under control. The rest of him knew no such restraint, though. His thick, muscled thighs flexed, thrusting his lower body forward, fucking, mating with, claiming her as his own. Her pussy clenched and groaned, squeezing against his cock as if desiring and begging for him to unleash his seed inside her.

She climaxed hard. Forgetting to breathe, gasping for breath, she grabbed his sides and latched onto his back with her fingers. Catching his fur, pulling at it, she opened her mouth wide and forgot everything entirely. Everett never ceased, always continued, on and on, coupling with her relentlessly.

It felt so magnificent and pure. Strange, that, with some monstrous, beast-cursed man riding atop her, thrusting into her, but her orgasm didn't care. It loved it, loved his cock, and desperately wanted more. Her pussy squeezed his shaft, hoping to drain him of his cum, but Everett had more stamina than that.

Her orgasm peaked, then tapered down, still wondrously delightful, but past its prime. She clutched onto him, squirming, digging into his flesh with her nails and needing more and more. As if intent on giving it to her, Everett leaned forward and drove his nose into her chest.

The honey glaze, the juice from the ham; he licked it all up. His need for her was voracious, and this was a part of that. His tongue roamed across her breasts, roughly cleaning her, drinking up her sweat and the mess from the food, delighting in it. Across her breasts, through the valley between them, alongside her nipples, and to the sides towards her underarms. Everything, all of it, all while he grinded and thrust into her.

Danya squeaked and simpered. Her orgasm returned, flaring up and pushing to the fore; not yet complete, but desperately needing to become whole. Everett thrust harder, once, twice, and a final time. Then he took her hard, claimed her for his own, finishing his sexual hunt by emptying his sticky seed inside his submissive prey.

She moved her hips to meet his final thrust, writhing against his body. He glazed her inner depths, thick and sweet. His cream filled her to the brim as he finalized their mating. Swift tremors of climax clenched and clutched against his cock, her body becoming a needy, desirous animal just like him. She rode him, pleasured him, took her pleasure from him, and knew nothing else.

When he finished releasing his seed inside her, he drooped down and to her side. His cock popped out of her with a shlick as he rolled away. Exhausted beyond belief, Danya wanted to simply lay there, but an urge overcame her.

Her body shook, trembling from the aftermath of their wild mating session. Lifting herself up with one shaky arm, she moved atop Everett and slid down his body towards his waist. She found his cock, still quivering and hard and covered in her arousal and his cum. Taking it in her hands, she licked around it with her tongue, tasting the mixture of their juices. He was sweet, so sweet, and she wanted more and more of him. Greedy and delirious, she licked his cock clean while tasting, then swallowing, as much of their syrupy mix as she could.

Everett collapsed, spent, laying on the carpet and letting her do what she wished.

In time, fatigue set in, and Danya squirmed up alongside him. She nestled into the pit of his arm, and, cuddled against him, dozing into a light sleep.

When Horatio returned with the next cart of food, he saw them on the floor and chuckled quietly. "I'll leave this on the table, Master Everett.

I'm certain you and the mistress will be hungry once you're both lively again."

"Yes," Everett said. "Good."

...

BEATRIX KNEW SOMETHING WAS HAPPENING. She could feel it in her bones, throughout her body, a shivering in her flesh making the fine hair on her arms stand on end. And, as well, something should happen, too. This year was the year that the century rose would bloom once more.

Magical, of course, and one of her specialties. It took a hundred years of nurturing to raise one of the roses to its full capacity, and then after that it would blossom forever with minimal care. Only once a century, though. But with a rose like this that was all she needed.

She could grow more if she liked, but the effort involved was a pain. What stopped most people was the amount of time the initial blossoming took. How could anyone know how long they would live? Most people never saw a hundred years of their lives pass them by, and so they couldn't very well grow a century rose on their own.

This led witches to stealing someone else's rose. Bribery, blackmail, coercion, and much, much more; abundant in the world of magicks and witchcraft, and all because of this one, single rose. Not every witch wanted one, but then the ones who didn't weren't worth the effort of caring about, either. As of now, Beatrix was the only witch she knew of who had attained the elusive flower.

She hadn't stolen it, either. No bribery, blackmail, coercion, or anything of the sort. She apprenticed with an elder witch before this and when her mentor was gasping, dying on her deathbed, the elder woman bequeathed her nearly finished rose to her pupil. Beatrix accepted it, more than grateful for this opportunity, and then her teacher died. With that, with the rose blossoming a few years later after being tended to for a century beforehand, Beatrix made her very first wish.

A common one, typical, but she wanted to live forever. The rose accepted, though it had a few drawbacks. Minor, nothing she couldn't handle, but she would need to deal with them for the rest of her life. And, now? Well, she was going to live for a very long time.

The rose blossomed more after that, and each century she gained the benefits of a new wish. More understanding, gaining knowledge, becoming better. Everything was good, except for last century's wish. Perhaps age should have made her wiser, but she'd been so irate, so full of wrath and anger, desiring absolute vengeance, that she did what she did without fully thinking it through.

The man deserved it, though. Everett thought he could seduce her? Whisper sweet words into her ear and lay her into bed, and then toss her on the streets like some common harlot after they slept together? Oh, no.

Except soon his curse would wear out. Or, it had the possibility of doing so. She had no doubts that a man like him might beat back her magic, but then again he might not. It hardly mattered to her what he did or didn't do, but she needed to get the rose back. This time, and all the next times, she wouldn't be so hasty with the magic it granted her.

Stepping into her house after a day of picking herbs, she swooped straight towards her looking glass. Staring into it, seeing her own lovely reflection, she admired herself for a moment. Bright, lustrous lips, red as sweet apples, with deep, mesmerizing brown eyes like an innocent doe. Blonde, of course, and gorgeous to boot. She'd assured her good looks with a wish from the rose long ago, and they never disappointed her. Enough of that, though.

Tapping on the mirror, reciting a brief incantation, the reflective surface of the looking glass swirled with trapped mist. The mist parted slowly, revealing the mansion's guest house. She kept the rose there when she left, because it seemed like the proper place. Everett fucked her in the rose's new home long ago, in the bedroom at the top of the stairs to the right. And, yes, there it was, floating calmly in a crystal display case.

Hovering over the rose, staring at it, Beatrix saw a girl she didn't recognize. Of course, she found herself barely recognizing most people, what with being hundreds of years old, but she thought she might find some family resemblance in the girl. Not at all, though, nothing. The girl stared at the rose as if in awe.

Where were her clothes? Not that it mattered much, but Beatrix didn't want her tampering with the rose and a naked girl inspired much more caution in her than one wearing clothing.

Everett, she thought. He must have seduced her. Despite the beastly appearance she set on him, the girl found him attractive in some way. Beatrix didn't blame her. She hadn't exactly made a point of making him unattractive so much as she wanted him to look like an animal. A wild, ragged wolf wearing men's clothing, in a manner of speaking. Not quite that, but the analogy suited her perceptions.

Ah, well, Beatrix would kill the girl. She needed to. The rose was too precious, and with this girl watching it like it was some trifling bauble or curious trinket, there was nothing else to do save to end her life and keep her from gaining the rose for herself. Beatrix had nothing against her or anything, but this was the way the world worked.

Except! Hm. Perhaps? She shifted her senses towards the rose, curious. Something about the girl, so naïve looking, innocent, sparked Beatrix's interest. She felt the rose's feelings and thoughts settle into her body as if they were her own. The rose couldn't smell, not exactly, but it could sense things in a different way. Beatrix filtered these sensations and translated them into more human-like concepts.

Ah ha! Yes! Oh, ho, how wonderful! Really, this was amazing.

Before coming here, the girl had definitely had sex with Everett. Nothing special about that, but the circumstances of their coupling worked in Beatrix's favor. Perhaps this girl wasn't exactly a virgin, as she walked casually while naked like she'd spent a time or two with a man, but Everett had been the one to steal her technical virginity. And--the best part of all this--she hadn't yet cleaned herself up afterwards. Not that she looked dirty. A bit worn, tired perhaps, but quite attractive and nubile. Beatrix could see why Everett chose this one.

And, Beatrix would choose her, too. A few magical cantrips, setting up her enchantments, and then she could borrow some of the girl's virgin blood and use it for her own purposes. Quite a useful reagent, that. She wondered how much she could gather, and what exactly she would use it for.

Probably, most definitely, to finish making Everett's life a living hell.

...

ALENA WANDERED THROUGH THE GUEST HOUSE, looking at each room with amazement. It was so wonderful! She loved it. She was so very glad that

Everett brought her here, since this was far better than the mansion in her mind. If she went to the mansion, she would need to share rooms with Danya. She'd be forced to see her sister wherever she went and be required to speak with her and be pleasant.

It wasn't that she minded doing these things, not quite. It was more that, after living with two sisters and her father for most of her life, she wondered how it was to live alone. To be by herself, just for a little bit. Of course, Everett didn't count in there, since he was a part of this. She was his and he was hers and she didn't think of him as a bother. Actually, Danya wasn't so much of a bother, either, but...

Alena just wanted to see how this was on her own. Maybe she would like it, and maybe she wouldn't, but she would never know until she tried. Right?

The only unfortunate part of the guest house was the dust. Everett either didn't clean often, didn't know how, or else he'd abandoned this home in favor of the mansion. Whichever, it didn't really matter. Alena knew how to clean, and so she immediately found a maid's closet and fetched a feather duster. She briefly contemplated putting on one of the maid outfits in the closet, too, but when she picked up a part of the ensemble it was frail and fell to pieces. The outfit would have looked so cute on her, though! She frowned, disappointed for a moment, but soon snapped out of it.

The front room of the house was the largest, and she dusted around the edges, then on to the den area, and finally a small dining table spot. She swept the feather duster across all of it, every nook and cranny. Clouds of dust swirled up, making her cough, and before she finished everything downstairs, she needed to escape upstairs in order to flee from the suffocating fog. This didn't usually happen, but she didn't usually clean places as completely abandoned as this one, either.

At the top of the stairs, she turned to the right and went into the first room she saw.

This one contained no dust or dirt. Strange? Yes, she thought, but there must be a reason. It was a bedroom, so perhaps that was it? Someone slept here--maybe Everett? Except, if so, why was the rest of the house so lax in cleanliness?

Alena sat on the bed, bouncing up and down on the cushions. It felt new, or at least newer, and without the wear and tear she typically associated with old furniture. The pillows looked nice, too. Jumping back, tossing herself fully onto the mattress, she lay her head on a pillow and spread her body atop the warm blankets. It felt so nice and wonderful and warm that she wanted to fall asleep right then and there. She thought she should do just that and rest a bit, then carry on, but something caught her attention from out of the corner of her eye. The closet door was cracked open by a bit and had a strange, pink glow shimmering out of it.

Alena rose from the bed and tiptoed across the wooden floor. The floorboards creaked, old and used, making her fearful. Would someone hear her? Except, what did that matter? It was Everett's house and he let her in here, so she had a right to stay. No one could tell her otherwise.

Her fingers wrapped around the edge of the door and she pulled it open slowly. The pink glow grew brighter, illuminating the closet and spreading into the bedroom. It twinkled and scattered across the walls and floor and furniture, leaving everything colored in rose hues. Even herself, her body, took on a different shade, pink and pretty.

Inside the closet--in fact, the only thing in the closet--was a vibrant, red rose. It lay in a glass display case floating in midair in the center of the room. No roots, no soil; nothing but the rose flower and its stem. Was it fake? She looked at it, wondering how it could have survived for so long inside a glass case like that. If the answer existed, she couldn't figure it out. Inspecting it closely, putting her nose up against the glass, she saw it had no thorns. And, also, now that she thought of it, how did the glass float like that?

Alena tapped on the case lightly. Nothing happened. She pushed the glass, thinking to move it, but it remained staunchly in place. When she tried to lift it from the bottom, it seemed as heavy as a boulder. No amount of pushing, prodding, or poking was able to move this case and this rose.

On the side, slightly hidden, was a keyhole, though. If she had the key, no doubt she could open the case and access the rose. Except she didn't have a key, now did she? In the bedroom, in the drawers maybe? The bedside tables or hidden within the bureau? She had no real reason to want the rose, but the fact that it was there made it a challenge in need of conquering.

A test, of sorts. No matter how little it made sense, she became determined to get at her new obsession. Unbeknownst to Alena, the rose was also growing obsessed with her.

She checked the bedside tables first. The top drawer had nothing in it but cobwebs, and the middle was the same. To get to the bottom drawer she needed to kneel, so she lowered herself quickly to check it. When she pulled on the handle, the drawer refused to budge. She pulled harder, but nothing, and finally she braced her feet against the base of the table and pulled with all her might while pushing with her legs. When she was about to give up, feeling no leeway whatsoever, the drawer slapped open with a pop, sending her flying backwards onto the floor.

Tumbling, crashing against the wood floorboards, Alena crumpled into a pile. She cursed and rubbed at her rear, which had hit against the wall. Besides that she was fine, but argh! How annoying.

In a pile on the floor, staring towards the

now open bottom drawer of the bedside table, she didn't realize it at first when something tapped her on the shoulder. When it tapped her once more, curious comprehension flitted through her mind. And then--wait, who was tapping her on the shoulder?

Startled and scared, Alena skittered across the floor and away from whomever was behind her. Though when she looked back, she saw no one. Peeking around the room, checking for signs of anyone at all, she still saw nothing.

Only when she squinted, confused and glancing towards the open closet door, did she see what had touched her.

The rose! Or, not quite the rose, per se, but an extension of it. The rose itself remained in its case, but sneaking through the keyhole was a vine. The vine grew from the stem, snaking out of its glass entrapment, then it widened to the size of her pinky finger and floated in the air where she'd just been sitting. The plant tendril faced her as if it was watching her. As she stared at it, it stared back, and then it drifted closer.

The viney finger stretched, growing, until it hovered in front of her face. Alena watched it, amused and curious. So this was what the rose did? Strange, that, but she liked it. It was interesting and she enjoyed interesting things.

The viney finger poked her in the nose, making Alena laugh. "Stop that," she said.

The vine backed away, startled.

"Oh! Oh no, I'm sorry. I didn't mean to upset you," she said.

Did it understand? This was magic, she thought, and so maybe it understood magically? What kind of magic, though? Was it alright to stay here, speaking with the rose, or should she figure out a way to escape? She thought--and she had no real reason to think this--that she should stay. If it meant to harm her, it would have done so already. And, what was the worst that could happen? The vine was so small that she could push it away and leave the bedroom if need be.

While she thought of these things, the tip of the vine shook. It shook and wriggled, then sprouted, blossoming into a miniature version of the rose flower in the case. Alena laughed, giddy and delighted.

"Oh! That's pretty. Is that for me?" she asked.

The flower gave a curt nod, as if agreeing with her, and then slithered forward. Alena moved close to it, elated with the fresh scented rose. She'd never known magic before except from the stories, and here in one day she'd seen two magical things! First, Everett, the beast, who was every bit as wonderful as she imagined, and now this lively rose.

There was something odd about the scent from the flower, though. Alena couldn't put her finger on it, but she thought it was a bit off. It did smell like a rose, but different, too. She moved her nose closer, hoping to figure it out, and at that very same moment the rose moved closer to her, too. Before she knew it, she had her nose pressed into the center of the blossom. A spray of pollen fluttered out of the flower, then onto and into her nose.

Alena sneezed. The force of it blew the flower back and the vine retreated to safety a few feet away. Alena sneezed again, and then a third time. Bracing herself against the wall, befuddled, she wiped her nose of pollen.

The vine floated in the air nearby, watching her.

The flower was so pretty, she thought. So delicate and nice and sexy. She wanted to kiss it and fondle it and touch it with her fingers, and...

What? Strange thoughts. A flower was a flower, and not much more than that. Beautiful, yes, but...

Her body warmed up, feeling hot and heavy. Her bare breasts felt tight and when she looked down she saw her nipples pointed straight out in front of her, stiff and aroused. For no reason she could think of, she let out a moan. It felt so wonderful to do, so she moaned again. With her back against the wall, she scooted her rear forward and spread her legs. Feet on the floor, knees in the air, Alena reached one hand between her thighs and teased along her slit.

Why, she wondered, was she so wet? Was it the flower, the pollen? Her fingers came away from her folds, slick and slippery. She smeared her arousal across her taut stomach and up towards her breasts. Without realizing it, she tweaked one of her nipples between her fingers and moaned again.

The flower on the end of the vine dropped to the floor. Still beautiful and lovely, but no longer attached. Alena crawled to fetch it so she could look at it. So cute and pretty and she wanted to keep it for herself.

The vine separated at the tip as she approached. First once, making two new vines, then each of those split, too. They split once more, leaving eight slender vines dangling from the end of the initial one. The plant grew and stretched until each of the eight vines was multiple feet long, hovering and twitching in the air as if they had a mind of their own.

Alena finished crawling towards the flower on the floor. Leaning forward, picking it up with her mouth, she started to crawl back towards the safety of her corner by the wall. The vine had other ideas for her, though.

One of the new plant extensions wrapped around her ankle and dragged her towards the other seven. Not harshly, and actually quite gently, but it pulled her across the floor nonetheless. Alena fell onto her back. Forced to look up, she saw what was going on. Except, what exactly *was* going on? This was so strange and new to her that she didn't know what to think of it.

The flower in her mouth fell away, landing

on the floor once more, but now with the vine taking up her thoughts, she forgot all about it.

Another viney tendril wrapped around her other leg by her thigh. The first tendril squirmed up her leg, too, and when both of them were in place by the core of her body, they pulled gently at her legs. Alena clenched her thighs shut, confused, but the vines insisted. Gentle tugs, light pulls, until Alena relented and allowed them to spread her legs.

Another vine moved in now. She stared at it, enrapt. It moved slow like a butterfly floating in a light breeze. Bobbing up and down, shifting closer to her, the third vine slipped towards her stomach and landed on her skin near the top of her pubis.

This rose, the vines, she thought they felt nice. They were soft to the touch, like ropes of silk, with fuzz on them like peaches. The vine on her stomach slithered towards her belly button and poked inside. It poked again, then again, kept poking. Ticklish, Alena laughed.

"What are you doing?" she asked it. "You can't get in my belly button."

The vine snapped up and looked at her. She watched it, thinking maybe it was confused. After a moment of critical thinking, the vine continued its travels up her stomach. It slinked and slithered, stretching and growing to allow it more exploration. Sliding further still, it slipped between her cleavage and onwards towards her neck. Not quite that far, though. When it reached the tops of her breasts, it curved around one of them, then more, until it wrapped around the entirety of her feminine mound.

Alena let out a lusty cry. Oh! She wanted this plant so badly. Was that wrong? She thought yes, maybe, except it didn't seem it at all. The plant, the rose, it seemed so erotic to her all of a sudden. Some illicit attraction, something she'd always known she desired, but never really understood it. But now? Oh, yes, she knew it. This plant could please her.

The vine wrapping around her breast squeezed, tightening her sensitive flesh. It stretched further again until the tip of the tendril poked up. It grabbed more, harder now, and the end of the vine slinked along the rest of the exposed skin of her chest. Alena squirmed against the sensation, but the vines holding her thighs kept her mostly in place.

Another vine wiggled forward, slow and steady. While the vine on her breast squeezed, it suddenly discovered her nipple as well, and the tip of the tendril grazed across her hardened nub. Shocked at the sudden sensation of pleasure shivering through her, Alena arched her back. The new vine used this distraction to slide beneath her and up past her shoulders, then on towards her nape. Alena moaned aloud, excited, and before she knew it the newest vine had wrapped itself around her neck.

The plant squeezed lightly, pressing against her throat. Alena froze, suddenly scared for her life, thinking she'd mistaken the plant's enthusiasm. It meant to kill her? Use her body as fertilizer?

A fifth vine snapped out, going straight for her free breast. It wrapped around her swelling bosom quickly, squeezing harder and tighter than the other. Then, not to be left out, it grew a longer tendril at the end and flicked her nipple hard. The other vine, the first to circle one of her breasts, continued to touch lightly against that nipple, no matter how hard and fast this new vine flicked.

This was all so strange and new to Alena and she wasn't sure how she should feel about it. On the one hand, it was wonderful. The vines felt so soft, even the one around her neck, and she liked them touching her. Especially the ones by her breasts. She didn't know why they were doing this, but she thought she'd very much like it if they continued. And what of the other vines? Did they want to touch her, too?

The sixth did indeed, and it slipped around her waist. The vines around her thighs, waist, and neck worked in unison and hefted her up and off the ground. They were strong, far stronger than she would have believed. They lifted her easily, holding her in the air and spinning her this way and that, slowly. As she rotated, floating, she spotted the last two vines.

They looked different now. Still mostly the

same, but thicker. They grew larger as she watched them, thickening to the width of her thumb after being closer to the size of her pinky finger, and then bigger still. One stopped once it grew to be about the size of her wrist, while the other halted at closer to half that width.

"Why are you growing?" she asked the vines. Neither answered, but she felt like asking them anyways.

The thicker vine moved towards the bottom of her foot, brushing against her sole. It tickled her and she laughed. Body jiggling from the laughter, squirming, still getting used to being held aloft, she wriggled in midair ineffectively. The vines held her tight and didn't let her fall, but with the strangeness of it she thought she might topple to the ground at any moment anyways.

The thick vine snaked up her calf and towards her thigh. It stopped when it met with the vine wrapped around the center of one thigh, but only for a second before it pressed onward. Up and up, closer to her stomach, and she thought maybe it would move towards the vine wrapped around her waist, but it didn't. She watched it, enthralled, curious as to what it would do.

It thickened more, but only at the tip. A strange substance oozed out of the top like thick nectar.

"Oh," Alena said, sad. "Are you hurt?"

If the vine understood, it did nothing to confirm her concern. Instead, the next thing she knew, it was pressing its tip against her pussy lips. The vine prodded and poked at her slit until it figured things out, and then, using its slick secretion and the wetness of her own arousal, it eased inside of her. Alena gasped and bucked her hips. Or she tried to move her hips, but the vine around her waist pulled her back.

The thick plant tendril delved deeper, exploring her darkest and most intimate depths. It bunched up, poking against her inner walls, then turned to push in further. Alena, shocked but delighted, clenched around the intrusion. It seemed that the more she squeezed against it, the thicker the vine became, too. Where at first it moved in a bumbling, confused fashion, it eventually grew so wide around that it only had one way to go; which was straight and further into her.

Once it tapped against her cervix, it had exhausted its options for advance, though.

The vine didn't like this. It retreated a few inches, then thrust forward again, meeting the same resistance. Alena squeaked, squeezing against the alarmed intruder.

"You can't go in any further!" she said. The plant disagreed.

It set into a rhythm, shifting back and winding up, then pushing in again. It couldn't move anywhere past her deepest depths, but it tried very hard. Soft, slick, with a hint of fuzz surrounding it, the vine pushed into her as far as it could go, over and over again.

It felt so strange and exciting. She didn't have experience with any cock besides Everett's, but she doubted any man would feel like this. The rose vine continued secreting viscous, sticky goop, lubricating her insides as it constantly struggled to push past her cervix. The slippery mess grew so abundant that it started leaking from her pussy and dripping down her floating body towards her ass, where it then dropped to the floor. She heard the sounds of it--drip, drip, drip like lusty rain--while the tendril assailed her body.

And the more she clenched, the thicker it grew! She tried to stop herself, not knowing how much bigger it would get, but the feeling of it inside her excited her too much. She un-intentionally squeezed and the vine shivered and thickened in response until she took control of her arousal long enough to loosen her muscles. Not for too long, though, and the inevitable clench returned, and the vine reacted once more.

When she tried to say something and explain to the plant that, yes, it could do this, but it shouldn't expect whatever it was expecting, the vine around her throat surprised her. It clapsed lightly, cutting off her breath so she couldn't speak for a second. That vine stretched, too, much like the ones currently flicking--one softly and one harsh--against her nipples. It grew, thickened, then pressed against her nose. It tried to enter her nostril, but it was too large around for that. Like a tracking dog sniffing out a hunter's prey, the vine tapped along her face towards her lips, then her mouth.

She tried to clamp her lips shut, but the vine hugged her throat harder. Not too hard, but enough that it made it so difficult to breathe that she eventually opened her mouth and gasped for air. The creeping tendril loosened then, which was something of a victory, except as it did this its tip thrust between her lips and into her mouth. It slipped in, secreting goo like the vine crammed into her core, and slithered across her tongue towards the back of her throat.

Oh! Oh no! A thought came to her. This was alright, despite it being completely unlike what she ever expected to happen when she entered this room, but it couldn't go further. Further being, in her mind, what the last vine must be for. She clenched her butt tight, intending on refusing it entrance. No, no, not there, and not ever, and...

The vines around her body wiggled and rotated her while the one between her thighs thrust into her, the ones around her breasts squeezed and flicked at her nipples, and the one in her mouth slipped closer and closer to the back of her throat. She saw the last one, poised at her rear, but it looked different now. A flower blossomed at the end of it, similar to the one that had gotten her into this mess. Pure white, completely void of color like an empty artist's canvas, the flower loomed below her crotch. It collected the dripping secretions from the vine thrusting into her inner depths.

At the base of the flower, one of the petals picked up a tiny hint of color. Barely anything, but it looked like it had small spots of red. She watched it when she could, but the plant flipped her around this way and that, every which way, never letting her stay in one position for too long.

She wanted to see the flower, to con-template it, but she couldn't think very well anymore. The vine between her legs slammed into her harder now, intent on trying to invade her womb, except it was growing far too thick. It stretched her whenever she squeezed against it, and by now she couldn't stop from clutching around its shaft. The arousal from the vines at her nipples and the vine shoving into her slit pushed pleasure into her body. She wanted to move and writhe and act like the sexual being she'd been when she was with Everett, but the plant didn't understand that.

She did manage to rock her hips a little, though. Not much, but just enough. The plant around her waist inched lower and lower with every movement she made, until she moved it to a spot that caused her to inhale sharply. Now, instead of it wrapping around her waist, she'd shimmied it low on her hips. The silken, fuzzy feel of it brushed against her clit, which only made her rock her center more and more.

When she inhaled, ready to let out a shriek

of pleasure, the vine in her throat wriggled in further. It pressed at the back of her throat, then stopped. She could breathe past it, but it was terribly difficult to make any sounds now. When she tried, her tongue licked against the underside of the shaft. In response, the tip of the vine shivered, secreting more ooze.

She swallowed it, tasting it. Her core clutched against the vine inside her and her hips wriggled, pressing the vine around her waist harder against her clit. The taste of the goop in her mouth drove her even further towards madness, too. She didn't know what it was, but it tasted like watery honey. Honeysuckle? Something like that, she decided. In an effort to get more, deliriously wanting it so badly, she licked at the shaft of the vine. It squirted more goo into her mouth and she swallowed it up.

The more she drank and tasted, the more aroused she became. It was so odd and awkward, but wonderful. Her body felt tingly and warm and amazing. The vine in her pussy kept stretching her, but the more syrup she drank from the one in her mouth, the more she wanted the lower one to dominate her. Further, yes, to gaping, she needed it to stretch her wide open and spill its goo into her. A continual squirt now, deep inside her body, as if it wanted to send forth its seed and pollinate her. She doubted this was possible, but it was a magical plant, so maybe? She knew, in the back of her mind, that this would probably be bad, but right at the moment she didn't care.

The plant squeezed her tight, pressed into her, shoved the thick vine into her cunt and let the slimmer one shiver and ooze into her mouth. Two more toyed with her breasts and nipples, while the ones by her thigh and neck and hips kept her shifting in perpetual slow circular motions. The flower one, whatever it was doing, must be some-where, but Alena was too far gone to care. Her body clenched and squeezed and tensed, taut, against the ministrations of the plant, driving her to the pinnacle of pleasure. She orgasmed hard, fertilizing the fecund plant with her climactic juices.

This, apparently, was what it wanted, but she didn't give it enough, not at first. It shoved into her, stretching her more, re-invigorating her orgasm immediately after she'd finished and bringing her to another. Then another, more. She felt like one huge mass of orgasm, a person made completely out of pleasure, as the plant acted with constant, calculated rhythm, forcing her to experience sensations beyond her regular com-prehension. She squirmed and bucked and writhed and licked and squeezed the rose vines, loving every moment of it.

Except, gods, could she keep this up? Could she keep going? Her body felt so tired, so physically exhausted, and she wanted to stop, but the vines wouldn't let her. They needed more from her, and her body gave it to them. How many times had she climaxed now? She lost count after four, and kept thinking four, except the last one had been four, hadn't it?

After the third four--at least the one she could remember being the third--she collapsed. Laying limp in the air, the vines holding her tight, she had no more to give this desirous flora. Fortunately that seemed to be enough for the rose, though. As she lay limp, a shivering bundle of woman pleasured to the extreme, the vines lowered her. Not to the ground like she expected, but onto the bed. They lay her head on the pillows and the ones binding her breasts released themselves and pulled back the covers. The vine between her legs writhed its way out of her and helped the other vines lay her to rest, concerting their efforts to pull the blankets up over her bare, shivering body.

They all slinked away, leaving her to sleep. She thought, for whatever reason, they looked pleased with themselves. Alena was rather pleased with them, too.

Shrinking after all the growing, the slippery vines retracted towards the display case and the original rose. She watched them leave, a faint smile on her lips. One vine vanished, absorbed back into the stem of the rose, and then another. The third, fourth, and fifth disappeared, too, then the sixth and seventh. The eighth was different, though. A vine, yes, but it was the one with the pure white flower on the end.

Except it was no longer white. The flower,

dark and rich, held a blood red color now. It stood in stark contrast to the pale, pink hues glowing from the rose in the closet. The petals of the flower shuddered, sneaking through the keyhole in the display case, and then all of a sudden the red flower vanished along with the rest of the vines. There was no trace of any magical occurrence afterwards, except for Alena's pleasure-addled self.

Maybe, she thought, it was a dream. If so, how should she wake from it? If she fell asleep in a dream, would she awake in the real world? She decided--mostly because she was now exhausted--that she'd try it. She got as far as thinking about sleeping before she passed into slumber.

...

BEATRIX LET OUT A MANIC LAUGH. HA HA! SO simple and easy. The girl enjoyed it, too, which made it all the more wonderful. She did seem nice, at least in the witch's eyes. Obviously watching someone orgasm over and over again constantly would make almost anyone look pleasing, but this girl had a certain knack to it. Not practiced or experienced, but that added to the eroticism. That girl was no hired prostitute feigning orgasm for the delight of her customers; she was the real deal. She enjoyed every moment of it.

And really, Beatrix didn't necessarily want to hurt her. In fact, she hadn't even wanted to kill her. And now maybe she wouldn't. The flower soaked up the inklings of her virgin's blood along with the sugary nectar secretions. Beatrix could use this to her advantage, exploit the ingredient in some elixir and figure out a way to give it to Everett so that he suffered through eternity. It was the least she could do for him after he'd fucked her and then tossed her aside. Honestly, why would he think it was a good idea to upset a witch?

Oh well. She had nothing against the girl. Maybe, actually, after this was finished, she would see if she wanted to apprentice as a witch. Beatrix had plenty of time to do it, so she might as well put forth the offer.

...

DANYA WAS PISSED. AT HERSELF, MOSTLY. She'd let Everett get the best of her. Again! She liked him, wanted him, and desired him so badly, but she couldn't give in so easily. She knew this, and yet she'd let him take her right in the middle of dinner. During dinner, even. And, gods, that was so amazing. She didn't regret it, not exactly, but she knew she shouldn't have done it.

He needed to know that he couldn't just sleep with her younger sister and get away with it. Or, to be more precise, he couldn't sleep with anyone besides Danya and get away with it. Either he wanted her, which he obviously did, or he didn't. If he did, then she required faithfulness from him. According to Horatio, this was Everett's tragic flaw, but Danya thought she could persuade him otherwise. She would tame this beast, teach him what he could gain from fidelity. He said he needed, and she needed too, but she needed to know that he wanted only her. He needed to want her so desperately that just the thought of her drove him insane. He should have no time in between imagining their next wild encounter to even think of another woman.

That was how Danya wanted it. She wanted Everett, but she couldn't act foolishly about this.

And, how could she teach him the consequences of sleeping around? She would do the same to him, that's how.

When she roused herself from a quick nap on the dining hall carpet, Everett was gone. Away again, with Alena? Maybe, but Danya didn't know for sure. She rose from the floor and sat at the dining hall table, picking at the roasted vegetables on a platter on the table. Horatio came out a few minutes after she woke and offered her coffee and dessert.

"I've made a delightful bread pudding and I have some hazelnut sweet cream that should mix wonderfully with the coffee," he said.

"I'd love both," she said, smiling at him. "Also, do you think you can show me to a closet with woman's clothing afterwards? I want to find something to wear. I'd like to explore the mansion, but I don't think it's proper to do it in the nude."

Horatio grinned. "Yes, of course, mistress. I shall see what I can do. I aim to please."

USED BY THE BEAST

ANYA DIPPED HER FORK INTO THE harvest pumpkin bread pudding and pulled a piece of it away. Dragging the morsel across her plate, running it through the syrupy juice lingering on the white porcelain, she let it soak in the sweetness before picking it up and dropping it into her mouth.

"Is the dessert acceptable, mistress?" Horatio asked.

"It's wonderful," Danya said. "I'm impressed with your skills in the kitchen."

"Thank you," he said. "Would you like to

know the secret?"

Danya nodded. Taking up her mug filled with hazelnut cream flavored coffee, she drank deeply. Horatio stepped forward and bowed low, whispering into her ear.

"The special ingredient," he said, "was made from the remainder of your orgasms atop the preparation table. I extracted the essence from the table and the kitchen tools."

Danya choked on the coffee, nearly spitting it out, barely managing to swallow it. Not that this helped much, oh no. She coughed, gulping down the hot liquid, sending the searing heat trailing through her throat and into her stomach. It settled there, a thick warmth, before mixing with the regular heat of her body and disappearing from her senses.

Horatio chuckled. "Is something the matter?"

Danya stared at the bread pudding, contemplative. "Well, it *is* delicious," she said.

"Indeed. I believe the Master will enjoy it. I'm sure he'll recognize the subtle flavor, at least. Shall I fetch him?"

"No need," Danya said, gritting her teeth. She pushed the dessert around the plate with her fork, toying with it.

She still couldn't believe it. Or, she knew she should have believed it, but why? Where had Alena come from? This was supposed to be for Danya, for her alone. She'd followed the Beast's note and come to the hidden mansion in the woods by herself. He'd kidnapped her and named himself as Everett and taken her atop the very dining table where she now sat, eating, but apparently that wasn't enough.

Alena, her younger sister, had intervened. Where had Alena come from, anyways? Danya still didn't know, still hadn't talked with her dearest darling sister. She had quite a few choice words for her sibling, too. Having caught her and Everett laying together, naked, on the mansion yard outside, left Danya more than a bit unnerved. At first she thought it was some odd hallucination, but, no, it couldn't be.

And Everett continued to leave her. After every time the beast-cursed man claimed Danya's body in order to defeat his curse, he left her soon after. Where did he go? The obvious answer was to Alena. He must have fucked her younger sister, too. Logical, no doubt, and it helped him alleviate his curse faster, but where did that leave Danya?

She refused to let him exploit her like that. True, she never thought she and Everett loved each other at first, but what about later? She was the one who would help him. She was the one who came at his time of need and accepted him and aided him in defeating the witch's curse and regaining his humanity. Except, no, that wasn't it at all.

Horatio explained it to her before, too. He told her about his master's proclivities towards casual dalliances. Danya wanted to deny it, she wanted to believe that years upon years of being trapped in his beastly form had changed Everett into something better, but apparently not. Still, that didn't make it alright for him to use her at his whim.

And where was he now? With Alena, no doubt. Danya intended to find them both and let them know exactly what she thought of this, too.

She nibbled on the bread pudding, thoughtful, forgetting what was in it. Horatio stood nearby to attend to her every need. She liked that, at least. No matter who Alena thought she was, the servants in the mansion accepted Danya as Everett's mistress. Or at least Horatio did. There were more she needed to account for, and she needed to do it soon.

"Did you find out about the clothes?" Danya asked.

Horatio nodded. "As a matter of fact, yes. Luck is on our side. After your most recent coupling with the Master, the mansion seamstress has returned. Her name is Taya. She's agreed to fit you for a dress."

"I see," Danya said. She stuffed a large chunk of bread pudding in her mouth and chased it down with a gulp of coffee. "Can you take me to her, Horatio?"

"It would be my absolute honor." He held out his hand to help her from her chair like a true gentleman. "Shall we?"

She took his hand and smiled. "Yes."

...

THERE WAS TROUBLE.

Everett smelled it, realized it, but it was too faint for him to fully recognize. His primal senses continued to dull every time he mated with one of the sisters. What started as a nose capable of smelling the tiniest minutiae became a still-powerful tool, but less sharp and more general; a dagger compared to a longsword. How long had he lived like this? How many years had it taken him to become accustomed to a new way of life?

Decades. Too many. He had been so lonely living in the mansion and had taken to wandering the forest in search of companionship. The deer fled from him, though. The wolves seemed his best option, except they, too, shunned his advances. They kept to their small packs and refused to accept him. And if they did, then what? He had no way to communicate with them

Now, he barely had a way to speak with Alena or Danya. He felt shoddy and lacking and unable to explain fully what he needed to tell them. There was more to this curse than even he knew, and Beatrix, the witch who cursed him in the first place, must have further plans. This was it, this year. If she wanted to spite him, to mock him for his inhumanity, she would show herself. Soon.

At least he knew the general direction of the

smell, even if he couldn't recognize the source. His guest home, where he left Alena. Was it small trouble? Was she hungry? There was food in the cellar there, packed away for the long haul. He would show her, feed her, keep her sated and safe. But then what?

Everett knew he should decide between them, choose one woman as a mate, except how? He enjoyed them both for different reasons, appreciated the nuances between the two. Not the same, no. Different.

He wanted them both as his mate. He needed it.

...

DANYA FOLLOWED HORATIO THROUGH THE wide halls of the mansion. They trekked along red carpets, past elegant wall tapestries, and up a winding spiral staircase. They moved past doors and windows and fancy displays of art on fine pedestals. She wanted to stop and sample the sights, to inspect everything that interested her, but she didn't have the time. Also, the fact that she stood naked and without a shred of anything to cover herself besides her hair gave her incentive to rectify this before sightseeing.

Later, when she had more time, she'd explore everything in Everett's mansion, but not now.

Horatio guided her through a servant's

passageway off of the main hallway, then into a wide open room. Wire dress dummies stood on wooden stands, cluttering the floor. They wore dresses and shirts and elaborate capes that flowed from their shoulders down to mere inches above the ground. One dummy wore a wedding dress with a long train trailing behind it. Bolts of cloth leaned against one wall, stacked and sorted by color and type. Tanned skins of leather lay in piles near the cloth, smelling faintly of stinging salt and bitter tannin.

A woman sat at a large sewing station, humming to herself. She spun thread on a sewing wheel with artful mastery. When Horatio walked in, she smiled and greeted him.

"Horatio, hello. Is this her? She's rather fetching," the woman said.

Horatio grinned. "Taya, meet Danya. She is the Master's new mistress. I believe she requires some clothing. Shall I leave her to you?"

Taya laughed. "It certainly looks like she needs something to wear, doesn't it? Yes, I'll handle her. Go, go, tend to your duties and I'll tend to mine."

Horatio nodded. "Here you are, mistress. Taya knows what she's doing. You're in good hands."

"Thank you," Danya said.

With that, he left her in the seamstress's care.

Taya finished up what she was doing and

stood. Danya expected someone far older, but this woman couldn't be more than a few years older than herself. Pretty, too, and probably with a lovely form, but she hid it beneath a frumpy smock. Taya's dark blond tresses lay curled beneath a cap with an assortment of needles fixed into it. Sewing needles, Danya recognized; all sorts and sizes for all different types of jobs.

Taya stepped up and took Danya's measure with a penetrative gaze. "You're tall, but not so tall. Quite a nice bust, too. Wide hips, good. Thin, but not too thin. You do eat, yes? Fairly well, I'd say, but you keep fit? Is that right?"

"I've eaten more lately," Danya said, remembering her last meal with Everett. He'd forced her to eat soup while he slavered on her breasts with his gritty tongue, then fucked her from behind while demanding she slice and eat the slab of pork on the plate in front of her. Then dessert later without him, but she hadn't had a meal that amazing in forever. Usually she cooked food for her sisters and her father, but it was more simple, easily managed fare.

"Don't go eating too much, or there's no use fitting you; you'll just outgrow it all. I'd say this is a good look for you, though. Hearty and comely. Good breeding stock, you might say. Nice child-bearing hips. I imagine Everett enjoys you." Taya winked at Danya. "Is it true what Horatio says? You're here to help revive the mansion?"

Was that it, she wondered? Was her only

purpose here to act as a partner for Everett in order to return these people to their previous lives? She wanted so much more from all of this, and it upset her to think that maybe there wasn't any.

"I don't know for certain," Danya said. "It all happened so suddenly. I'm still trying to figure it out."

"Understandable," Taya said. "Come, come here. I'll get my measuring tapes and see what sort of measurements we're working with."

Danya followed Taya through the room to the corner where the seamstress had been working at her spinning wheel before. She stood, unsure, while the slightly older woman fetched through a teensy desk in search of the tapes.

"This has happened before," Taya said. "Just so you know. You aren't the first."

"What do you mean?" Danya asked.

"Do you love him, is that it? Everett, I mean. The Master is a kind man for the most part, but he's callous and disregarding, too. I doubt he understands what he does most of the time. A pity, really." Taya swooped over with a measuring tape in hand and tapped on Danya's arms. "Up you go. Yes, just like that."

Danya raised her arms in the air and held her chin up high. No matter what this woman said, she wanted to believe something else. Whatever everyone thought of Everett, it couldn't be true. Or, it couldn't be true now, right? Except she'd seen him with Alena. Their sweat-soaked bodies pressing together, clearly in the aftermath of some erotic encounter.

"He's bedded women more than once in the past. Common women from the village nearby, which I imagine is where you're from? The upper class, too. He adores holding parties and passing out wine freely, then whispering lovely words into lovely ears. That's how we came to this mess, I'm told." The seamstress began taking measurements.

"There's stories," Danya said. "I don't know how truthful they are. I haven't asked Everett."

"Truthful enough, I'd say. There was a witch, Beatrix. A nice, kind woman, for the most part. She helped us plenty around here. Lives in the woods awhile away, or she did. She magicked up the mansion, the whole lot of it. There's magic everywhere. Still works, too."

That was odd, Danya thought. Why would the witch leave the magic if she cursed Everett. "Maybe she can't remove it," she said.

"Oh, Beatrix can do what she likes. She's crafty enough to be one of the only witches with a century rose, so I don't doubt she can remove some simple magic from a mansion if she wants. But, no, look."

Pinching the flimsy tape between her fingers and holding it in place around Danya's hips, Taya lifted her other hand in the air and waved it about. Her fingers danced as if they were playing at the piano. Danya watched her, curious.

And then, all of a sudden, one of the dress

dummies came to life. The tripod stand it stood on curled its legs and started walking towards the seamstress, while its shoulders bobbed up and down like one would see with a regular person's gait. It maneuvered towards the woman with the measuring tape and stopped right in front of her.

"You see?" Taya asked. "There's more, too. But why would Beatrix leave us with magic if she despised us so much? Oh, no, I doubt she hates anyone but Everett. Perhaps she hates you now, too, since you're working at undoing her spell. I don't envy you for that, though who knows what she's thinking? She's immortal, you know?"

Danya gulped. Simple magic, obvious magic, but the implications of what Taya said weighed heavily on her, the girl who was merely a merchant's daughter the day before. "What did he do to her?" she asked. "The stories don't say. They only mention a curse."

"What did he do to her? What do you think he did? What he does to every pretty face. Oh, Beatrix adored Everett. Being a witch doesn't make you any less foolish in regards to love. Everett saw her as another conquest, and quite a lofty one. Who wouldn't? It's not every day you have a chance to fuck an immortal witch, now is it? And so he did what he does. He slept with her and then pissed her off. The morning after, while she wandered down from his bedroom to get breakfast, he informed her that he needed her out of his mansion within the hour because he had guests

141

arriving."

"Oh," Danya said.

The seamstress was still taking her measure, but the tape was getting tighter and tighter. Taya pulled it tighter still, squeezing the measuring tool against Danya's bare skin. She wrapped the tape around Danya's backside and back to her front, constricting it around her model's bare clit. Danya gasped and squirmed and Taya slapped at her breasts to keep her from moving, but that only made her fidget more.

"Stand still!" Taya said. "Fucked by our master and you can't take a little tension on the old love button there? My gods."

"Please," Danya said. "I don't like this."

"You know what? I don't like it, either. Cursed because of some folly done by the man who runs the house, while I didn't do nothing to help him? Then brought back, just like that. I was trapped in a dress dummy for all those years, sitting there, waiting. Do you think Beatrix is just going to be done with it and forgive us all? Doubtful."

'I don't see--" Danya started to say, but Taya wrapped the tape around her back and pressed it hard against her breasts, squeezing them together. The tape lay directly on her nipples, which quickly jutted out in reluctant arousal at the abuse. "I don't see what that has to do with me," she finished saying, her voice shaky.

"The way I see it, maybe I'll just stop it all

now. If Beatrix comes and finds out I've helped keep Everett cursed, that's sure to count for something, right? I'll just hold you here and hide you and stop Everett from fucking your plump cunt. A good idea, don't you think?"

"You can't," Danya said, trying to sound braver than she felt. "I'll stop you. I'll fight."

"See, that's the thing, isn't it?" Taya grinned. "The dress dummies aren't the only magic here. I actually asked Beatrix to do something special for me. Usually it's for children, but the occasional uppity lady or fidgety gentleman needed it, too. Let's see if I..."

Danya jerked free from the measuring tape and bolted for the door. She'd wanted an outfit to keep herself off of open display to Everett, but now it seemed silly. This woman, Taya, was far too volatile. Danya should have realized it, shouldn't have preemptively judged based on her experiences with Horatio, except it was too late for regrets. No, all she needed to do was leave here and run somewhere else. She could find clothes in a spare bedroom, perhaps. Most were tattered and moth-eaten in all likelihood, but there must be something.

That was her plan, but it didn't work quite like she expected. She barely made it a few steps away before her feet refused to move. They clung to the ground, thick and heavy and feeling wooden. Then the rest of her body followed suit. Her knees locked into place, keeping her standing upright, and her hips froze so she couldn't bend forward or back. Her arms dropped limply to her sides, clattering against her body, while her neck swiveled and leaned slightly forward. Danya blinked, unmoving, unsure what had happened.

"The idea is," Taya said, "that if people move too much, I can't get good measurements. Sometimes you just tell a person to stop moving, but it don't always work. Beatrix listened to my argument and offered a solution. Basically, if someone moves too much, I threaten to turn them into a mannequin. And if they keep moving, then I do it."

Danya forced her gaze lower. Yes, it was true. Her body felt wooden and her limbs looked like they belonged on a ball-jointed doll. She could blink though, and a quick test proved she could open her mouth, too.

"You can't do this," Danya said. "I'll scream."

"Who are you going to scream to? Who knows where Everett is. Horatio's off doing errands, too. Oh, I'm sure he'll come back, but why shouldn't I just gag you, stuff you under some cloth, and be done with it?"

Danya didn't know. She didn't understand this. What had she ever done to this woman. What had she...

"I'm only playing with you," Taya said, laughing. She wandered in front of Danya and caressed her hand along the girl's new doll-like body. Danya felt it, through magic or whatnot, but she couldn't move to do anything about it. "I'm not going to hurt you. I really won't. Do you think I went too far? It's hard, you know? Trapped for a hundred years without companionship. I wasn't ever very companionable in the first place, but..."

"Please, will you let me go?" Danya asked.

"Horatio told me about what happened in the kitchen," Taya said.

Danya paused, then nervously said, "What of it?"

"I've always wanted to. To do that. Not to me, but to someone. I deal with stuffy women barging into my studio and demanding things of me, and do you know how tempted I was to just change them into mannequins with the magic Beatrix left here? Not just that, oh no. And I'll let you go, yes, but..."

"But what?"

"I don't care what you say, you can't change my mind. I don't care what Everett does, either. If he kills me, oh well. But I'm going to do it, and you can enjoy it or not. *I'll* enjoy it either way."

Taya lifted Danya up and dragged her towards a waist-high stack of leather. She tossed her atop it and moved her so she was laying on her back. All Danya could do was watch her body doing as this woman wanted. Taya shifted Danya's legs into a lewd, spread display, then moved her wooden hands so they lay atop her breasts.

"Are you comfortable?" Taya asked.

"Does it matter?" Danya asked.

"Well, I suppose not. Shall I explain this to you then, this fantasy of mine?" Taya offered her a toothy grin. "In my mind, it goes like this. A haughty young lady comes in demanding things of me, and I get so sick of her that I change her into a mannequin. And she screams, oh yes, except I don't care. What I do next is, I magic a few of the dress dummies, much like Horatio enchanted the rolling pin, and they fuck her while she's trapped there with no way of escape."

"And you, of course, are her," Taya continued. "I have your measurements and the spell should wear off around the time I'm done fixing up a dress for you. I'll give it to you once I'm finished, but until then..."

Taya waved her hand in the air and conjured forth a wooden dress dummy. The inanimate thing swaggered forward, almost as if it knew what she wanted of it and found great joy in its prospects. Taya held the measuring tape in front of it, near where its crotch would be if it had one, and measured a few inches, then more.

"Eight?" she said, looking to Danya.

Danya watched as the dress dummy grew a wooden penis to match the end of Taya's measurement: eight inches. She gulped and ogled the thing.

"Thicker, shall we? And longer, I think. Do you suppose ten is alright? Hm."

With expert measuring skills, Taya shifted the measurements of the magical cock. It still looked wooden like a rolling pin, but it was thick now and longer.

"This isn't any fun, though," Taya said. She squeezed the cock in her hand and it changed. No longer as wooden, more pliant. The wooden cock bounced in front of the dress dummy like a real man's cock. The head at the end of the shaft shifted into a resemblance of the real thing, too.

Danya gulped and stared at it, unsure what to make of this. Taya slapped a hand on Danya's crotch and toyed with her folds.

"You're wet, dear," Taya said, laughing. "You don't have anything to be afraid of. I've done this myself, actually. It's strange and different. Exciting. You can't move, but your body will still mostly work like it's used to. That includes here--" The seamstress slipped a finger inside Danya and wiggled it around, then popped it out. "--and here." The woman grabbed Danya's breasts and squeezed them.

While her body felt heavy and ungainly it only added to her sensation. When the woman touched her breasts, they wobbled back and forth, slow, like chilled bowls of jelly. And, oh hell, when she'd slipped a finger inside of her...

It felt like Danya's entire body was tense, already in the throes of climax. Tight, constricted muscles squeezing against the cock pounding inside her, milking it for all it was worth, except there was no cock. Just a finger, nothing more, and Danya wasn't even climaxing, but the feeling and sensation...

"Just lay back and enjoy yourself and give me a show. I'll make you a dress that's more than worth it," Taya said. And with that she left, returning to her spinning wheel and studio corner.

Danya followed her with her eyes, watching the woman stroll towards her work station and sit down on a stool. Taya picked up a spool of thread and pulled a needle from her cap, then set herself to the task at hand.

And the dress dummy approached. Its painfully throbbing cock, harder than any cock had a right to be, bobbed up and down in front of it as it wobbled towards Danya's body.

"Oh, before I forget."

Taya was speaking, Danya realized, but all she could think about was the head of the cock now parting her labia and pushing into her.

A bolt of cloth unraveled itself at Danya's side. It fluttered out and up, catching her eye, then a pair of scissors soared forth and snipped off pieces of the fabric. Two wide pieces, each with four snips on the end. The cloth fell to the ground, and the scissors along with them, but not for long. Quivering on the floor, snaking their way towards the dress dummy, the pieces of cloth climbed up the wooden stand and to the shoulders of the dummy, then attached themselves to the sides like arms. The snips formed fingers, which immediately grabbed Danya's wooden thighs and held them hard.

Everything felt so strong and powerful. The tight feeling in her thighs contrasted heavily with the soft touch of the dummy's cloth hands. It held her firmly and pulled her towards it while wobbling forward at the same time, hastening the process of impaling her on its cock. Danya bit her lip, finding it difficult to think properly.

The pulsing wooden cock trudged through the tunnel of her slit, forcing its way towards her deepest depths. While it looked and felt more like a real cock now, it was smooth to the touch like the polished dining hall tabletop downstairs. Changed into the shape of a doll, Danya couldn't move, couldn't squeeze against the intrusion inside her no matter how hard she wished for it. Except *everything* felt like a tight squeeze to her now, beyond her control, consistent and thrumming.

As the dress dummy thrust into her, Danya moaned out her lust. Off to the side, sewing her dress, Taya watched, rapt. Danya felt a quick burst of shame and embarrassment, but not for long. The dummy pounded the rest of the way inside of her, filling her to the brim, and then slowly pulled out.

Danya glanced down her body, looked at how she was being used as a fuck toy for this animated dummy. Curious, enchanted, she noticed her clit popping up, hard, like a marble. It looked so much more prominent and aroused than she could ever remember it having looked before. Taya must have noticed where Danya's gaze was, because no sooner than she thought it, one of the fabric arms shifted from Danya's thigh to her clit.

The fluttering fingers flicked at her pleasure pearl like heavy feathers. The smooth cock continued to pull out of her arousal-slick folds. The tensing, the pressure; it was too much.

Danya wanted to grab her breasts and scream and moan. She wanted to wrap her legs around the dummy's rear and pull it back inside of her and hold it there, to feel its cock dwelling deep between her thighs and inside her. She wanted it to cram itself hard into her, to grind the head of its polished cock against her smooth inner walls and use her.

But she couldn't. Her hands lay on her breasts, but she couldn't move them. She felt them there, thick, holding her wobbling bosom, but there was no way for her to tweak her prominent nipples or put on a show for the dummy. Not that the thing needed it, but the idea excited her. She couldn't wrap her legs around the back of it, couldn't pull it further into her. She couldn't do much of anything.

She could scream, though.

She let out a loud moan as the thing pressed inside of her again. She wanted to moan more, again, except she forgot how. Her thoughts lay scattered in her mind, blocky and incoherent, distracted by the sensation of her tensing pussy squeezing the dummy's cock without her permission.

She felt an orgasm building within her

through the squeezing, but it couldn't shove itself to the fore. Pursing her lips, Danya tried to excite herself further with thoughts and ideas. She remembered Everett shoving her breasts into the table and taking her from behind, rutting with her in the dining hall like she was a bitch in heat when she first entered his mansion. The wood of the table had been smooth like her breasts.

The dress dummy rolled her hard clit between its cloth fingers, joining in and helping coax her orgasm into existence. It didn't help, though. She felt it, clenching contractions wanting to spasm throughout her body, but the wood and magic refused to let them through. Her body clenched harder of its own accord, smashing pleasure against her resistant flesh over and over, but still nothing.

The dress dummy picked up speed. While Danya desperately tried to achieve climax, the dummy slammed its cock into her over and over again. Each time it jostled her atop the pile of leather. Her immovable arms jumped and clattered against her chest, inadvertently rubbing against her nipples and making her pleasure all the more excruciating. The dummy's fingers slapped against her clit, waving back and forth like the merchant's shop sign outside her father's store on a windy day.

One orgasm or five, maybe more, they built up inside of her and demanded she let them loose to wreak havoc upon her body, to transform her into a twitching mess of sex and flesh, but she couldn't. Her mind desired it, desired it so badly, but her body refused to accept this.

She didn't know how long this went on. Hours, perhaps, or maybe just minutes. Each agonizingly pleasurable thrust from the dress dummy sent her into inane utterances and lusty moans. She closed her eyes and focused, concentrating deeply and attempting to overcome this block on her climax, but none of that worked.

Danya heard the clicking sound of shoes walking across the floor towards her. She opened her eyes and tried to understand what was going on, but it was so very very difficult. Taya held the most beautiful dress Danya had ever seen, showing it off to its new owner.

"What do you think?" Taya asked.

Danya stared at it, mesmerized. In her pleasure heightened state, the dress looked extravagant and beautiful. It was as if the ecstasy in her body brought the dress to a higher state of beauty just by existing in close proximity to the sex-crazed person before it.

The cloth was pale blue. The dress dummy's cock shoved all the way inside of her. Danya tried to reach a hand out for the dress and one of her fingers wiggled while remaining on her breasts.

The dress had one shoulder strap, keeping the other shoulder bare. With glittering gems sewn into the decolletage. Danya squeezed hard against the cock inside of her, or she meant to. Everything clenched all the time now, but she felt a faint tremor, her body listening to her command and clutching against the wooden shaft ever so lightly.

An enhanced bust, corset sewn tight so as to show off Danya's chest. Tight around the waist, too, then flaring out wider by the hips and leaving a silken trail flowing down to the floor.

Her body cracked. That was the only way she could think to describe it. She heard a strange sound like shattering ice on a winter lake, and then more, further, until her body exploded into shards of pleasure.

Regaining her previous form, fully human and able to control herself at will, she descended into the pits of passion. Her orgasm--or five, or more--split through her body, no longer walled off and separated from her like before. The dress dummy pounded into her over and over, needy, while Danya trembled in climax after climax upon its wooden rod.

She raked her nails across her chest and squeezed her breasts roughly, reveling in the *life* in them. No longer wooden, now hers again, and she wanted to feel every part of them. Confused, curious, one hand jerked towards her clit and rubbed furiously. Too hard, possibly, except, no, not hard enough. Restrained and unable to touch herself before made everything so sensitive and wonderful now. She clenched and climaxed upon the dummy's cock and forced more and more pleasure through her bewildered body.

She only stopped when she grew too tired to continue. Taya stood there, smiling, clearly enjoying the show. The wooden dummy had lost its liveliness some time ago, though Danya didn't know when. It stood before her, slumped, with its cock half sheathed inside of her, coated in her creamy juices.

Danya felt wooden again now, but for a different reason. She could move, but she was too tired to move. She lay against the leather, silent.

"I can see why Everett likes you," Taya said. "He is somewhat of a beast, it's true, but he's not a bad man by any means. I wonder if Beatrix will find it in herself to forgive him. I wonder if he's changed. Or if she has."

Danya was too tired to theorize. She lay there, staring at the ceiling, following the cracks and lines with her eyes.

"You can lay there for a bit," Taya said, draping the dress across Danya's chest. "I have a lot of other work to do, though. Rest up, then I'll help you dress and you're on your own."

...

BEATRIX WADED THROUGH THE CLUTTER covering the floor of her house. She had the miniature rose now, with the virgin's blood extracted from that girl in Everett's guest home. What a show that was, too. She'd quite enjoyed watching the girl writhe in the air while held up and spun around by the vines sprouting from her century rose's stem. Trapped, helpless, and utterly at the whim of the plant. Though the girl did enjoy it, so there was that.

Anyways, Beatrix had business to attend to. What should she do with her new reagent? Blood had many uses, and virgin's blood even more. She thought she should find a spell that specifically required deflowering a virgin, though perhaps she should settle for a more powerful version of a common blood spell?

Possession, maybe? She could take control of the girl's body and use it to do her bidding. Perhaps simplicity was the easiest thing here. Grab a knife, seduce Everett into bed, then stab him in the heart. The idea held a certain amount of allure to the witch, but it seemed too common and trite.

Shrinking Everett to nothing? Perhaps if she transformed him so his body was the size of her pinky finger she could keep him trapped in a bird cage forever more. Or swallow him whole and deal with him like that? But, ugh, while she knew some witches wouldn't hesitate to do this to their enemies, Beatrix felt squeamish even thinking it.

Truth be told, she didn't even want Everett dead. She wanted him to suffer forever in torment and rue the day he'd shunned her, but she didn't want him to die. Or, she wanted all this until he apologized. Was that too much to ask? She wouldn't ask, because he should know and should do it unbidden, but the principle of it remained.

A curse? Another curse? Control. Pain. Minor magic, so she doubted she would do it, but perhaps it might amuse her to block him from ever maintaining an erection again.

Or perhaps a summons. Yes, summoning a creature from the dark beyond sounded like just what she wanted. Nothing too terrible, but a ghast to follow Everett around and torment him. This, she thought, seemed like her best choice, because if for some reason he managed to undo her beast-curse, he'd still need to deal with the supernatural being haunting his mansion. A spectral creature to instill fear in those inhabiting the place. And perhaps they'd flee, running off to somewhere else, leaving Everett alone and afraid.

Beatrix thumbed through the books on her bookshelf and snapped up one dedicated to summoning magic. She scanned through it, hoping to find something delightfully fearful.

And... yes! A vampir. Children of the Dead, many called them. They weren't any such thing, though. Malicious creatures that roamed the night in shadowed forms and caused mischief by levitating objects around and clattering them through a house. They had screams like exploding firecrackers and loved rich opulence. Of course they did require blood to sustain themselves, but mostly they preferred easy prey like squirrels and rabbits. Some ancient vampir preyed on humans, but she wouldn't summon one of those.

Everything was in order, and with that

decided, Beatrix set to work. She snatched up a piece of chalk and drew a summoning circle on her cluttered floor, then plucked the various required reagents off her shelves. And, for the final step, she skittered towards her looking glass and fetched the sanguinary rose filled with the girl's virgin blood.

Beatrix scattered the ingredients into a bowl and then tossed the rose in, too. Casting a quick cantrip, she formed a circle of flames in the air that descended upon the bowl. The reagents caught fire, bursting into a rush of glaring orange flames, and that was that; a vampir should rise from the summoning circle to do her bidding.

Except it didn't end up working that way.

A giant, blindfolded man shimmered into existence in the center of the circle. The folded black wings on his back unfurled and slapped against the shelves on Beatrix's walls, sending the contents crashing to the ground. The man wore no shirt or shoes or gloves of any kind. The only thing covering his ruddy body was a tattered piece of cloth wrapped around his waist like a skirt or a kilt.

He stood and surveyed his surroundings. This wasn't what Beatrix wanted, but as long as he wasn't some powerful demon or other celestial being, the summoning circle should keep him trapped until she commanded something of him.

"I don't require your assistance," Beatrix said, keeping her voice firm. "Begone."

"No mortal commands Pinem'e," he said, his voice booming through her house and nearly shattering her windows. "I see your thoughts, though, witch. They interest me. In repayment for bringing me into your world I shall destroy the man you hate, but that is all. You may be next. I have yet to decide what I shall do here."

Pinem'e crouched low, tensing his legs, then he bounded off the floor and thrashed his wings, flying straight through her roof.

Beatrix stared at the empty summoning circle, blinking. Pinem'e? No, it couldn't be. That wasn't the spell she'd cast, not at all. Why would she ever want to summon one of the fallen angels? *How*, even?

Belatedly, she realized her folly. She hadn't just used virgin's blood in her spell; she'd used a part of the century rose, too. She should have extracted the blood first, but in her rush for vengeance, it seemed unnecessary. And most times it would have been, it should have been.

What had she done? Well, Everett was most assuredly dead now, no matter what else she did. Not her preferred choice of action, but she couldn't very well stop it. The only thing left to do was fetch the rose from the guest house bedroom and then leave. No matter what Pinem'e wanted, he shouldn't be able to remain outside his celestial plane for long with the paltry amount of reagents she'd used for the spell. A day or so, but no more.

Beatrix sauntered over to her looking glass, planning on simply pulling the rose through it. She'd set this up ages ago so that anything within the rose's glass box could be grabbed through the mirror, or she might place something in the box from her side of the mirror, too. Among other things, it acted as a good precaution for thievery.

She tapped the glass and watched the mist inside ripple away like a drop of water splashing into a puddle. It cleared, and there sat the box, but...

Where was the rose?

Stuck inside the keyhole of the box lay the key. Hadn't she destroyed that? Except, no, apparently not, and the twisted key had opened the box. Who stole her rose, though?

That girl! Argh! Beatrix screamed out her frustration.

She couldn't lose that rose. Most of the time she wouldn't worry, except a fallen angel was one of the few things that could completely obliterate her century rose. And why would he *not* do that? Or he might use it to sustain himself in this world for a longer time, too. The small portion of the rose she'd given him in the summoning might keep him alive for a day, but if he consumed the entire thing who knew how much time he had? Years, decades, more?

Beatrix sprinted out her front door and whistled for her horse. After a few seconds, the beast cantered towards her, whinnying and stamping the ground by her feet.

"Yes, well, we need to go," she said.

The horse gave her a curt bow of his head.

...

ALENA AWOKE TO THE BLARING LIGHT OF imminent sunset. Hues of orange and gold streamed through the shaded window and assailed her vision, forcing her to acknowledge them. She blinked away her sleep and opened her eyes, looking around.

She felt physically exhausted and sore all throughout her body, but a good kind of sore. It was almost as if she'd spent the day running errands and helping her father in the shop, moving heavy items and doing hard work. Exercise fatigue was good fatigue, and she didn't mind it too much.

Also, she felt mentally invigorated. Where was she? What was this? She wanted to know and experience it and learn everything she could. She'd always loved schooling, but she hated how they told her to learn specific things. She was sure she'd get to those things eventually on her own, but she wanted to discover more about what intrigued her first.

And her current situation definitely intrigued her.

Oh, yes. She remembered it all in vivid detail. The plant, the sex, the sweet taste of its nectar gushing into her mouth and its seed seeping between her feminine folds. Was that a dream, though? Odd, and not something she'd usually do, but she slipped a hand beneath the bed covers and ran a finger across her glistening slit intending on tasting her arousal. Faintly sticky, like watered honey, she relished in the joy of teasing her body before moving onwards with her plan. Her fingers toyed with her clit and she stuck one, then another, inside of her. Hard, fast, again, gathering her lustrous arousal, then using it to coat her labia and spread the smoothness across her clit. She gasped, oversensitive and sore.

An orgasm overtook her like an unexpected flash of heat lightning in the middle of an otherwise clear summer day. Alena fingered herself furiously, surprised at the sudden gush of pleasure but wanting to prolong it as much as she could. She shifted uncontrollably on the bed, leaving a line of slick arousal on the sheets wherever she moved. Her orgasm flared up higher, reaching the pinnacle of delight, and she arched her back and stared mindlessly at the ceiling. Her body bent to her will so wonderfully and she wanted more, but she couldn't continue.

She crashed onto the bed with a thud, falling limp, twitching. The blankets scraped lightly across her clit, making her fidget at the pure sensation of it. She lay there, confounded, but completely and utterly amused.

How had that happened? So fast and quick and strange? She didn't know, but she wanted to find out.

And then she remembered what she'd intended to do in the first place. Slow, cautious, feeling like she should rub herself to climax once more but denying her urges, she made a smooth trail with her fingertip from the bottom of her slit to right below the hood of her clit. Pulling her finger away before she changed her mind, she brought her hand to her mouth and licked at her own juices.

She tasted sweet and ripe like fresh-picked peaches. Alena stuck her entire finger in her mouth and sucked away her arousal. Swirling her tongue to taste all of it, not leaving so much as a drop, she lay languishing on the bed while enjoying her honeyed arousal.

She'd never done that before, and she'd never really thought to do it, either. It seemed odd, but interesting.

It was the plant, she decided. The flower from before with its pleasing odor and shimmery pollen. When it puffed the powder into her nose, it must have done something to her. An aphrodisiac of sorts, some kind of pheromones. Not only did they make her irresistibly aroused, but the sensation lingered in her body and made her feel devious. She wanted to smear her slickness all over her slit and her stomach and coat her breasts in sticky arousal, then plump up her bosom in her hands and lean down and lick the liquid off her own chest, teasing her nipples with her tongue if she could.

She wanted to abandon herself to pleasure. She wanted to stay in this bed, forever, and masturbate herself into a state of transcendental bliss. She wouldn't just feel pleasure, she would become pleasure, and drift away to another place entire. By her own magic, by the magic of her body, by...

Alena snapped herself back to reality. No, that couldn't happen. But, yes, it must be the plant. When it filled her with its viscous nectar, it must have instilled something in her. Fermenting, alcoholic and intoxicating, the honey-sweet sap had brewed inside of her and made her mind think strange thoughts.

This might have upset her, except Alena had a brilliant idea. The rose, yes, she needed it. She needed the petals and she needed its juice. Her own sweet arousal was enough for a little while, but she needed more, and for quite a distinct purpose. Ignoring her desires, tossing the covers up and throwing herself off the bed, she scrambled towards the bedside table. The bottom drawer remained agape from before the plant had taken use of her body, from when she'd struggled to open it.

She peeked inside, hoping beyond hope to find what she thought was there. Lowering her head to inspect it closer, looking in every corner, she knew it must be here. The key that opened the floating glass container holding the rose had to be here somewhere.

Except it wasn't.

Alena cursed, enraged, and felt pangs of ecstasy shooting through her body. Apparently it didn't matter what kind of excitement she felt, just as long as it was exciting. She spasmed on her knees, barely managing to refrain from shoving a hand between her thighs and stroking her clit. When the spasms subsided, Alena yanked at the drawer, frustrated. She pulled the entire thing out and threw it against the wall, glaring at it as the front of the drawer broke off and clattered to the floor beside the rest of it.

Then, there, right in front of her, hidden on the floor beneath the bottom shelf, was the key. Alena snatched it up quickly and hopped to her feet. She wanted to shove the key inside her slit and between her folds and feel the cool metal against her hungry inner walls, but, no.

No, no, no, no.

She hobbled towards the glass display case in the closet. Lowering the key to the keyhole, she managed to slip it in and turn it; though, oh, it was so dreadfully difficult. Her hands shook, her whole body shook, and she wanted nothing more than to return to the bed.

She needed the rose, though.

With this rose, and the allure of her glistening folds, she could lure Everett into eternally loving her. If he so much as licked at her slick slit, she knew he'd become drunk off the sweet taste of it. More, more, he would need more, and Alena would gladly give it to him. Anywhere, everywhere, with his head stuffed between her thighs and his mouth latched onto her pussy.

And she'd make a tea from the petals of the rose and offer it to him. Once he drank, he, too, would know what she felt. An uncontrollable urge for pleasure, except why must they feel it alone? They needn't, she thought. With both of them aroused, they should serve each other well.

She imagined herself laying back while Everett stared at her, drool dripping down his lips and onto her stomach and her chest. His thick, protruding cock ready to slam into her folds, and in her mind he wasted no time doing it. And while the rose affected him, his masculine cream would taste like the sickly sweet seed from the plant's vines.

A constant cycle, over and over. When he stuffed her with his cum, she'd scoop it out and eat her fill. Then, while they readied themselves once more, Everett could gorge on the slick arousal gathering between her legs. They would feed one another in constant amorous pleasure until one or the other eventually ran out, and then, laying in a mess wherever they were, they would both feel eternal, constant, and endless love for one another.

Alena *would* win. She plucked the rose from the now open glass case and tucked it behind her ear. With this rose, no matter what her older sister, Danya, tried, Alena would overcome it and become Everett's sole mate.

They would marry, and have children, and fuck, and enjoy fine dining and fancy ballroom dances. Carnal pleasure followed by culinary delight, and oh so much more.

Stealing away from the room, her feet pounding on the floor, Alena ran to find Everett. Whatever happened, she needed to get to him before Danya did.

...

PINEM'E FLEW HIGH ABOVE THE TREES. HE SAW the mansion amidst the woods and descended towards it. Landing upon a balcony ledge, the fallen angel ripped open the flimsy French doors and stepped inside.

Pinem'e surveyed his surroundings: a library.

...

DANYA STOOD IN FRONT OF A BODY LENGTH mirror. The dress Taya made for her was beautiful. Or, technically it was already sewn, but the alterations the seamstress did to fit it to Danya's form made it look wonderful on her. She spun around, letting the skirt of the dress swish outwards.

Taya nodded her approval. "Very good. It's a lovely dress. Not that you needed one. I'm sure Everett wouldn't mind if you walked around naked, so long as you submit to his cock whenever he likes. And speaking of..."

Everett stood in the doorway. He looked

less beastly now, though only slightly. Shorter hair covered his body, and he had a smoother jaw than before. If he shaved himself completely and put on a suit, she thought he might look like any other rugged gentleman.

"Danya, you," he said. "Beauty." He admired her for a moment, then said, "I need speak with." Everett cleared his throat and furrowed his brow. "I need to speak with you."

Danya stared at him, unsure. Should she go to him? Accept him? Except why? She needed him to realize that no matter what he used to do, she wouldn't be that for him. She refused to acknowledge herself as some common breed mare for him to stuff his cock into and cum inside, no matter how much she enjoyed it.

"I don't care what you two do," Taya said, "but close the door on your way out. I have a lot of clothing to finish. Everything is ruined, and I have to mend it before the others come back alive. Shoo, shoo." The seamstress pushed Danya lightly, urging her towards the door.

Danya went. The pale blue dress hung low to the floor, hiding the fact that she wore no shoes. Taya was a seamstress, not a cobbler, so she couldn't help her there. Danya walked past the exact dress dummy she'd just spent carnal moments with, glancing at it out of the corner of her eye, and then moved onwards towards Everett.

He held out a hand for her and she took it, letting him escort her out of the seamstress's studio.

Closing the door behind them, he walked her a short distance across the hallway towards one of the large mansion windows.

"Danya," he said, ogling her. His hands grabbed her hips and he dug his fingers into the fabric of her dress. Not enough to rip it, but it worried her. He pulled lightly, lifting, bringing the skirt of the dress up to just below her knees. "Beautiful."

"Everett, stop," she said. Placing a hand on his chest, she pushed him away. Not hard--though it wasn't as if she could push this beast of a man away if he didn't want to move, anyways--but enough to presumably get her point across. "No more. I know what you're doing and I refuse. I enjoy it. I enjoy you. But I won't let you use me. I know Alena is here and I know what you've been doing with her."

Everett smirked at her, some beastly and wicked grin. She held her hand against his chest trying to halt him, but he ignored her and pressed forward.

She couldn't hold him off. To keep distance between them, she backed away. Everett refused to let her go. A predator stalking his prey, he backed her against the wall outside of Taya's room and leered down at her.

"Danya jealous," he said. "I come to speak about Danya sister, Alena. I understand. Danya jealous."

"What do you mean?" she asked.

It was difficult to figure out what he meant, especially when he kept pushing against her. Her arm bent, hand still pressed against his chest. His hot, heavy breath fumed from his mouth like thick smoke, fogging up her vision. He grabbed her hips once more, but this time when she pushed against him he didn't let go.

"No," she said. "Everett, stop. You're using me and I understand it's to break your curse, but I won't. You need to understand that..."

He pulled at the dress of her skirt, bunching it up in his fingers. Inch by inch, up and up, he pulled her skirt away and revealed her calves, then her knees, the middle of her thigh, and further still. He lifted it up, despite her protests, until he had a clear view of her bare crotch. Everett stared at her slit, sniffing her arousal.

Why was she aroused? Dammit! She needed this to stop, needed him to understand, but her body refused to accept her wishes. His fingers tightened on the dress, nails pressing hard against the fabric. Everett wore nothing in terms of clothes, had no way to hide himself.

His cock slowly rose, twitching and growing and stretching. She stared downwards, ashamed, watching his erection rise.

"Please," she said, begging him. Begging him for what? "Don't rip the dress. Please don't. We need to talk."

Everett nodded. "I understand. We talk."

He understood! Yes, this was what she

needed. He must understand, of course, but she understood how it might be difficult for him, too. Alone in the woods for all these years, seeking a mate, and it must have been a very hard life.

Thinking of how to explain the situation to him, Danya didn't realize exactly what he was up to. Everett's hands cupped her ass and lifted her off the floor. He stepped forward, pressing her back against the wall, holding her aloft. His cock bounced up, tapping against her slick folds. He lowered her onto his erection, quick and deliberately. Only when he was halfway into her did she realize what he was doing.

"No!" she said. "Everett, stop this. I mean it!"

"We talk," he said, continuing to lower her onto him. More, three quarters of the way, then entirely. "You tell me. We talk."

Danya shivered, too distracted by the pleasure to keep up her willful refusal of him. He pushed forward more, closing the gap between their bodies. The soft fur on his stomach tickled against her clit and caused her eyes to clamp shut as she bit her lower lip.

He lifted her off of him, then back down. "What is it?" he asked. "What is problem for Danya?"

"You don't--fuck!" She couldn't concentrate.

"I fuck," he said, laughing. "We fuck now."

He lifted her up and down his cock, using her for his needs. Baring his teeth in some display of dominance, he growled at her slightly. Her eyes shot open and she stared at him, wide-eyed.

"I want more," she said. "I don't just want..."

"More?" Everett asked. He held onto her ass firmly and thrust up into her while pulling her down onto his cock. Faster and harder now. More.

Danya trembled. The corset of her dress held her breasts in place under normal circumstances, but as it was they jumped and bounced, smacking against each other with every thrust from his cock. Everett's balls slapped against her ass, and his fur-covered abdomen caressed her clit. She grabbed his shoulders and let out a string of verbal nonsense.

"What Danya mean?" he asked, never stopping.

"Fucking! Dammit!" This was too much; he was too much. She felt herself losing control, felt her body betraying her further. "I don't want to be your toy!" she screamed before the idea eluded her. "I want to be something more!"

Her body thrashed against his and her legs kicked at his sides, frustrated and enraged. Everett ogled her, leering at her bouncing breasts. Leaning down and forward he licked her chin and her neck, scraping his rough tongue against her smooth flesh. He thrust into her harder now, barely lifting her up and off his cock before pulling her back onto it.

"I want more, too," he said. "I like Danya."

She came. Not as hard as before since she

still felt weak from the abuse Taya put her through with the dress dummy, but still satisfyingly strong. Her inner walls clenched against Everett's rigid cock, begging him for his seed. She'd said words earlier, begged him to stop, but now her body was begging for him to fill her?

She didn't really want him to stop, but she wanted him to understand. She wanted him to...

Everett let out a shattering roar. The sound echoed through the empty hallways and down the stairs, then back up and returning to them in a hollow approximation of its initial glory. Back and forth, rattling Danya's senses, reverberating through her ears. Losing herself to the harsh overload of physical and aural sensation, she bit her lip so hard that it started to bleed.

Just a little bit, a small drop of blood. Everett sniffed it, sensed it. He stared at her and kissed her, reveling in the tangy taste of iron and life essence on her lips. She kissed him back, desired him. She had never felt like he really wanted her before, loved her, but now she did. Was it her blood feeding his primal lust, or was there more to it, too?

She didn't care, refused to worry. Everett slammed hard into her and held himself there. Danya squirmed against his cock. She felt the telltale signs of his impending climax as his shaft surged with strength and flexed against her body's convulsions. His seed streamed up and into her, filling her, then spilling out slowly.

Her dress. It was ruined. She'd worn it for less than ten minutes and now it was ruined.

Except, no, Everett held her skirt in his hands, bunched up still and above her waist. Yes, he held her ass in his hands, too, pulling her hard against his cock as he emptied his creamy load inside her, but he was mindful of her dress.

As he held her there, both of them coming down from their climax, Danya saw something out of the corner of her eye. A ruddy skinned figure walked down the hallway towards them. He wore a dark feathered cape, a blindfold, tattered cloth pants and nothing else. His unseeing gaze met her own, harsh and unforgiving.

"Everett," she said, barely able to speak. Chill sweat brought goosebumps to her flesh and she shivered in his arms. "Everett, look. Someone's there."

The beast-cursed man turned to where she was looking and saw the ominous figure approaching. That wasn't a cape, she realized. He had wings. The dark-winged man took one more step before he disappeared entirely.

Or, he didn't disappear, but he *ran*. The demonic figure dashed down the hallway faster than Danya could follow with her eyes. She saw him when he arrived, though. He stood right behind Everett, arms upraised, hands grasped into a double fist, ready to smash her beast-cursed lover's head.

Danya screamed. Everett's cock tensed

inside of her, pressing against her, but then it was gone. He threw her to the side, away from him, then bolted in the other direction. The winged man's pounding assault slammed into the wall, sending forth shattered bits of wood and plaster.

"Danya!" Everett hollered. "Run!"

Danya ran. Her fingers pulled at the carpet beneath her and she scrambled on hands and knees away from the Demon and the Beast. Finally managing to catch her footing, barely capable of standing, she staggered away from the pair. Briefly glancing over her shoulder, she saw Everett grappling with the monster. The winged abomination reared back his head, then crashed forward, butting his forehead against Everett's. Blood seeped from a splitting wound in her lover's brow.

Danya screamed, cried, grabbed at the wall. Her feet felt non-existent as she stumbled and ran away. She fell, picked herself up, and hobbled towards the staircase. Downstairs, to Horatio, to...

Who was going to help her? Who was going to help Everett? What was going on? What was happening?

Danya panicked and reached for the banister of the staircase, but she reached too far. With unsure footing and her wits burnt and gone, she flipped up and over the railing. Down, she tumbled, through the center of the spiral staircase. One leg smacked against the polished wood of the banister as she fell, sending her spinning.

This was it. All of it. Everything. Finished in the blink of an eye. Just like that.

...

ALENA HEARD THE SCREAM AS SHE RAN through the outer mansion grounds in search of Everett. He must be inside, maybe with Danya. That ruined her plans, but she could adjust them.

And another scream. Her plans could wait. Who was that screaming? It sounded like her sister, except why? What was going on?

Ignoring the seething arousal spreading through her body, feeling it worsen as she sprinted and her thighs rubbed against one another, she headed for the front door of the mansion. Darkness settled, only the barest glimpse of light remaining from the receding sunset. The mansion windows lit up with lanternlight, casting an eerie glow upon the outdoor paths.

Alena dashed through the garden and towards the trees outside the dining hall windows. She spared a quick glance at the spot where Everett had first claimed her virginity. The grass lay slightly matted, showing a scant imprint of her and Everett's coupling, but it would look fine by the time morning came.

Alena hurried, bare feet stomping against the grass, her thighs burning with exertion and a need for pleasure. She wanted to wrap her legs around Everett's waist and hold him so his cock dug deep into her, and...

Another scream, quick and fading. This one different. Something had happened to Danya and she'd stopped screaming halfway through it. Alena gained a burst of speed, adrenaline spiking through her body. She dashed to the huge front doors of the mansion and pulled hard on the heavy handles.

The doors opened slowly, refusing to hurry for her. The hinges creaked and groaned and cried out.

Alena rushed inside once she'd opened the doors enough to squeeze through. She didn't bother closing them, merely left them open. Something horrible was happening and she didn't have time for proper etiquette.

...

BEATRIX ARRIVED AT THE OUTSIDE GATES TO Everett's home. They were magic, she knew. In fact, she'd enchanted them herself. Manipulating the spell, she forced the gates to open for her and her horse. The magic lock clicked, then the gates began to bend outwards.

She heard the faintest hint of a scream from inside the mansion as she rode the horse at a canter down the hard-packed path to the front doors. From far off, she spotted a naked woman opening the doors and slipping through. The woman wore a bright red rose behind her ear, treating it like a casual accessory or some piece of cheap jewelry.

Beatrix pushed the horse into a gallop. The animal bolted forth, heading straight for the door.

She *would* get her rose back.

...

AT THE FOOT OF THE STAIRS, RESTING ON A pedestal, was an ornate candelabra. By magic, it lit up when the light grew sparse outside. It had five candles in it, and the wick on each caught flame one by one. First the left, then the next, the middle, another, and the final one on the right.

The candelabra also contained another light. As soon as Everett came inside Danya, the hidden light trapped within the candelabra sputtered forth. It grappled with its confines and shimmied up and out of the center candle, finding freedom in the open air. The wisp of light sparkled, then grew, shining bright, until it took the form of a young man.

The young man had just enough time to brush down his pants and fix his finely sewn shirt before he heard the scream. Looking up, he saw her. The screaming woman crashed into the banister, then fell over it. He ran forward just in time to catch her before she thudded against the ground.

Snarls and roars sounded from upstairs. Not a great place to be, he decided. Hefting the woman over his shoulder, he hurried away from the rough noises happening on the second floor.

Well, this wasn't his idea of a good re-start to life, but he'd take it. Whatever was going on upstairs could stay upstairs for all he cared. Why bother with that when he had some comely lass in his arms? And, yes, she was unconscious at the moment, but did it matter? His hand crept under her dress and up her thigh towards her rear and her crotch. He fully intended on going further, toying with her femine charms, but then he felt the heavy goo leaking from her folds and down her thigh.

He sighed. "Really, now? Really?"

Maybe he'd have his way with her, anyways. She did owe him, afterall. Otherwise she'd be dead. Right?

Where to, where to? Ah ha!

The wine cellar.

...

PINEM'E SENSED THE WITCH WHO SUMMONED him standing outside the mansion in the woods. He turned his head towards her, curious. He could not see her, but he knew she was there.

The man she hated punched the fallen angel in the jaw. Pinem'e glared, angry. Red smoke trailed from his nostrils.

When he turned to finish the man, to end him and remove him from this mortal coil, the man was gone.

Pinem'e refused to acknowledge this. He

gathered his senses and prepared to hunt.

BOUND BY THE BEAST

ANYA AWOKE TO THE SICKLY SWEET and acrid smell of pungent breath mixed with alcohol. Her vision was blurry and her body felt uncertain and unsure, like some newborn foal, but she forced herself to remember and to recover. At least she tried to do these things as best she could, though her mind barely wanted to cooperate.

"Great," a man's voice said to her, slurred. "I was tired of drinking alone. Let's get you drunk, too, so we can get to fucking."

Danya blinked once, then again, and finally

she could see straight. Sitting across from her and leaning against a wine rack was a rugged, some- what handsome looking man. He looked to be about her age, maybe a little older. To be honest, he somewhat reminded her of Michael in a way, though she didn't know exactly how. His manner? Yes, maybe, or maybe it was just the fact that he was drunk. Michael loved being an idiot and drinking, so they both had that in common at least.

"Where am I?" she asked him.

"Where's look like it?" he asked, his sentence as garbled as his voice. "The wine cellar. Duh."

Everett hadn't brought her to this room in particular, but she remembered how he went to fetch a bottle of wine after she first arrived. This must have been where he'd gotten it from. And how old were these wines, anyways? If the rumors were true, Everett had been beast-cursed almost a century ago. They were either very good, or very bad wines by now according to that logic.

From the sloshed look of the man across from her, potentially they were the former.

"I'm Peter, by the by," the man said. "I saved you, you know? You were a'right falling from the stairs, but I went up and caught you. You owe me your life, that you do."

He couldn't be so bad then, right? Danya smiled. "Thank you, Peter. I'm Danya."

"Fuck if I care what your name is. When are you gonna give me my reward? I thought about fucking you while you were sleeping, but where's the fun in that? Boring, that's what that is."

"I..." She didn't know what to say to that. "I don't think that we should? I appreciate your help, but..."

Everett! Besides the fact that she wanted to be with Everett, she remembered exactly why she'd fallen from the second floor in the first place. Some hulk of a man with tatters for clothes and a blindfold covering his eyes had accosted them outside of the seamstress's room. Everett fought him, and Danya ran, but now what? Where was the wine cellar compared to the stairs and the second floor? And where was Everett? Was he alive, or...?

"You're probably fucking the Master, huh?" Peter asked. "Makes sense. That's why I'm back, I reckon. Good deal, really. It'll be much better once we start doing the rootsie-tootsie, though. Then you can go back to whatever the hell you want to do. What do I care?"

He was more than a bit drunk, of that she was certain. Peter wobbled side to side, sloshing his wine bottle drink to and fro. A splash of it cascaded up out of the bottle and landed on his thigh, leaving a trail of red wine on his brown pants. It looked almost like a blood stain in the dim light of the wine cellar, which reminded Danya of Everett and the demon fighting. Not good thoughts, no.

Peter plunked his wine bottle off to the side,

then shakily rose from the floor. Standing up and looming over her, he grinned. Leering at her, watching her, he shambled forward.

Danya didn't know what to do. What did anyone do in circumstances like this? Peter was inebriated, but he was her savior, too. She wanted to thank him, but not in the way that he wanted; did she have a choice, though? She didn't even know where she was or how to get out of here, and before she could think of anything more, he was upon her.

Stumbling, he fell atop her, pinning her to the ground. Drunken lips kissed across her cheek and throat and he grabbed for her breast. She still wore the beautiful pale blue dress that Taya custom-fitted for her. Peter wrenched at the bodice of it, pulling the fabric down to reveal her bare breasts, then he slobbered his way from her collarbone to her nipple.

Danya froze. This was more than out of the ordinary. She'd had sex with men before, for favors or for fun, but she'd always been the one to offer first; or at least she had a choice in the matter in some regards. She didn't *need* to do it, not necessarily, but she benefited from it. This, though, it was different. Peter saved her, and for what? Because he wanted to fuck her, of course. She didn't even know him!

He snaked a hand beneath her skirt and drove it between her thighs. His fingers pulled and pinched at her labia and she twisted and squirmed, trying to get away from him.

"Peter," she said, urgent. "Peter, we can't. I'm Everett's. We're a couple, somewhat. Peter. Peter, we can't."

"Is that who you were fucking before I found you?" he asked, digging two fingers into her slit. "I'm not all that fond of the whole sloopy seconds or whatever the hell they call it, but makes no matter right now. Might be good for lubrication, am I right?"

He pushed his fingers deeper inside of her., using Everett's remaining seed to further his cause. Danya bit her bottom lip, ashamed and embarrassed. She didn't want to do this, didn't understand any of it, and yet for some reason that spurred her body's arousal onwards. The idea of this man using Everett's cum as slippery grease in order to fuck her better was both sexually intoxicating and morbidly horrifying all at once.

A crashing footstep thudded against the ceiling. Danya glanced up, frightened. The ceiling was made from the wooden floorboards of whatever room lay above them, with faint slits between each slat of wood and streams of light shimmering into the cellars. Through a knothole in one of the floorboards, Danya recognized the ruddy-hued skin of the monster that had attacked Everett.

Oh gods, they were going to die, weren't they?

Danya leaned over to whisper to Peter. "We

need to be quiet. We're in danger."

Peter rolled his eyes at her while suckling on her breast and fingering her. He tore himself away long enough to whisper back, "Spread your dirty legs and I'll be as quiet as you fucking want."

Too loud! Danya panicked and glanced up, but the demon above didn't seem to notice. He stomped forward, tentative and slow as if he were trying to figure out where to go.

Danya had no other choice. She hated this, felt like she would never do it under normal circumstances, regardless of her reputation, but it needed to be done. Pulling her dress up and revealing her crotch, she gave Peter a show. He nearly laughed in delight at her wanton approach, but she slapped a hand over his mouth before he could. Twisting beneath his hulking body, she squirmed to display her ass to him. He didn't need much more than that.

Ripping open his pants, making far too much noise for Danya's comfort, he pulled out his erect cock. She expected a little more than that, but, no. Peter charged forward, grabbed her hips with one hand, rubbed the head of his cock against her folds with the other, then thrust into her.

Danya gasped; or she almost gasped. She caught the noise in her throat, choking on it. Peter ground his hips against her, digging his cock into her as far as he could, then he pulled out quick and slammed back in. The sound of flesh against flesh clapped and echoed through the wine cellar.

The noise! Fuck! He needed to be quiet. Danya mentally screamed at herself and him, but she didn't dare risk making more noise than necessary. Trying to calm Peter down, she pushed back against him, but to no avail. He pounded into her, relentless. The sound of his cock squelching into her pussy, aided and abetted by Everett's personal lubricant, blared through the cellar, alerting any listeners to their presence.

Above them, the floorboards shook once more. Dust and dirt sprayed onto them as the monstrous demon stomped and searched for his prey barely ten feet away from where Peter frantically drove his cock into Danya's reluctant body.

She needed to finish Peter fast, then shut him up. Clenching and squeezing against him, pushing back more, she tried to coax him to orgasm as quickly as she could. Unfortunately the alcohol gave him more stamina than he might have otherwise had, and he kept thrusting away, happily oblivious.

The terror of being found, the wrongness of being with this man in this way, and the urging from her body; it caught up with her. She clamped her lips together and clenched her teeth and her face wrinkled in something akin to pain. She wasn't in pain, though, oh no.

Forced and horrible climax ripped through her, making her spasm and shake. Her inner depths convulsed around Peter's cock and offered him even more lubrication. The sounds of their fucking grew louder and louder still. Goaded on by her climax, Peter grinned and shoved himself inside of her, pushing and pinning her to the ground. His cock grinded against her inner walls as she grabbed at him with her orgasm, and then suddenly he was cumming inside of her.

Thick, naughty seed splashed into her abused cunt. She felt so debased and wrong, but what did it matter? She would live, they would live, and now there were no more noises to give away their hiding spot.

Or so she thought. Peter grunted loudly, claiming her with his cum. "Fucking hell-o!" he yelled in triumph.

The monster above them had been moving away, but he must have heard Peter's sexual victory shout. He stomped, ran, stomped. Then nothing for a split second. Danya glanced up, confused, but it didn't take long to realize what had happened.

The thing above them jumped high into the air and landed on the floorboards, bent over like a cannonball. Shoving the entire force of his body into his attack, and using his feet and one fist to lead the way, the demon smashed through the wood. The ceiling above her shattered into a splintering rain with the demonic entity charging through the middle of it. Once he landed, he rose to standing, then glanced around with blindfold covered eyes. He stopped when he was staring straight at Danya and Peter.

She shoved the drunken man off of her and clambered to her feet. The demon-beast strode forward, seemingly intent on inflicting some horrific pain upon her, but he found Peter first.

Danya screamed. She screamed and then she ran. She didn't stop running until she reached the edge of a staircase leading upwards. Racks of wine and rows of kegs, and more and more, but if she climbed these stairs and escaped from this terror, she was free from it all.

Maybe she wasn't free forever, but she'd be free for now at least.

Glancing over her shoulder, she looked to see if Peter had managed to escape. Unfortunately, he hadn't.

The otherworldly creature held Peter in one hand, picking him up by the collar of his shirt. He stared at the man, or at least what approximated to a stare with his blinded eyes, and surveyed him. Whatever he saw, he didn't seem to like it. He flung Peter aside and behind him and the drunk man crumpled to the ground. That's when the demon turned his attentions towards her.

The last thing Danya saw before she frantically pounded her feet up the stairs was the demon approaching her and Peter struggling to get to his knees.

...

THE GIRL WHO HAD STOLEN HER ROSE WAS gone. Beatrix cursed her luck. She should have tried to stop her when she first saw her scurrying into the mansion. It was too late now, of course. Some spell or other might be able to find her, but she didn't have the patience or the time to sit still long enough to prepare one. The fallen angel, Pinem'e, was on the loose, and if he found the girl and the rose, that was it.

She briefly wondered if the dark being would even recognize the significance of the magical flower, then dismissed the idea as idiocy. Of course he would. Any lesser creature might never realize it, but Pinem'e wasn't one of the named fallen angels for no particular reason. Only fools and madmen--and, she supposed, accidental imbeciles like herself--would have ever summoned forth something like him in the first place.

And once they did, Pinem'e was all but assured to wreak the most absolute and utter destruction that he could. Presumably one needed to do some terrible things to be excised from the greater heavens, and he'd definitely done them. Expecting anything lesser of him now was foolhardy at best.

It behooved her to find the girl and the rose as quickly as possible, to waste no time, so Beatrix attempted just that. Dashing through the mansion halls, fleet-footed and alert, she glanced this way and that, hoping to catch sight of the girl or the demon. In all likelihood, Pinem'e had no interest in her as of now, but that didn't mean he wouldn't turn on her later. Especially if he'd already killed Everett.

She reached the dining hall where remnants of some meal lay strewn across the table. Someone had taken up a plate and ostensibly thrown it against the wall, leaving shattered pieces of white porcelain and sticky debris of glazed ham strewn across the carpet. Other than that, no one was here. She sidestepped the misplaced meal and continued onwards, but something stopped her.

Down the hall, far off and away but easily recognizable--especially to her--stood the Master of the Manse. Everett, fur-covered body and all, limped towards her. He had a small gash in his upper arm that he held with his other hand. It didn't look deadly, or at least not from what she could tell, but she was uncertain as to the qualities of this fallen angel's attacks. Did he possess poisons or diseases? Preferably not, but who knew?

Oh, hell. She couldn't risk it. Frustrated with herself, perturbed that it even came to this, she walked down the hall to greet Everett. He didn't notice her until she was quite a bit closer, but once he did he lifted his head up and snarled at her, his beastly hair bristling on end.

"Stuff it," Beatrix said. "I've come to help you."

Everett stared at her, confused. "Beatrix? Why? How..." He struggled to speak, but he held off until he could put proper words to his thoughts. "Why are you here? How did you get here?"

"I rode my horse," she said, matter-of-factly. "I'm here because of the thing that attacked you, most likely. Where is it?"

"You..." He paused to think. The pain in his arm seemed to be his main distraction. "You sent it?" he asked.

"Listen," she said. "It was an accident and I didn't mean to, but, yes, if you want to split hairs, I did in a way. What of it?"

He growled and looked ready to pounce and maim her, but as soon as he moved his shoulder he winced in pain. "Kill," he said. "Be done with it. Kill me."

She sighed. This wasn't going at all like how she'd hoped or preferred. And, thinking about that, what did she hope to gain from all of this? What were her preferences? She just wanted him to...

She knew what she wanted, but it didn't matter. If wishes were horses then beggars would ride, and all of that. Idiotic proverbs and useless idioms, to be certain, but she didn't have time for dreams. There was nothing but her, here and now, and Everett bleeding out on the hallway carpet.

"Let me see your arm," she said, stepping forward.

Reluctant, eying her with guarded intent, Everett moved his hand away and showed her his injured arm. She stared at the nasty gash, frowning. It didn't look so terrible, but without quick work, he'd no doubt be injured for the rest of his life. Full range of motion might not be necessary for everyone, but for the Master of the Manse, any such frailty would be inexcusable weakness.

Muttering a curt incantation, Beatrix waved her hand over the wound. Lively green fog flickered from her fingertips and settled into the cut, clearing away any risk of infection. Reciting her spell for a little longer brought forth sparkles like starlight, which fluttered down to Everett's injury and stitched the flesh back together. After all of half a minute or so, his arm looked mostly as good as new, albeit with a marked loss of beast-cursed hair covering a raw pink patch of new skin.

"There," she said. "Perfect."

He glanced at her, quizzical. What was that incessantly horrific look on his face? He looked something akin to grateful and bewildered and she didn't like any of it. If he just hated her again, treated her horribly, then she'd be happy to go on her way and be done with this.

Everett opened his mouth to speak. The barest beginnings of a word of gratitude left his lips right before the both of them heard a woman screaming. Down the halls to the right, the other way from the stairs a little ways in front of her. Near the larders and the wine cellars? A quick spell to enhance her senses told her she was correct.

"We go," Everett said. "Come, Beatrix."

As annoyed and frustrated with him as she

was, when he grabbed her hand to lead her along, her heart skipped a beat. What use was that, she asked herself? None, nothing. She should slip away from him and go find the girl and her rose.

Unfortunately, she didn't. She rushed down the mansion halls and towards the storage pantry with the half-uncursed Everett.

...

ALENA WANTED TO FIND EVERETT. SHE WANTED to find her lovely Beast so very badly, and yet where was he? She didn't know her way around this place, so she could hardly expect to find him right off, but that didn't mean he wasn't here. She wouldn't give up. She needed to see him. If she offered him herself, her body and her love, and seduced him with the magic from this pretty little rose, then everything would be wonderful.

She touched her ear, and along with it the rose she kept tucked behind it. It lay there, the petals resting near her temple. Perhaps she should have done up her hair before chasing after Everett, but she hadn't had time. Would he prefer her this way, though? Naked, bounding through his mansion, with tousled, sex-messy hair and a beautiful flower tucked in her ear. She thought she must look like some wild child of the woods, and seeing as Everett was her beast, it surely suited. Together they were primal, like human lust and nature's instinctual need combined.

She wanted Everett to find her and take her and mate with her, howling at the apex of his climax like some voracious wolf. He needed, he'd said to her before. Yes, and she wanted. Together they would satisfy all of their necessary desires.

Stumbling through the mansion halls, lost and alone, she grew impatient and upset. This was not how it should go. She had an idea of it, a picture in her mind, but the reality was nothing like it. Perhaps it was a bit too much to ask to expect to find Everett immediately upon entering his mansion, but she thought she should have seen him within the first five minutes. He should smell her, catch the scent of her excitement and arousal, and come to her.

She grew tired of running and trying to find him. An open door up ahead distracted her, and she walked towards it and stepped inside. It was an overlarge bedroom bigger than the entire first floor of her family's quaint apartments, she noted, and with a man standing near the bed. He had his head bent down, presumably admiring one of the pictures resting in an ornate frame upon the bedside table. When she entered, breathing hard from exertion, his ears perked up and he tilted his head to the side and looked over his shoulder at her.

Alena caught some of her breath, but she lost it as quickly as that. The man in front of her was the most gorgeous and handsome specimen of masculinity she'd ever seen, with unruly dark hair and a playfully sinister gleam in his eyes. He crooked his lips up, seeing her naked, and laughed.

It was Everett. She recognized him immediately. Human now, no longer beast-cursed, but none of that mattered. He was hers, here, and in a bedroom for the both of them. Her image of their reunion was so certain and sure before, but now she realized it wasn't. This was how they should meet, here and now, and while he currently wore clothes and she wore none, they'd both be naked soon enough.

She would lay splayed across the bed as he grabbed her thighs and buried his face between her breasts, singing his praise of her with his lips and his mouth. He'd torment and tease her, tempt her to the edge of pleasure and insanity, then lure her back just enough before doing it all over again. And she'd offer him the rose, seduce him with its magic. Together, one, they'd couple, fuck, rut and mate, make sweet, sensual love, all of it. On the bed--his bed--right here and now, for all eternity.

Perhaps not exactly forever, but, oh, she wanted to. If they could, if it was possible, she wanted to love him with all of her heart and soul and every single minuscule piece of her, ad infinitum; forevermore and another day on top of that.

"Miss," Everett said, bemused. "Are you in need of attire?"

She shook her head and grinned, silly and nymphish. "Everett, let's make love right here. I want you so badly. I haven't stopped thinking about you."

He blinked, then frowned and shook his head. "Ah, you have me mistaken, sweetling. My name is Dante."

What game was he playing with her? She didn't like it, whatever it was. Why would he lie to her about this? Did he think she didn't recognize him now that he'd regained his humanity? She stepped closer to him, tentative, sparing surreptitious glances towards the bed.

"Everett," she said, her voice a sultry whisper. "Please? I've missed you and I want you to make love to me. Or, if you'd rather, we can be rough. We can fuck if you'd like. I don't even care. I just want you inside of me."

Dante, or Everett, or whoever this was, stepped towards her and put his hands on her shoulders, holding her at arm's length. "I do apologize for whatever notions my brother's put in your head. You seem like a nice young woman, disregarding your lack of clothes. I can't in good faith accept your request, though. I'm not Everett, and I don't wish to couple with you based on a lie."

"Why are you doing this?" Alena whined. "Why can't we?"

"Do you want to know something?" he asked.

Yes, she did. She wanted to know everything about Everett, no matter if he didn't want to be truthful with her right now or not. She nodded fast.

"This is silly," he said. "Perhaps I should let it go, really. Who knows if this will last, though? My brother's slept with you, I'm sure, and parts of the mansion are coming back to life. I'm here, now, aren't I? But will I be able to stay?"

She didn't know what he meant, but she listened with rapt attention.

"My brother is a nice man, but drawn towards whim and fancy. He does as he likes half the time, and what he needs to do the other half. Unfortunately what he likes to do is seduce sweet young maidens such as yourself, with no regard for their well-being. I hope you understand. It's not that he has no respect for you, but he never thinks about it."

"I don't understand," she said, shaking her head. "Everett loves me." He might not, she knew, but she wanted him to. If she wanted it enough, would it become true?

"Does he?" the man in front of her asked. "It's possible. Perhaps he does. I'm too afraid to go see him, myself. I'm nothing, you know? We're brothers, but he's the Master of the Manse and I'm nothing but his servant. The eldest gets everything, and the younger nothing. He's..." Dante choked on the words. "He's offered me girls like you before. His leftovers, he said. We're similar in looks and build, and in the dim light no one would notice, but I can't. I couldn't then, and I can't now."

A silent, isolated tear dripped down Alena's

cheek and she stared at this man, Dante, entirely unsure of everything all of a sudden. She wanted and needed. The rose had made her aroused beyond belief. And yet, that wasn't everything, was it? Was want and need and arousal the only way towards love, or was there more to it than that? She didn't know. She didn't know anything, she realized.

She didn't know if this was Dante or Everett, and she didn't know if she was truly in love. It seemed foolish and sophomoric now that she thought about it. They'd fucked outside and Everett had taken her virginity, then carried her away towards his guest home. Not his real home, oh no. That was where Danya stayed. Danya got everything, really. Their father preferred her older sister and let her tend his shop alone. Alena merely got a pat on the head and was told to go out and do as she wished. Why bother herself with the store?

She was old enough, though. She was an adult and she could have adult responsibilities. That's what she wanted. She wanted to know maturity and be older. Just a little bit, just enough, but she felt like she desperately needed it or else she didn't belong anywhere. She was nothing, lesser, and that faint glimpse of tender affection that Everett offered her made her think that perhaps she was something more.

Perhaps not, though. Perhaps she was merely a shadow, forever getting in the way, relegated to nothing, just like this man said he was.

"Are you really not Everett?" she asked him. She needed him to say it again, needed him to tell her once more.

"I'm sorry," he said. "I'm not. I truly am his younger brother. I'm Dante."

She smiled and held out her hand for him to shake. "I'm Alena."

He watched her, confusion flittering through his eyes. Moving one hand from her shoulder, he took her offered hand in his and shook it. "It's a pleasure to make your acquaintance, Alena," he said.

"Can..." She felt so silly and childish for this, but she said it anyways. "Can you kiss the back of my hand?" she asked. "As if I were a lady? I know I'm... well, I have no clothes, and you're fully dressed, but can you pretend?"

He grinned, then lifted her hand to his lips and kissed the back of it. "You're rather odd," he said. "It's nice, though. I like it."

"I'm a little tired. I've been running. Do you mind if we sit? On the bed? Shall we talk? Do you like to talk? I've never really talked much with a man before."

"Oh?" he asked. "Really? Yes, let's sit, shall we? What do you mean you haven't talked with a man before? That seems like something everyone does."

Yes, well, it probably was. She knew others who did. Unfortunately no men talked with her. Or, they talked enough to coax her somewhere private, and then there was no more talking going on. She liked it, or she used to. It was fun taking them in her mouth and feeling wanted and needed, or stroking them in her hand and watching the way their faces scrunched up so delightfully.

They wanted her then, if only for a few minutes. It made her feel special... if only for a few minutes.

None of them talked with her, though. None of them cared. No one had ever denied her in regards to sexual dalliance. She'd only ever had actual sex with Everett, but still. No one had ever agreed to just sit and talk with her, especially when she was already naked. It sort of felt nice. It was enticing in an entirely different sort of way.

She wanted to test it. When they seated themselves on the bed, she glanced at Dante and batted her eyelashes. "Can I kiss you?" she asked.

He pursed his lips and frowned. "No, I don't think that's a good idea."

Oh! It made her laugh. She scooted closer to him and rested her chin on his shoulder and stared at him, curious. He was a curious and interesting man, wasn't he. And *handsome*, too. She wanted to touch his cheek with her fingertips, so she did.

"Alena..." Dante said, furrowing his brow. "We can't."

"I know," she said. "I just think you're very nice. You have soft cheeks."

"Thank you," he said curtly.

Before either of them said anymore, a strangled scream echoed through the outer halls and rebounded into the room. Alena knew that scream. She'd heard it somewhat recently, too. While her father mindlessly ate dinner and she teased her younger sister about cats or yellow elephants over a half-eaten plate of food, she'd heard nearly that exact same scream.

It was Danya.

"That's my sister," she said, confused.

Dante frowned. "Come, sweetling. That didn't sound good. I fear there's magic running amok and we'll need to deal with it sooner rather than later. I can feel it."

"You can feel magic?" she asked in awe.

"Somewhat," he said with a shrug, leaping from the bed and taking her hand in his. "My soul was trapped within a suit of armor for decades, so there's a certain... resonance, if you will? I don't know what's going on exactly, but I know it isn't good. Something is wrong."

"Oh," Alena said. She didn't know what to say to that. Being able to sense magic sounded so interesting and wonderful. She wished she could do it.

"Come," Dante said once more, tugging on her hand.

They went off in search of Danya and the reason for her scream.

...

DANYA RAN DOWN THE HALLS IN SEARCH OF somewhere safe to hide. Was anywhere safe, though? This thing, this dark and ruddy skinned man with black-feathered wings upon his back--he obviously wasn't human, and so could he find her no matter what? Was he like Everett, with a sharpened sense of smell? If so, he had plenty of scents to follow her by. She had the disturbing mix of her own forced arousal between her thighs, Everett's semen, and Peter's wicked cum inside of her, callously dripping down her leg and onto her beautiful dress.

The dress was ruined, but if this dangerous monster caught up with her that would be the least of her worries. Could he smell her? Could he smell all of it? Could he, perhaps, smell her fear? The idea disturbed her. He shouldn't be able to see while wearing that blindfold of his, but obviously he could in some way. How, though? Was it something else? Something entirely beyond anything she could ever understand?

Danya wasn't anyone important. She was the daughter of a lazy, flighty shopkeep of no renown, caught up in some grand scheme of magic and witchcraft, lured here by a Beast who shouldn't even exist outside of rumors and legends. Perhaps she was dreaming all of this and when she woke everything would be fine.

She doubted it, though. Dreams weren't this real. Even nightmares weren't this frightening.

Dashing through the halls, she passed by

two larger doors. Glancing over her shoulder, she didn't see the demon chasing her anymore. This was good. She'd escape in here, shut the doors behind her, and wait for him to pass her by. Opening the doors, she intended to do just that, but out of the corner of her eye she spotted the dark and ominous figure of her pursuer patrolling towards her.

The room no longer seemed safe, not by any stretch of the imagination. Large and open, with a ceiling stretching probably as high as the second floor of the mansion, and with little to nothing in the way of a place to hide. She couldn't go in there.

Abandoning the doors and fleeing onwards, she ran further down the halls.

...

EVERETT AND BEATRIX ARRIVED AT WHAT USED to be the pantry of his mansion. It contained all sorts of dried foods, magically preserved by a spell she'd cast so long ago. It had sustained him all these years and kept him fed. Occasionally he'd tried cooking, but his bestial instincts and wild mannerisms made him impatient in the way of culinary artistry. He never much liked to cook in the first place, and doubly so now.

He thought he might want to try it again, though. Not immediately, as there were far more pressing issues commanding his attention, but later. With Danya, with...

Danya was nowhere. She'd screamed, he was sure of it, and he'd vaguely caught her scent as he rushed here with Beatrix, but now there was nothing. He had mated with the willing sisters too much, and lost almost the entirety of his beast-cursed senses. He held on to a little, and he still had some of his strength and most of his ridiculous looking fur, but that was it.

He should be happy to finally be close to becoming fully human, to return to his regular body. The more he strayed from his beastly aspects, the less of a chance he had to save Danya, though.

Judging by the ruined remains of his pantry and the splintered and gaping hole in the floorboards leading into the wine cellar, Danya might no longer even be alive. Before, he would have been able to smell her blood and her shattered body, but currently all he could smell was the thick scent of spilled wine from the broken bottles below him.

Beatrix scanned the area, then sighed. "Nothing," she said. "No one's there. Pinem'e is gone."

"Who?" Everett asked.

"One of the fallen angels with a name," she said, as if this made any sense whatsoever. "I inadvertently summoned him when I meant to bring forth a vampir to torment you."

Everett grunted. He knew what a vampir was, at least. Nothing near as powerful and dangerous as this Pinem'e that Beatrix summoned, but frustrating and annoying to deal with nonetheless.

"I don't know what more to do," she said. "The only thing we *can* do is keep running through the mansion trying to find them. I doubt I can do much of anything once we do. If I could have, I would have stopped the dark angel before he left my summoning circle."

Everett nodded. Beatrix might be a spiteful woman, but she had no real reason to lie to him right now.

"I don't care what you think of me, Everett, but I don't partake in dark and disturbing rituals like that. I want you to know this. You may think I'm horrible because of what I did to you, but in all honesty I think you deserved it. Did everyone in your household deserve the same? No. I'm some-what ashamed of that, but I was angry and what's done is done. It's far too late to do much about it anyways. You look like you've been doing a fine job of breaking the curse on your own."

He winced, remembering Danya and Alena. Beatrix might not know the exact specifics, but she knew him before he became cursed, and she knew what it took to break the curse, so of course she must know about his sexual escapades.

"The only person who might have a chance at doing anything right now would be a member of the clergy," the witch said, thinking aloud. "Maybe not even anyone current. I doubt we have time to rush into town and find someone who has experience with demons. It's unlikely we'll be able to find someone and get back in time before Pinem'e's destroyed your mansion and killed everyone left in it. He might chase us, though. Or, you, more like. Luring him into town might be even worse."

Everett thought. It was easier to think now, though he was still growing accustomed to real, logical acumen. It took time, but it seemed like one of those things where once you knew it, you could always do it.

He thought, and then he knew. "I have," he said. More. Say it. Correctly. You aren't a beast any longer, he reminded himself. You've almost freed yourself from this curse. "I had a member of the clergy within my household," he finished. Beatrix would know this, too. "He was one of the best and had experience with demon exorcism. We never needed to rely on him for that, but my father insisted we keep safeguards just in case."

"Yes, well, I was such a safeguard once upon a time, now wasn't I? Look what good that did you?" Beatrix laughed at her own joke, then stopped abruptly. "Is he revived? Father Auguste?"

It was certainly possible. Possible, and yet he doubted it. He should've known of Father Auguste had been revived before now, unless he returned after his most recent coupling with Danya. Even still, if Father Auguste came back then, he likely would have immediately recognized the presence of a demon within the mansion and done something about it. Seeing as he hadn't, and Everett had passed by the small chapel room in the mansion many times before his most recent dalliance, it seemed unlikely the priest was back.

"No," he said. "I don't think so."

"A great lot of good that is, then. We could bring him back, of course. If there was a woman here for you to fuck. It's a gamble, but it's better than any other choice we have. Not that we have..." She paused.

Everett blinked at her.

She blinked at him.

"I guess we could," she said, muttering.

He cocked his head to the side and regarded her oddly. "What?"

"Are you an idiot?" she asked. "You bring people's souls back from the objects I put them in by fucking a willing woman, right? I'm a woman, aren't I?"

Everett cleared his throat after nearly choking in surprise. "Beatrix..."

"I'm willing, alright? I'll do it. What other choice do we have?"

He wasn't entirely sure what happened after that. Something primal and base within him took control. To be honest, he did like Beatrix. He liked her before and he'd admired her from afar. It was silly and dumb at the time, and he knew nothing could come of it, but then... there was a faint spark of possibility.

He'd watched Beatrix attending her duties around the mansion for years, always thinking of her more as a guest than anything else. She was a servant of sorts, but not at all the same as anyone else within his family's service. Powerful and strong, an immortal witch, and more than somewhat untouchable because of that. He honestly never thought of her as sexual, though he'd privately fantasized about it on more than one occasion. What need did a witch have for sex, especially one that would live forever?

Oh, he was wrong, though. A few strong glasses of wine and some sweet words brought Beatrix to his bed. The experience was both oddly unsettling, and deliriously amazing all in one. Beatrix was unapproachable, and so no one had bothered approaching her. He found out that this made her all the more willing and eager. She enchanted him that night, literally, and they coupled, bodies entangled together, for hours and hours. He couldn't stop, and didn't want to. Whenever he spent himself inside of her, he remained erect and ready to go again, and so they did.

She had a sparkle in her eyes then that he'd never forget. It pained him to remember it now, because he knew he'd hurt her so much. The whole scenario scared him, though. What good was that to admit? He was the Master in charge of this mansion, and long ago he'd been important. Nearly a King, or at least a prince, a powerful lord, destined to rule this area. He wasn't allowed to be scared, especially of one of his servants.

Those exact thoughts were what led to his downfall. To be honest, he considered stayed in bed late that morning and cuddling with Beatrix, treating her more like a lover than a tramp, but he couldn't. Or, he didn't think he could. He needed to show himself that he was still in charge, and unfortunately at the time that involved humiliating Beatrix. He'd waited until she came down for breakfast, then informed her she needed to leave because he had guests. A witch wasn't proper company for the people he planned to play host to, so she needed to go back to her hovel or hut or whatever dirty, desolate place where she lived, and leave.

He had no guests coming. He didn't know exactly where Beatrix lived. He didn't know that she really did live alone in a small house that could probably use a little cleaning. She wasn't a person to him and she didn't have true feelings or emotions; she was immortal and a witch, existing beyond all of that. She was so much more than him, but in his position he could never admit it, and so he'd berated her and tried to cast her down in order to elevate himself back up again.

It helped that he had a reputation for casual dalliances and fooling around. He never really loved any of the woman he slept with, though he was fond of many of them. Unfortunately fondness couldn't solve the question as to whether he could take them as a wife; and regardless of what he felt, he knew he couldn't act upon it. He couldn't marry some lowly servant girl, nor a lesser woman of nobility. He especially couldn't marry a witch.

That was all in the past, though. And what of now? He supposed it didn't matter what he did or who he married. He was still the Master of this mansion, but what use was that? He had no control, no power. The world had forgotten him long ago and he'd become some whispered rumor, the beast-cursed man who angered a witch. That was all anyone would remember him for.

He was still that, and currently he was rutting with that very same witch off to the side in the destroyed remnants of his pantry.

Beatrix held her dress up near her waist, giving him easy access to the core of her body. Wild, sniffing, losing himself in her intoxicating beauty, he moved forward with reckless abandon and buried his erect cock between the beautifully plump folds of her pussy. He thrust deep, pounding into her, taking and claiming her. She had bound him as a beast, but he was in control right now.

Beatrix was always beautiful. It was magic, he knew, but that didn't make her flawlessness any less attractive and arousing. Everything about her appearance was perfect, as she'd wished it so hundreds and hundreds of years ago. He never asked her exactly how old she was, but he knew of her magic and her rose. He knew she kept it in his guest home where they'd fucked so very long ago.

He even knew some of her wishes

Extraordinary beauty, immortality, and his curse. The century rose only fully bloomed once every hundred years, and offered a single near-perfect wish at the same time. With those three wishes, Beatrix was at least three hundred years of age, but for all he knew she could be many hundreds more than that, too.

It didn't even matter. She was as perfectly nubile and beautiful as if she'd just turned eighteen. Her femininity, those clean-shaven and kissable lower lips just begging to be savored with a tongue and licked and caressed and touched, looked pristine and unused as if she were a virgin. Hundreds of years of knowledge gave her plenty of experience in her version of sexual witchcraft, too. He didn't think that was magically endowed, though he never asked and couldn't know for sure.

She was tight around his cock, then and now. He pressed far into her, feeling her clutch and squeeze against him. It was perfect, almost too perfect; custom-fitted just for his shaft. The first time they'd had sex, he lost himself completely with one thrust. She'd giggled at that, sticking her fingers between her legs and feeling his seed seep out of her. He apologized--it was embarrassing and despite what anyone ever said, he honestly had never done something like that before--but it didn't matter. She'd just winked at him and wiggled her fingers, making his softening cock jut back up to full attraction.

She felt the same now as she did then. Her inner walls caressed and massaged against his throbbing shaft as if she were teasing and caressing him with her fingers. He groaned, relishing in the sensation. It was perfect, and yet there was no love here. There probably never was any love, either. It was fun, yes, and he'd enjoyed it before as he enjoyed it now, but that was it.

That never meant he needed to be rude to her, nor that he needed to humiliate and embarrass her. Even if she was a one night stand, she was a person and worthy of respect. He'd never thought of this before, but after a century of complete isolation, he had a lot of time to think.

"Everett," Beatrix whimpered. Her body grew hotter around him and she squeezed harder against him. "I'm... I'm going to..."

He grabbed her hips and pounded into her. He wasn't going to last much longer. This wasn't an extended thing, anyways. Out of necessity, they fucked, in some random, nonsensical hope that their coupling would revive Father Auguste and give them a means to end the fallen angel's rampage.

He wanted to be considerate to Beatrix, though. If that was the only thing he could do to make any amends, he would try. He could have ignored all of this and let her perfect body have its way with him and his seed in mere seconds, but he forced himself to prolong it enough to give her pleasure, too. Was it worth it? Did she care?

He thrust, hard, in, out, over and over, barely able to contain his lust and pleasure. His cock felt so sensitive, especially at the tip, and he could barely hold back his climax. Then Beatrix screamed out in ecstasy and her body convulsed hard around him, milking his cock of its cream. He was so lost in lust and pleasure that he barely realized the difference between his and her orgasm. With every twitch and throb of his cock as he released his seed inside of her, her body responded with greedy, spasmic tremors, pulling more and more from him.

He didn't know how long it went on, nor what became of either of them afterwards. Crumpling atop her and burying his face in her hair, he breathed in deeply of her scent. Beatrix smelled lovely. She always smelled lovely, though.

Nestling against her sex-worn body, he whispered into her ear. "Beatrix, I'm so sorry for what I did all those years ago. I was a fool and an idiot."

"Yes," she said, whispering. "You were."

He could feel her heartbeat in her throat as he pressed his head against the side of her neck. "We can't be together and it scared me."

She breathed in deep, then out again. "Everett, I knew how you treated women before any of that. I never expected something serious to come of it. That wasn't what it was about. You might have been cursed to look like a beast, but people always treated me like one. I'm beautiful. I made certain of that. I have powerful magic. No one ever treated me like a woman, though. I was considered fearsome and horrifying and the only reason anyone bothered to put up with me was because I offered them some of my magic. Otherwise, they wanted nothing to do with me and hoped I would go away."

It was probably true. He couldn't say it wasn't.

"Maybe that would have been the only night," she said. "Maybe we never would have done it again. I *wanted* that night, though. I wanted to be a regular woman, if only just for a little while, and when you approached me, well... some wishes aren't possible, no matter what kind of magical powers you have. You did grant my wish that night, but then in the morning..." She trailed off.

"I'm sorry," he said again.

"I never intended to marry you. I might've been your mistress if you asked and we remained discrete, but other than that... obviously you have obligations. I just wanted to feel normal and be treated normally, that's all."

"I'll try to make amends," he said. "I owe that to you. If we make it out of this, if Father Auguste is revived, then..."

"He's not," Beatrix said, flat and monotone. "I'm sorry, Everett, but this was for naught. Father Auguste wasn't brought back."

"We..." He choked on the words. "Again...

we can..."

"We don't have time," she said. "As much as I enjoyed it, that took far too long as it is."

This was it, then? They were done for? What could they do now? Fight, run?

The only thing he had to look forward to was his regained humanity. After coupling with Beatrix, the remainder of his curse was fading away. His fur vanished, replaced by tanned skin, and his mind felt less muddled and primal. He could think, understand, and comprehend so much more. His speech felt odd, but he didn't feel stupid when he talked.

Unfortunately that was literally the only thing Everett had going for him at the moment. Besides the fact that an angel cast down from the heavens was on a mission to destroy him and perhaps his entire household, when he glanced up after seeing something out of the corner of his eye, he noticed Danya standing on the outskirts of the destroyed pantry. She was staring at the sexual aftermath of his and Beatrix's foolhardy plan, both of them laying on the floor in blissful afterglow, spent.

Danya watched him, aghast, mouth open, gaping.

...

ALENA AND DANTE DIDN'T FIND DANYA. As they rushed down the halls towards the source of the scream, something stopped them. Wide open and alluring, two large double doors called to them in the middle of the hallway they traversed. If they looked inside, surely they'd find Danya. This was what Dante said, at least.

Unfortunately that never happened, for a few reasons. The foremost of which was the human-looking creature roaming through the opened room, with dark black wings, little to speak of in the way of clothes, and a foreboding sense of wrongness surrounding him. Or at least Alena assumed it was a him. He had a muscular chest, chiseled and perfect like some man out of a romance story book. She couldn't see his eyes as they were covered by cloth, but she thought they might be pitch black and wanting.

When she and Dante stopped to peer into the room, perhaps to find Danya there, the thing glanced their way. It stopped, stared at them, and then it dashed forward. Dante flung her to the side, defending her from being hit by the creatures attack. This didn't help him, though.

Once she regained her composure after the sudden escape, she looked up to see Dante wounded and grappling with the demonic man. One of the man's clawed hands had raked down Dante's arm, leaving painful, red bleeding gouts of jagged flesh and ripped cloth. Dante warded him off with his other arm, but just barely.

Alena screamed for the thing to stop, to stop attacking Dante, to stop... to just stop. She screamed so loud that she caught its attention. Dante spun away and freed himself from their wrestling, but not for long. The demon had no interest in screams and he chased after Everett's younger brother once more.

Where were they, even? Alena didn't know. Granted, she didn't know anything about this mansion. The room was overlarge, with a ceiling twice as high up as she thought it ought to be. Slick, wood paneled floors stretched from wall to wall beneath her feet. They looked perfect for dancing, she thought. Maybe this was a dancing room?

Perhaps, yes. It seemed to have some other occasional use, too, though. She watched as Dante escaped towards a rack near one wall and fetched something from it. A sword? Not a large one, though, but smaller. Thin, with a rounded pommel; a fencing sword. He parried a wrathful blow from the demon, then stepped to the side and delivered a counter attack. The demon blocked it using the edge of his wing and a spray of dark feathers splattered into the air before fluttering to the ground.

They moved, the pair of them, fighting, this way and that. Dante had expert precision and grace and managed to dodge and parry most all of the demon's attacks, swerving to riposte when possible. Anything that he couldn't prevent, he minimized, just barely slipping to the side, letting claws rip his clothes instead of his flesh. It worked, or so it looked, but the demon didn't appear close to stopping anytime soon, and Dante didn't seem anywhere close to defeating him, either.

A stalemate, perhaps, except how long could that go on? Alena doubted it would work forever. One or the other would tire, and presumably Dante would be the one to do it first.

How had this happened? She didn't want this. She'd come to the mansion to find Everett, to seduce him with this rose, and yet none of that happened. That was fine, she thought. It was alright, because... because perhaps she shouldn't have done that. She knew this now, knew the folly in her oversight. She wasn't exactly thinking clearly, and the rose didn't help. Even without the rose, she might have been blinded by other new sensations.

But Dante was nice, too. She didn't know if he was very nice, or if he was very nice for her, but he was nice. She liked him and she wanted to find out exactly how nice he was and if he'd spend more time with her. Except how should he do that if he died here and now? He couldn't, and she didn't want that, and...

Fretting and worried, she toyed with a few strands of hair. She still wore no clothes, but this seemed somewhat inconsequential and unnecessary to think about at the moment. What use were clothes when a demon wanted to kill her? She touched at the side of the rose, remembering it resting there behind her ear. As soon as she did, the demon stopped and glanced her way.

The dark being had been crashing down upon Dante and pressing him towards a wall, but when Alena toyed with the rose he leaped backwards and stared t her. Caught off guard, Dante hesitated, confused, but then he rushed forward to engage in combat once more. The demon batted him aside, sending his sword flying to the other end of the room. Weaponless and otherwise defenseless, Dante prepared for the worst.

His enemy seemed disinterested now, though. Alena's fingers kept playing with the rose, unbidden. She was nervous, and doing nervous things, except her thoughts kept switching to this and that and now she felt strange, and what was that lightheaded feeling glazing through her?

The rose sensed her thoughts; or, more like, it wanted to change her thoughts. It had a purpose before, given to it by the witch, Beatrix, and it saw a chance to fulfill this desire once again. Alena knew nothing about any of this. The demon sensed it, though. The magic from the rose lured it in.

The demon took large, soaring bounds, striding towards her. He crashed against the floor, sending his one piece of tattered clothing fluttering up and revealing his masculine center. Growing and stretching, jutting out from the side of his loincloth, she spotted his cock.

It looked dark and wicked, rippling and grayed with a thick tinge of purple from the throbbing veins surrounding it, reminiscent of runes surrounding a circle for witchcraft. The demon confronted her, stood before her, and threw his loincloth aside, tossing it to the ground. She gasped at his audacity and gaped at his erect cock.

She wanted to scream and run, but the rose muddled her thoughts. Tempted by seduction and lust, she crawled across the floor to the aroused demon and ogled his masculinity. Slow, tentative, she reached for his erection and slid it between her hands. The demon wasn't slow, nor tentative. He grabbed the back of her head and forced her open mouth to take him in.

Alena spluttered and gagged, feeling the head of his cock thrusting between her lips and hitting the back of her throat. It hurt at first, but she wanted it for some reason. Why did she want it? She didn't know, couldn't have said. The demon sneered down at her, watching as she greedily slurped and sucked on his cock. He pulled out and let her savor his taste, grinning as she ran her tongue alongside the pulsing, runic purple veins of his shaft.

She'd wanted to be fucked before. She wanted Everett to take her like some beast while she used the rose to seduce him. Dante had distracted her, made her feel differently for a moment. Not now, though. The rose used its magic to bring her mind back to where it was. Perhaps this demon wasn't Everett, but he seemed beastly enough, and in the end what did it matter? Sex was sex; a cock fitted tightly into her cunt.

Alena had the barest inkling of these thoughts before she succumbed to the inordinate amount of lust and lascivious need that now pounded through her mind like a sexual headache.

...

DANTE GAPED AT THE SIGHT BEFORE HIM. THE demon had... stopped? Stopped and rushed that sweet girl, Alena. And then he... they were... what?

He didn't understand any of this. Magic was involved, he knew. What sort? Was she a witch? He hadn't sensed it before, or at least he hadn't thought she was a witch. She still didn't have the precise magical nature of a woman of that sort, so he wasn't entirely sure what she was, but apparently she controlled some spellcrafting abilities.

Then he realized it and recognized it; the rose. He'd thought it a mere decoration before, but now he knew better. That was Beatrix's rose, and extremely powerful. Alena must have inadvertently cast a spell. Without a witch's experience or similar magical ability of her own, her thoughts would twist in upon themselves and the rose would give them form.

She'd wanted his older brother. In all likelihood, if she'd realized it before, she might have accidentally used the rose's magic on him instead of Everett. Dante had stopped her without realizing it, but now there was no more stopping.

He couldn't do anything about this, as frustrated as it made him. He watched the girl taking the demon's cock within her mouth and pleasing him. The demon grabbed at her hair and tugged hard, forcing his way far into her throat. She choked and sputtered, sending dribbles of saliva down her lips and onto the floor.

He couldn't watch this. This was horrible. But what could he do? If he attacked, the lust-driven creature might kill Alena. She was defenseless, currently only protected because of her innate sexual prowess.

Beatrix was here, though. And his older brother, Everett. Perhaps between the three of them they could...? What? Would they even acquiesce to working together? Beatrix had no reason to, but she wasn't some cold-hearted monster, either. Surely she wouldn't want an innocent woman to get hurt because of this. Right?

He needed to find both of them and rush them here to save Alena. He doubted he could do anything else to help.

...

DANYA WAS NOTHING. SHE HATED HERSELF. How could she ever have let this happen? Or, she knew how; she knew exactly how. She'd been lulled into some false sense of need and longing that never existed. Having Michael do it was one thing, or needing to sell her body and her love as necessity dictated was another, but this...

It was too much. She couldn't handle it any longer. Everett acted so plainly before, so obvious. He wanted, he'd said. *Needed*, even. She thought he meant that he wanted and needed her, but in actuality it was all for his curse. He needed and wanted to deceive her, to fuck her like some wild animal. He was the beast in all of this, and yet he treated her like one to accomplish his goals. And, well, he'd done just that, hadn't he?

She hadn't seen all of it, if they'd been at it for long, but she saw the last part. Everett looked so satisfied and content, and at the same time frantic and excited. He pushed hard into the woman beneath him, whose beauty was somehow incomprehensible and incomparable, and coupled with her in desperate need.

The woman looked quite satisfied with this arrangement, too. Granted, she kept her clothes on, but somehow that added to the inherent wrongness of the whole situation. If she'd been naked, Danya might have been able to accept it more, but as it was the illicit pair seemed to want to finish fast and hide their iniquity from the entire world.

Perhaps full nudity wouldn't have helped, though. With just some of the woman's body on display, and not even the entirety of it, she looked more glorious than Danya could ever imagine looking. She liked the way she looked, or she thought she did, but now she felt entirely inadequate. There was no way she could become anything like that, and so she was useless and worthless now, wasn't she?

No one cared about her, though. The roughly fucking pair finished their dirty misdeed. Everett sank himself deep into the woman, pressing hard against her body, and Danya watched as they both twitched and spasmed and tensed in some obvious show of mutual satisfaction. Both of their faces twisted into ecstatic agony, heightening their beautifully erotic appearances. If Danya were an artist, she would paint this, and through time eternal it'd probably be a masterpiece acknowledged throughout the entire world.

It didn't matter how good they looked while doing what they did, though. It mattered that what they were doing was not what they should be doing. More to the point, they both didn't seem to care at all about any of it, but Danya did. She felt embarrassed and humiliated for allowing herself to become duped by this man in beast's clothing.

Even worse, he wasn't even the Beast of legends anymore. After this current sexual session, his body changed with a sense of finality. Perhaps the mansion wasn't entirely fixed, but Everett was. His fur shed away from his skin, drifting to the floor, featherlight, where it vanished in a puff of dust, never to be seen again. His eyes switched from an aggressive yellow to a more mild hazel, and his body overall became softer. He still looked strong, fierce, and dominant, but no longer like some cross between a human and a wolf.

Danya hated him. She hated herself. As she stared, gaping at the two of them, Everett glanced up and looked her way. He caught her watching them, but it was too late now. What would he say about it? She didn't care. Refusing to accept letting him see her cry, she spun on her heels and hurried off.

There was a demon somewhere within the mansion, but she didn't care now. She could die. It could destroy her. As long as it took away her pain and torment, she'd barely bother herself with the after effects. Why should she care, anyways? If she were dead, she didn't need to worry about anything.

Everett came, though. Oh, yes, of course he came. What did he want from her now? To stop her, trap her, keep her in some cage, bound to his will, to fuck and rut and mate with as he wished? The thing that upset her the most is that she'd probably like it. She wouldn't like the fact of it, or him, but he was good at what he did in regards to his sexual experiences, and he could satisfy her body whether she wanted it or not.

The idea of that bothered her to no end. She'd rather die than to accept a life as some pleasure slave; forced to give and receive enjoyment at someone else's whim.

Everett put an arm on her shoulder, calm and soothing, but she didn't want any of that. Danya tried to move away, to slap his hand and keep him from touching her, but he grabbed her waist and held her tight. He pulled her towards him and spun her around and she balled her hand into a fist and punched at his chest.

She hit him in the chin, too, then gasped. She'd never hit a man like that, never punched one. He frowned at her, staring blankly, but doing nothing about it.

She hit him again, this time with an open hand, slapping him hard on the cheek. He winced as her palm smacked against his jawline.

"I hate you," she said. She wanted him to know this because he needed to know it. He needed to let her go so she could leave right now and either die or pretend her life wasn't made of collapsed debris and shambles.

Everett choked. "Please don't cry, Danya. I... let me explain."

"I'm not crying!" She probably was crying, but what did he care?

"I needed to. It was the only thing I could think of."

"Oh, is that it?" she asked. "That's how all men are, aren't they? I don't know what to do, so, sex. That's it, isn't it? You just can't think of a thing to help or do or believe in, and so you just want to fuck someone, because you feel like you're fucked. Well, you know what? I don't want to be fucked, Everett. I want to be special. I thought maybe I was, and I thought that despite everything I'd heard about you, and what I'd seen, that maybe I could convince you I was special, but obviously I'm not."

"You..." He paused to think and scrunched up his brow. "You are special. What do you mean? I never planned any of this to hurt you. It's so hard to explain. I don't know how."

"I'll explain it for you," Danya said. "I saw you with my sister outside the dining hall window. I would've appreciated it if you didn't have sex with her at all, but even doing so somewhere entirely away from exactly where I was would've been nice. Did you think of that? Of course not. Every time you wanted to couple with me, you left afterwards, too. Every single time. Where were you? With Alena, no doubt. For your curse, right? Oh, poor you, Everett."

"I might have felt sorry for you," she continued, "except from what I've heard, you deserved it. You think that women are your playthings, don't you? You're worse than anyone ever, you know that? I used to think Michael was terrible, but at least he makes his intentions known." Mocking him, speaking in as gruff a voice as she could manage, she said, "I need," and finished by lewdly cupping her crotch like he'd done to her in the foyer when he first brought her here. "Do you know how I feel right now about all of that? I feel sick and disgusted for falling for your deceit. I hate you."

Everett opened his mouth to speak, but no words came out. He didn't have time to think of any before that cursed woman from before came up alongside them, smiling in greeting.

"Hello," the woman said, more to Everett than Danya. "Who is this?"

Danya turned on her; she was a woman scorned, enraged, and not at all happy. "Who am I? Who the hell do you think you are? I don't like you, you... you unattractive and unpleasant wench!"

It was a lie, of course. Or partly. Who knew if the woman was unpleasant, but she wasn't unattractive, not in the least. Danya didn't like her, though, and that was the only part that seemed pertinent at the moment.

The woman didn't care, though. She smirked, some amused and entertained expression, then said, "I'm Beatrix, the witch. The very same who cursed Everett into his beastly form, actually."

Oh, Danya thought. And then she said it as well. "Oh."

"A pleasure to make your acquaintance," Beatrix said, curtseying.

Danya couldn't curtsey with Everett's hands on her waist and shoulder, but she wouldn't have anyways. "You don't scare me," she said. "Do you think that you can? I don't even care. I'm not. Curse me and turn me into a frog. It doesn't matter anymore."

"I don't want to curse you," Beatrix said.

"Then why are you here?" Danya wanted her to go away. She wanted everyone and everything to go away. She wanted to huddle up in a corner and tuck her knees beneath her chin and sit there quietly and let her mind wander, contemplating everything and nothing. She just wanted to be left alone, but she never had a chance at it.

At home, she didn't. Here, she didn't. With her family, she never had privacy when she needed it, and whenever Everett left her by herself here, she didn't want him to. She felt spoiled and rotten for wanting something more, for wanting exactly what she wanted, but how could she want anything less?

"Everett is a fool and a cad," Beatrix said. "He's not entirely intelligent most times, especially when it comes to women. He's somewhat of an idiot in those regards. Give him a sword or bring him out hunting and he's impeccable, but women are an entirely different breed of animal, don't you think? Unfortunately, he's terrible at that, though he does have his charms now and again. He's more than pleasant in a few ways."

"I don't want to hear this," Danya said. "I already know he's awful but I don't want to hear about his... his abilities..." His *charms*, how *pleasant* he was. How skillfully he could thrust his cock inside of her wet and wanting pussy and bring her to the precipice of pleasure, and then over, while barely even trying. Maybe he was good at sex, but that didn't make him a good person.

"While I profess I did enjoy myself while

you were watching us, and I imagine Everett enjoyed himself as well, we were partaking in that endeavour as a means to hopefully revive a member of his household, Father Auguste," Beatrix added, "who should be able to exorcise us of some issues we're all currently having,"

Oh. That somewhat made sense. It still didn't make Danya feel any better. If... if that was necessary, Everett could have come to her. She would have let him, would have gladly accepted and allowed it and would have felt even more ecstatic knowing that they might bring an end to a problem through their coupling. But... no, he hadn't. He'd abandoned her, went to the first available option. And if the witch, Beatrix, wasn't here, then what? If Alena was closer, would Everett have gone to her instead?

"Well, you know what?" She said this to Everett, not Beatrix. She didn't want to speak to either of them, but she especially disliked the witch, regardless of her logical explanation. "I gave Horatio a blowjob earlier," she said, matter-of-fact, smirking. "Also, he gave me more than one orgasm with his magical kitchen implements. And your dressmaker, Taya? While she crafted this very dress that I'm wearing, I let her fuck me with a wooden dress dummy. Also, Peter and I had sex in this wine cellar before the demon destroyed it. I don't care one bit about you, Everett."

Everett frowned at her words. He frowned and then he kissed her. Placing one hand on the small of her back and the other near the nape of her neck, he bent forward and thrust his lips against hers. Danya's lips parted in surprise and she let out a slight gasp, but he kissed it away. She struggled against him once she regained her senses and pushed and slapped at his chest, but he refused to release her or her lips.

He kissed her with wild, reckless abandon and some primal, thoughtless lust and need. It.. it seemed more than that, though. It seemed aggressive, and yet scared? Not a distinct, trembling fear, but a worry of loss. A loss of what? Her, of course, or that's what her mind wanted to think, but she couldn't let it. It didn't make sense. None of this made sense.

Barely a few days ago she'd been working away at her father's shop, blissfully unaware of all of this. It bothered her, and the work was for nothing half the time. Working just to stay alive, to sustain herself and her sister—and, while she hated to admit it, her father, too. She hated it, hated all of them, but not really. She hated that she hated them and she didn't want to hate them, but it hurt. Everything hurt. She just wanted something, some place, just for her. She wanted someone to share it with, but no one ever wanted to share anything with her.

Everett kissed her, though. He wanted her. He *had* wanted her before all of this, too. He knew about her and Michael in the woods, but that was before. Everett had followed her, perhaps stalked her, and entered into her room without her knowing. To sniff her panties, she remembered. How silly and weird. It made her want to laugh and cringe all at once. He liked the scent of her? It was somewhat erotic and arousing when she thought of it, though. His primal, desirous nature sending a thrill through his body when he caught a whiff of her sex.

And his letters, his flower. He sent them to her. Not to Alena. Alena existed, yes, and of course he'd fucked her, but... why was Alena even here? She didn't know and hadn't talked with her sister since seeing her outside, but that part made little sense to her.

Everett kissed her and she kissed him back. Grabbing at his forearms and digging her finger-nails into his skin, she kissed him hard and with a longing she hadn't known existed. Her nails pierced his new, softer and more sensitive human skin, sending thin rakes of blood down his arms, but neither of them seemed to care.

"I'm sorry, Danya," Everett somehow managed to say in between their fervid kissing. "It's been so long. I've been alone for so long and I couldn't bear it anymore. I didn't think. I let greed and lust control me, because I wanted to be human again, but I hurt you because of it."

Danya kissed him, kissed him again. Licked at his lips and teased the lower between her teeth. Then she pulled away from him and stopped, affected, shyly laughing. "I've been sort of naughty, too," she said. "I *am* upset at you, don't misunderstand, but I've done so many dumb things, also. I know this sounds foolish, but sometimes everything is so difficult. Life and everything and I just want someone to help me and to be there and I didn't want you to go away.

She felt stupid. Stupid, yet hopeful. Was this some ruse again? Was she opening herself up to more pain and hurt and heartbreak? Should she end this or proceed? And then what? Was that it, would she attain her happily ever after, or was it impossible now?

She didn't know the answers to any of that, but at least Everett seemed different. *Different in a way*, at least. Michael would never apologize to her. No other man cared about her after she joined them in sexual dalliance. They fucked her, and perhaps treated her nicely, but they didn't want more. Everett said he wanted more, and he apologized, but was it real? She didn't know if this was what she wanted or if she was setting herself up for destruction.

Before she could give away any chance at leaving, at freeing herself from the shackles around her pounding, clenching heart, before she could just spit out the words and tell Everett that perhaps she might want to love him, heavy footfalls rushed down the hallway. The thick thuds of pounding boots against carpeted floors approached quickly, and within a moment's notice someone else joined them, breathing heavily.

Danya turned, then nearly fainted. Everett, or someone who looked very similar to how he did now, stood there, hands on his thighs, catching his breath.

Beatrix raised one eyebrow. "Dante?"

Everett frowned, then let Danya go and approached the man who might as well be his twin. "Brother, what is it? You've returned. What's wrong?"

"The..." Dante said. "A girl. Alena. With the demon. She's..."

"Is my sister in trouble?" Danya asked.

The man nodded. Having caught his breath, he stood up tall, shoulders squared and steady. "She's safe for now, though I fear she won't be for long. The winged creature rampaging through the manse has her in a situation unsuited for discussion in front of a lady's ears."

"Does she have the rose?" Beatrix asked, frantic. She rushed forward and tugged hard at Dante's shirt sleeve. "Dante, does she have my rose?"

"Yes," he said, nodding. "Unfortunately, yes."

...

ALENA'S LIPS SLID UP AND DOWN THE DEMONIC figure's cock, moving easily now that she'd been doing this for awhile. Her jaw hurt, but that seemed unimportant. Why was she doing this, though? She didn't know, but the idea of it, the mere thought of pleasing this ruddy skinned and rugged figure, aroused her so much. The wet, slick lips between her legs pummeled her with blissful sensation whenever they slid together as she moved to better accommodate the cock in her mouth.

The demon before her wasn't fully satisfied though, oh no. He grabbed at the back of her head and forced her onto his shaft. She gagged in response, unable to take the entirety of him in her mouth, but this only seemed to goad him on. Her strangled, choking throat convulsed and pressed around his cockhead, teasing and enticing him into further rough behavior.

It reminded her of an orgasm, as if her lower lips were kissing around his cock and her inner depths were clenching in ecstasy, except not. Choking was dangerous, potentially lethal, and she knew this, but for some reason her mind refused to accept it. Instead, she giggled, her body thrumming with excitement and her overstuffed mouth and throat humming around the demon's erect intrusion.

"Enough," he said, his voice reminiscent of a butcher slapping a thick slab of meat atop the chopping block. "Pinem'e will sate himself inside of you, girl. You shall know the insanity brought about by my angelic seed. Truly, it is a gift."

So this man was an angel? She wondered about that, because he didn't seem like any sort of angel she'd ever thought of. Granted, she'd never met an angel before, and only knew about them from vague stories or imagined pictures but he seemed unlike any of that. Forceful, rough, crude and unsettling.

He pulled her off of his cock and pushed her to the side. Staggering on unsteady legs, Alena toppled sideways. Pinem'e caught her, but only in order to flip her around and press her to the floor. Pinned against the smooth wood of the ballroom, Alena struggled to move.

One of the demonic angel's hands pushed between her shoulders, keeping her upper body trapped against the flooring, while the other worked at spreading her legs. Alena flailed help-lessly, caught between fear and lust and uncertain of any of this. What was going on and why did she feel like this? She wanted him to thrust inside of her, to take her, claim her as his and fill her with his seed. She wanted him to use her and abuse her greedy, wanton cunt with his thick, celestial cock.

She wanted all of this, but she didn't. She wanted Dante to come back and she hoped they could go somewhere to talk. She'd like to find a dress to wear, because it seemed entirely in-appropriate to waltz through the mansion naked, especially when almost everyone else wore clothes. The demon behind her, sliding his cockhead up and down her slick folds, he didn't wear clothes, but she didn't want to talk with him, either.

She wanted him to fuck her, rut inside of

her, pound hard into her, break her.

She didn't want him to do any of that. These thoughts confused her.

He pressed past her folds, defiling the barest beginnings of her slit, and then he shoved himself the rest of the way inside of her in one powerful burst. His cock slammed against her cervix, making her yelp, but the demon didn't care.

It felt so painful and wondrously good that Alena didn't know if she could take it. Her whole body groaned in exertion, stuck to the floor like some butterfly specimen in an entomologist's collection. Her pussy wrapped around his cock, squeezing and clutching it, desiring it, and her tongue lolled to the side, unsure if it wanted to remain in her mouth or slip out in a pant.

The fallen angel pulled out of her, then thrust back in. Thankfully she pulled her tongue back into her mouth before he did, because otherwise she might have bit into it.

The pain and agony of his size made her wince in instinctive knowledge and fear, but for some horrible reason it blossomed into pure, pleasant sensation after a brief glimpse of torment. It hurt so much and felt so good and she doubted any of this made sense, but she wanted it to stop and wanted more of it at the same time.

The demonic being slid her across the floor like some child's ragdoll, abusing her body and her sex with his strength and his cock. He pounded into her until she pushed up against a wall, where he paused for a moment before returning with renewed invigoration. Sharp, fast, constant, needy and necessary thrusts, he pushed her to her limits, over and over again.

Alena didn't know if she had limits anymore. This was so far above and beyond anything she'd ever experienced. Granted, before Everett, the most she'd ever let a man do was use his fingers on her, or occasionally his mouth, but still. Everett was rough, but far more gentle than this.

This was...

Her body protested against the demon's cock while at the same time absorbing his sexual essence. While the demon grunted and groaned, mating with her, Alena whimpered and moaned beneath him. Her body needed him, clutched him inside of her, tried to squeeze him out and pull him in, and then she shivered in climax. A chill, harsh feeling swept through her, soon replaced by an overbearing warmth and joy. Her stomach tightened, abdomen taut and tensed, body clapping against the wooden floor.

Her orgasm streaked through her, wracking her body in agonizing ecstasy. She clenched her teeth together while the demon took his pleasure from her, and then a second orgasm thrashed into her, too. More, again, she couldn't stop, and the vile creature behind her refused to stop, either.

Alena gasped, trying to breathe. She felt breathless and scared and wanting more and more.

She felt as if she were drowning beneath thick and heavy waves, trying to catch her breath in the water, and when she opened her mouth for air, the scorching feeling of liquid filled her lungs and overcame her. Except instead of that, instead of swallowing water and losing herself within it, she was drowning in a sea of orgiastic pleasure.

It caught her, pulled her, the demon's undertow of phallic submission. He was grabbing at her ankle and making her drown, but making her want to drown at the same time.

No. No, she didn't want that. She didn't want to die, and she didn't know if she could live. Her hands grabbed at the floor, ineffective. She wanted Dante, or Everett, or even her sister. She wanted Danya to come to her and cradle her like she'd done when they were both younger after their mother left. She wanted her father to love her again and to stop acting a fool and treating her like some curious babbling child. She wanted so much, and yet she couldn't have anything.

The demonic fallen angel devoured all of her feelings; hope, despair, worry, love, everything. He devoured her emotions and digested them, then spit them back out at her in the form of pleasure and ecstasy. He fed them to her forcefully, through his cock into her cunt, and he loved every minute of it.

Alena didn't know if she really liked it, or if some magic had overtaken her. Any time she attempted to think about it, the idea slipped away from her and another climax threw her body into a fit of orgasmic tremors.

Blinking, nearly caught unaware, she glanced up and saw people standing in the nearest doorway, staring at her. It was everyone, all of them. Dante. Then Everett, who was human once more. Danya wore a pretty pale blue dress, and looked so lovely. A true angel stood beside them, with hair like spun gold and a dress sewn of midnight and moonlight.

...

DANYA WATCHED AS THE DEMON FUCKED HER sister. It shocked her into inaction, and she didn't know what to make of it. When she'd seen Alena with Everett, it enraged her, and yet now she only felt pity and sorrow. The demon had Alena thrust up against a wall, forever pounding into her with his maliciously engorged cock. Alena had looked like she was trying to do something, trying to clutch at the floor to pull herself away, but that didn't last for long. Instead, she lay there, nearly limp except for the strained shaking of her pleasure-riddled body.

It upset Danya to see her sister this way, as some plaything for a man not of this world. Everett was one thing, and she wouldn't tolerate that either, but at least he'd treated Alena with some modicum of decency. She'd seen them together, Alena crawling up Everett's body and laying atop him, watching him fondly. Alena looked almost happy then, in some odd, perverse sort of way.

She didn't look happy now. She didn't look unhappy, either. She seemed lost, abandoned, and in need of something more.

Everett and Dante strode towards a rack of swords, each of them grabbing one and wielding it aloft. They returned to Beatrix's side, consulting with the witch.

"Where is the rose?" Beatrix asked.

Everett growled. "We don't have time for that."

"Listen to her," Dante said. "You never listen to anyone, and now isn't the time."

Muttering, frustrated, Everett acquiesced.

"It's not for my own gain," Beatrix said. "Although I do want it back, as it's mine anyways, but if I can get the rose, and if it's matured enough, we might be able to..."

The demon spotted them then. Alena had seen them the entire time, kept looking at them with a blank, listless expression. The demon had alternate ideas, though. Pulling his cock from Alena's pussy, making a squelching, shlurping sound as he did, he wiped his shaft across her rear, then left her laying there. Regarding the four of them near the doorway, Pinem'e offered a curt bow of his head before rushing towards them.

Perhaps rushing wasn't the correct term. Danya noticed him tense, the muscles in his legs flexing hard as he readied himself to pounce, and then he was there, upon them. Nothing in between, or at least it barely seemed like it. Pinem'e appeared and then he attacked. Everett and Dante fended him off with their swords, fighting side by side. They tried to separate and trap the demon between them, but they barely had the skill necessary to parry his oncoming blows.

The two brothers managed, though. They shifted and sidestepped and countered as best they could, until it almost looked as if they were fighting on even ground. Even, yes, except for the fact that there were two of them and only one of the dark angel. They should have been doing better. They should have been...

"Come," Beatrix said, rousing Danya from her gawking stare. "Attend to your sister and I shall fetch the rose. I'll guard you both as best I can."

Danya ran. She ran towards Alena, rushing to her side. Kneeling beside her, she smiled, though she only felt fear, not happiness. Alena smiled back, barely able to grin. Her younger sister reached for her, and Danya scooped the girl into her lap, cradling her head there like she'd done when they were both much younger. Whenever Alena was sick or upset at the loss of their mother, Danya used to make soup and they'd sit in bed and talk and tell stories.

That was so long ago, though. Years and years. They'd grown apart, hadn't they? They talked at dinner, and occasionally throughout the day, but nothing like back then. They didn't lay in bed together and cuddle and soothe each other. Alena was never very good at it, anyways. Danya smiled, remembering it. It didn't matter at the time, though. Danya liked taking care of her sister, because in a way she found it comforting.

It made her feel important and loved. She knew why their mother left, and how their father had driven her away, but the abandonment hurt nonetheless. She and Alena had made a silent promise to one another never to leave the other behind, and yet they had, hadn't they? What of their younger sister, too? What did Felice think? Was she lonely as well? Was she gone, lost, and alone?

Danya bent low and kissed Alena's cheek. "I love you," she said.

"Can we have soup?" Alena asked, choking on a laugh. "It's silly, isn't it? I used to love when we would sit in bed and you'd bring two bowls of soup."

Danya smiled. "It wasn't much more than broth and some noodles, you know?"

"I liked it anyways."

Beatrix arrived, running towards the two sisters. In her hand, she carried a rose. It glimmered in the light of the high-ceilinged ball-room, glistening with fresh dewdrops. Danya almost thought the rose was crying in a way. Were they tears of happiness or depression? She didn't know.

Alena held her hand out towards the rose, reaching for it like some fond, ungraspable memory.

"To make a long story short," Beatrix said, "every one hundred years, this rose grants a wish. In a few moments I can use it again, but I don't know if the magic of it will be able to banish the demon. I've never tried. I might seem powerful to you, but I'm nothing compared to some. I... I languished. I liked remaining in this mansion and tending to people. I didn't want them to fear me, so I kept my magic contained and I lacked study for more. I know more than enough, but I don't know if I know enough for this. I'm just..."

Danya didn't know what to tell her. Beatrix might only know some magic, but Danya knew none. She didn't know if it was enough, or what was what, or how any spellcasting worked. She was simple, wanted to be simple, and yet none of this was simple.

Beatrix smiled sadly. "The best I can do is try..." Her words trailed off and she wrinkled her nose in thought. "I know what to do," she said.

The witch didn't elaborate. Danya held Alena and they both watched Beatrix as she turned to face the demonic creature battling Everett and Dante. The celestial beast had them on the defensive, bashing through their sworded defenses and slashing at their hands and arms and chests. Not enough to do much harm yet, but the brothers were flagging and didn't look like they could continue the fight for much longer.

Beatrix touched the dewdrops from the rose, then recited a short spell. Finished, she said, "Matilda, I need you. I'm keeping my promise. Come back, please. You can live forever."

The dewdrops flickered with ephemeral light, sparkling and releasing a brilliant luminescence. Danya stared in awe at the brightness of it; enough to transform the decently lit room into some extravagant, wondrous affair. She wasn't the only one who became attracted to the rose's luster, though. Across the room, caught in his battle with the brothers, the demon craned its neck to the side and glared at the new light.

Pinem'e broke off from fighting against Everett and Dante and rushed at the witch. The two brothers struggled to chase after him and stop his headlong rush, but they were losing before and they weren't in any shape to begin winning now.

Dashing at Beatrix, the fallen angel readied for an assault against her. Before it could, though, something peculiar happened. The dewdrops from the rose clattered to the ground, splashing against the wooden floor. Where they landed, a radiant sapling sprouted, growing roots within the very floorboards themselves. Accelerated, its growth transcended any normal tree, and it bent and bowed, thrusting upwards and towards the high-topped ceiling of the ballroom.

It grew directly in front of Beatrix, acting as

somewhat of a barricade against the dark being. The witch murmured to herself and worry creased her brow, but for now they were safe. The tree spread outwards, growing wider at the base, inching upwards slowly, then surpassing that speed and rising in leaps and bounds. Branches sprouted leaves of gold and silver, and the bark became a brassy hue. Once its upper canopy touched against the ceiling, it stopped.

Dante and Everett caught up with Pinem'e in the interim. They engaged the demonic beast on the other side of the tree, keeping it busy and away from Danya, Alena, and Beatrix. Danya didn't quite know what use a tree was, especially against a fallen angel, but it did look pretty. Perhaps it was a holy tree? What did Beatrix say before she summoned it forth?

The bark in the tree split, forming a hole. Or, more precisely, somewhat of a doorway. Danya peered inside, curious. There was starlight and emptiness on the other end, with a hint of more. More what? More everything. Indescribable and unfathomable, there lay an entire world of amazement inside the gateway within the tree. From the edge of it, standing just past the precipice of this world and that, stood a young woman.

As easy and simple as that, the woman stepped through the arboreal door and into the ballroom. The tree groaned and shivered as she walked through, clamping its bark shut once she reached the other side.

"Matilda," Beatrix said, breathing a sigh of relief. "Thank the heavens, it worked."

Matilda ogled Beatrix and cocked her head to the side. "Doesn't look like this was your first wish, hm? Prettied yourself up some, have you? Immortal now, I suppose? How long has it been? The immortality I can understand, but really now, you needed to beautify yourself before bringing me back from the dead?"

Beatrix fumbled with her hands, flustered. "We don't have time for this."

"Who are these girls? Why's one of them naked?"

Behind the witch and the woman she'd brought back from the dead, the tree of life trembled and the floor beneath it quaked. The sounds of swordplay and claws clashed on the other side. The tree cracked in the middle and Danya thought it might open a gateway once more. To summon forth more people from the land of the dead? But, no, it didn't. It cracked, and then it *shattered*, sending metallic bronze splinters crumbling to the ground. Leaves of gold and silver fell from the air above, floating like autumn down to the floor.

The barricade between the women and the men fighting Pinem'e was gone. The beast noticed this and leered at them, snarling in lascivious satisfaction.

"Well, fuck," Matilda said.

It was so ridiculous and out of place that Danya wanted to both laugh and cry all at once. This was their savior? This woman? What was she, and what use did she have? Why did Beatrix summon her? Danya didn't know a thing about witchcraft, but this hardly seemed like the answer to their problems. It hardly seemed like the answer to anyone's problems. Did they really need one more person to feed the savage fallen angel's bloodlust? Was another death necessary?

"Blood could seal it," Matilda said quickly.

Beatrix nodded. "They haven't been able to cut it, though. I thought of that, but I couldn't do it on my own, anyways."

"Who do we want to seal it in? One of the boys? They look grown up now, don't they? So cute! I remember their grandfather. Great-grandfather? How many 'greats' should I add? How long have I been gone?"

"Matilda!"

"Oh, hush." Matilda deftly dodged to the side when the demon pounced towards her. "Feisty thing, ain't it?"

"Matty, please!" Dante said. "Help Beatrix!"

"I'm doing it! I can't just make magic out of nothing, you know?"

Danya fumed with unrepentant anger. She held her naked sister in her arms, dealing with the aftermath of being ravaged by some monstrous entity, and here everyone was, doing nothing about it. It all looked flashy, but for what? What use was any of this? Nothing, none, never. Magic was pointless, she thought. It seemed wonderful from the outside looking in, but once she gained a better taste of what it could do, she disliked it. A pie made of pure rhubarb might look delightful and lushly red, but it would pucker your lips and leave you sour with just one bite; which was exactly how she felt about this magical business right now.

Alena mumbled, whispering to Danya. "I think that woman's a witch," she said.

Danya stared at the newcomer, not convinced. "How can you tell?"

"I don't know, but she moves differently. A normal person can't move like that."

The demon slashed at Beatrix, who gained the protection of Everett's sword at the last moment. Warded off, Pinem'e went for Matilda once more. The woman just shifted away, like before, but she didn't *step* to the side exactly. Danya blinked, unsure. For all the oddness of it, it seemed like Matilda was *pulled* away, like some living marionette being controlled by invisible strings.

"We can't seal it in anyone without some of its essence," Matilda said. "So either someone cuts the thing and we collect a bit of its blood, or we sit around and let it kill us."

"Yes!" Pinem'e shouted with ravenous glee; the first words it had spoken in a long while. "Death reigns supreme. The archwitch speaks pleasing words to Pinem'e. Let slaughter define you and sate my every desire before the consumption of your flesh and your magic sustains my existence."

This was it, Danya thought. They were going to die.

...

ALENA SHIVERED AND NUZZLED CLOSER TO Danya. She was so cold and worn. The fallen angel had... it had done things to her. She didn't know what to make of that. It felt wonderful at the time, but currently she felt abused and debased. Was this her lot in life, then? To be used as some toy for whomever wished to pleasure themselves with her body?

She'd kept her virginity, hoping to hold it for someone special, and none of that had worked out. Before that, she understood men weren't entirely interested in every part of her, but she did like their interest in some of her. She wanted more, and hoped to find it in someone. She hadn't found it yet, but Dante, maybe... and...

Except, perhaps not. Not now. Not ever, even. She'd taken the demon's cock in her mouth right in front of the man she wanted to impress, and for what reason? None that she could think of, except she enjoyed it. She was worthless, completely helpless and useless, barely more than a tight fitting sleeve for whatever cock that wished to stuff itself between her lusty folds.

Danya was here, though. Danya held her like when they were little, caring for her. Alena loved her sister so much right now, but she knew it was all for naught. They would die here, destroyed by the fallen angel, Pinem'e. She wanted it to be swift. She hoped that he would end their lives without hesitation, because elsewise he might...

He might use her again. Torment her and force pleasure through her body. Make her tremble and quiver in orgasmic glee while he pounded his monstrous, darkly ominous cock inside of her body. If he filled her with his seed, what then? Could she become pregnant from it, completely defiled, some breedmate for vile, wicked ends?

The idea of bringing offspring like Pinem'e into the world, the very concept of becoming a mother to vicious evil like that, it shook her to her very core and filled her with dreadful, self-injurious thoughts. The only thing keeping her somewhat sane at the moment was the knowledge that Danya was here, holding her, silently telling her that everything would be alright.

The battle between the demon and the two brothers raged on, but Dante and Everett wouldn't be able to hold him back for much longer. Even Alena, who knew barely anything about fighting, could tell that neither of them was capable of winning this. The witch and archwitch, Beatrix and Matilda, barely seemed competent now.

If Alena knew strong magic such as they did, she'd know what to do. She'd do it without a second thought, perform the rites through in-stinctive memory, and seal away the demon with barely more than a thought. Something pricked at her mind, like a needle stabbing at her ideas. She winced and clenched her eyes shut, but the pain vanished as quickly as it came.

"Oh," Matilda said somewhere far away and close all at once. "The thing was having sex with her?"

"Before you came back," Beatrix said. "Yes."

"You should have said that."

"What do you mean I should have said that? What use is it? I don't want to embarrass the poor girl."

Matilda lifted her nose into the air and sniffed. "Ah. Not perfect, but it should do."

This was her they were talking about. Alena frowned, humiliated. Yes, well, she'd fucked some evil creature, and what of it? She couldn't very well change that now, and she wanted to forget it. If this ended well, she might be able to, but...

"We don't need blood," Matilda said. "Any liquid essence will do. The fallen angel's seed would be best, but his precum is fine, and the girl has plenty of that sloshing around inside of her. Mind, this means we'll need to seal it in her, because..."

"We can't seal one of the named fallen angel's inside of a regular girl!" Beatrix protested.

"Bebe, you're being daft again. It's

endearing, but not now, alright? The girl has plenty of aptitude, and you should be able to tell. She'll be perfectly fine."

Beatrix muttered to herself. "She did manage to use the rose."

"Ladies," Everett screamed. "Please!"

"Yes, if you--" Dante parried one of Pinem'e's attacks, but just barely. Barely, and not enough. The demon's claws sent the man falling to the ground and his sword clattering away. Dante's eyes widened and he scrambled for his weapon. He wouldn't make it in time, though, and his attacker knew it.

The fallen angel grinned with malicious intent and jumped up high, planning to land on and rip through Dante with the full weight of his body and powerful hands.

Matilda appeared alongside Beatrix, some fast blip of speed transporting her from one space to another. The archwitch grabbed her cohorts hands tightly, nodded fast, and then they both began to chant an incantation. Midair, the demon's eyes darted towards the recital, then back to Dante. Pinem'e landed on the man's midsection, then lifted up a sharply clawed fist, aiming to pummel through the younger brother's skull.

The witch's incantation quickened, faster, then finished. The demon's fist grazed Dante's ear, but then it froze. Caught by some invisible force, Pinem'e struggled to free himself and finish his deathly chore, but to no avail. When he realized he couldn't do this thing, he fought just to move, but that didn't work, either. Then he tried to speak.

As soon as he opened his mouth, the air came thrashing out of his body. He shriveled, his body pulling in upon itself, shrinking. Further, more, over and over, muscles and bones popping as they shifted out of place. The fallen angel's physique shrank further, all resemblance of any potential humanity disappearing into some tiny ball of dark celestial energy.

Molded by witchcraft, Pinem'e became a living orb, as smooth and small as a marble. That wasn't the end of it, though. Void and stars and blackness filled the animated marble, then it sped towards Alena. She gasped, breathing in the essence of evil. It stuck in her throat, choking her. Frantic, Danya screamed, squeezing her sister and shaking her and...

Alena swallowed.

...

THE DEMON'S ESSENCE ENTERED ALENA'S MOUTH and pushed at the back of her throat. She choked and coughed and sputtered. It reminded her of when his cock was between her lips, prodding past her resistance, forcing her to breathe around his shaft. And then, with that, every time she swallowed, the convulsing pressure from the muscles of her throat massaged and teased against Pinem'e's insatiable cockhead.

That seemed to please him at the time. When Alena did nearly the exact same thing now, the living orb slipped down her throat as easily as that. She swallowed hard, consuming it. As it trickled into her stomach, it melted away into creamy nothingness. It reminded her of--and this was perhaps crass, and unsuited to the odd anxiety and fear she now felt, but--it reminded her of when she'd given men pleasure with her mouth and then swallowed their seed afterwards.

There was a certain amount of satisfaction to be gained from the look on a man's face whenever she did that. Currently she had no man to garner such favor with, though. She saw Everett and Dante watching her with morbid fascination and horror, while the two witches stood to the side, pleased with their work. And where was Danya? Behind her, yes, holding her, and...

The orb containing the demon's essence settled into the pit of her stomach, but that wasn't it. It melted and spread further, tightening her body and her core. She felt worried and wonderful, as if she was about to orgasm. Odd, that, but it suited her at the moment. It reminded her of times when she'd let a man lead her towards a corner nook in a small shop and hike up her skirt while toying with her folds. He slid his fingers along her slick lower lips before pushing hard into her. When she would go to gasp, he clapped a hand over her mouth and quieted her.

All of this while in a shop that anyone

might walk into at any moment. They never had, and her temporary lover brought her to orgasm in a matter of minutes, but she thought most of that was from the forbidden nature of what they were doing. If someone caught them, if someone saw... then what?

Everyone saw her now, but she felt nearly the same as then. Her body tightened, tense and uneasy. The demon's essence pushed through her, towards her impassioned core, lighting her body aflame with dark arousal. Her pussy thrummed, practically vibrating in her mind. The hood of her clit clamped down hard on the hidden pearl beneath it, pressuring her to acknowledge the pleasure it wanted to give her. Her breasts felt so sore and sensitive, but alive and wonderful, too.

She wanted more. More than this, and more than she could ever imagine.

The delicious essence coursing through her wanted to give more to her, too.

Her body spasmed in some unidentifiable ecstasy. She felt alive, as if throughout the previous eighteen years of her life she'd never been anything more than a non-existent thought. Sensuous light surrounded her, dim and dark but luminous to her eyes. She saw everything as black, except different shades and colors of black, as if this were a thing that existed regularly and everyone might perceive as normal.

Alena knew it wasn't normal, but she didn't care.

Tight, orgiastic climax crashed through her very being. Her inner walls tightened and clamped, pulling at some invisible object pressed inside of her. She screamed aloud, but more out of lust than from pain. Oh, yes, there was a little pain, but of a good kind. Stretching her, reshaping her, re-imagining her into some new and exciting creation.

She breathed heavily, breasts bouncing on her chest. Her eyes glanced down somehow, somewhere, and she saw how pert and perky her chest was now. She'd never been unattractive, or at least she never thought she was, but now her breasts looked marvelous. Two hardened little peaks for nipples pointed outwards upon her beautiful bust, just begging to be licked and sucked.

She would do that herself if she could, but she couldn't. Instead, her hands sought out her nipples, and she pulled and teased at them. Oh! It felt so nice. So different. Her body liked that. It was her body, yes, and yet she felt like it was someone else's, too. Strange, perhaps, but it didn't matter right now.

Shimmering dark scales, like a pair of tight lady's gloves, covered her wrists and the back of her hands. Not on her fingers, nor much further past her forearm than her wrists, but the scales shimmered and glowed like brilliant gems. Alena stared at them, rapt, while tweaking her nipples between her fingers.

And more. Oh gods, there was so much more. Sensation shimmied down her stomach, pulling inwards here, then out there. Her hips widened, broader, begging for a man's hands to grab onto them and fuck wildly into her. She wanted this, yes, and yet the men in front of her weren't willing to do it. Taking matters into her own hands, she plunged two fingers deep into her slit. Her pleasure roared, increasing tenfold, but she only managed two deep thrusts of her own before her body trembled in spastic pleasure.

Writhing on the floor, letting the demon's essence metamorphosize her, Alena basked in her newfound glory. This was magical and interesting, and wasn't that exactly what she'd wanted when she arrived here?

Mmm~yes.

...

DANYA NEEDED TO LEAVE. IT WAS ONE THING to have seen Everett and Alena basking in the afterglow of their sexual escapades, but it was quite another to be holding onto her younger sister as she delighted in some strange form of witch's magic. Was it dangerous, though? Was this alright?

She didn't know. She didn't understand. The fallen angel was gone, vanished, swallowed by Alena, and everything seemed fine now. Fine, yes, except for the desirous twitching of her sister's face, and the way she spasmed in glee, seeming to do so at the merest thought of excitement.

At first Danya thought Alena was hurt somehow, but when she started pulling at her nipples after scaly, feminine gloves sprouted from the skin on her hands, Danya decided maybe she was fine. Mostly... that was her sister, and...

Strange. It was strange, and she needed to separate herself from this. Perhaps she'd make soup, prepare a spot on a quiet couch somewhere, and...

Was that possible? What had the witches done to her? She didn't want Alena gone. She wanted her here again, her sister to take care of, and she wanted everything to be happy. If she needed to go back to her father's house and her otherwise miserable life in the horrible town she grew up in, she'd do it. If she needed to... if...

"I'll speak with her," the archwitch said, noticing Danya slinking away from her sister's transformation upon the ballroom floor. Matilda walked up to Danya and smiled. "Shall we go?"

"Is she alright?" Danya asked, sparing a glance towards Alena. "Will she be fine?"

"Yes," the archwitch said. "It's just the transformation. The effects are different depending on the person and the process, but not too much. Within a few minutes, she'll settle down, and then everything should work out."

"Should?" Danya asked.

Matilda shrugged. "Well, there's a chance

that she'll become some sex-crazed succubus fiend, but that's not too terrible, is it?"

"What?" Danya gasped, then repeated the word, shouting. "What! What have you done to her? What's going..." The world vanished, replaced by something entirely different. "...on."

She and Matilda stood in a bedroom somewhere entirely separated from the overlarge ballroom. It looked like this new room was in a tower, high up and aloft, peering out over the forest and surrounding countryside. Danya recognized some of the area as the land around Everett's mansion, but she didn't recognize this room, nor did she remember any towers here or anywhere near here.

"Beatrix's room," Matilda explained. "From long ago. I used to tell her it was silly to take up tasks like this in places like these, but she always wanted to be a good witch. Who wants to be a good witch, I ask you? Not that I want to be an evil witch, mind, but I'd rather be an interesting witch. Good people hardly ever do interesting things, though on occasion they might."

"What are you going to do to me?" Danya asked. "Are you going to kill me?"

Matilda blinked. "The idea hadn't occurred to me. Do you want me to kill you?"

Now Danya blinked.

"I might have been wrong," the witch admitted. "Good people may do interesting things. This has certainly been interesting, hasn't it? I don't know exactly what went on, and previously I might have enjoyed siding with one of the named fallen angels, but there's something to be said for allying with an underdog, don't you think?"

"A what?" Danya asked. No one here was a dog of any sort. Unless... did she mean her and Alena? The sisters? Dogs, like bitches in heat, ready for mating with the mansion's brothers, treated to scraps and...

"Get those thoughts out of your head," Matilda said, frowning. "The person who is expected to lose. That's what that is; an underdog. It's just a term. Looking into the future is difficult at times, but I liked to collect new phrases when I could. It's not so hard, that. People in the future have such strange ways of saying things. It's fun to learn them and use them, then no one knows what you're talking about."

"Oh," Danya said. She didn't understand any of that, nor why it should be fun to speak when no one understood you, but she also wasn't a witch, so maybe that was a part of it.

"Anyways, as I intended to do, I'll explain your sister's predicament. Pardon Beatrix and I for not being able to perform the spell as properly as usual, but we didn't have much time and I haven't worked alongside her in centuries. I hope you'll forgive us that."

"Alena will be alright, though?"

"After the transformation, yes. She'll be a succubus, of course, but that's not the worst thing ever. A bit of magic here and there, probably wings. Those scales you saw. I find them pretty, myself. Centuries ago, however long I've been gone, some women used to enjoy wearing similar attire to events. Somewhat scandalous, you know? Copying the style of a sexual demon and attending a dance like that? Oh, I wonder what they did afterwards, with the men they coaxed into their bedrooms? Hm..."

"If my sister is going to be a demon, I hardly think she's going to be alright."

"Half of a demon," Matilda corrected. "And as long as she isn't a crazy person, she'll be fine. Anyone with any decent amount of magic can control themselves easily after learning how. Of course, when she dies or is killed, Pinem'e might become freed, but as long as that doesn't happen anytime too soon, Beatrix and I can teach her how to subdue his soul."

This sounded terrible. Why did this woman think it wasn't terrible. Danya frowned and fretted, fumbling with her hands.

"If we'd used his blood," Matilda said, "it would have been worse. Blood is a painful reagent most times, typically reserved for malicious spells. It depends on where the blood is from, of course, but most blood is used for evil intentions. If we'd attained some blood and sealed the named fallen angel within Everett as an example, he'd be wracked with pain for many minutes, barely able to contain it. Horrid screams and clenched teeth, awfulness, all of that. Not good."

"Since we used the demon's sexual essence," the witch continued, "it's different. Angels, especially ones that have fallen towards demonic existence, are somewhat lascivious. They feed off of strong emotions, like anger and hatred and fear. But also, they can cause these, and lust, too. Anything strong and powerful, and..."

"If blood causes pain, because bleeding involves injury and hurt, are you saying that... my sister..." Danya stopped talking and gaped. Oh gods, this... this was not good. This was...

"There's really worse things in life than being brought to magical orgasm and kept that way for multiple minutes, you know?" Matilda shrugged. "Ten minutes at the most, I imagine. It won't be much longer than a quarter of an hour, at any rate. She'll be tired after, of course, but that's how that goes."

"I need to leave," Danya said. "We need to leave. Just... just take it out of her. Put it somewhere else. Send us away. I promise we won't bother you or anyone here ever again. Just... please? Please don't do this to my sister? She hasn't... we haven't... I never wanted this. I just wanted..."

"Oh, bother," Matilda said, sighing. "I thought you'd understand, but I suppose not. Sleeping it off should help."

"I can't sleep!" Danya screamed. "How do you expect--"

A spell. Danya realized it a little too late. Matilda waved a finger through the air and slumbering dust fell upon Danya, knocking her unconscious. She teetered and wobbled on her feet, suddenly desperately tired.

"--me... to..." Somehow she managed to finish part of her sentence before toppling onto the bed and falling into a deep and dreamless sleep.

...

ALENA LAY ON DANTE'S BED, LINGERIE-CLAD, marveling at the ceiling. He had paintings up there, somewhat. They weren't real paintings, nor were they colored like she normally expected, but there were lines drawn here and there, connected into shapes, moving this way and that. They reminded her of clouds or constellations, where the person looking at them got to determine what exactly they were. She liked them.

Dante sat nearby, reading. Alena moved to watch him instead. She wondered about Dante. Was he like the ceiling, the lines? What was he exactly? And what was she, too?

The witches explained it to her, but it seemed a little silly and fantastic to her mind. She was a succubus? Or partly one. Not bad, though, oh no. She didn't want to be bad, anyways. Alena just wanted to be herself, truth be told, though she wasn't entirely sure what that was, either.

She wanted to test something. Would it

explain more about who she was? Perhaps, but perhaps not.

"Dante," she said, catching his attention.

He glanced up from his reading. "Yes, Alena?"

"Can we have sex?"

"No," he said.

She giggled hysterically, rolling on the bed. One of her new wings creased and bent on the bed cover, causing her to wince in pain and stop her laughter.

Dante set his book aside and rushed to her side. "Are you alright?" he asked. "What were you laughing for?"

"I forgot I have wings now," she said. "It just hurt a little. I like to move them, but I think I should put them away for now."

Concentrating on the odd new muscles located somewhere along her back, Alena focused and pulled her gossamer wings inwards. They shrunk, moving closer to her body, then blended into her skin. On her back, patterned and dark like ink, lay the imprints of her wings. The witches told her she could pull them in and out of her skin like that, forming something akin to a primal tattoo, but a part of her, too. Living, different, existing in a sense unlike anything any other human could ever know.

Alena grinned at the idea. Oh, she was different now, yes. She liked the thought of that. She didn't want to be too different, but she wanted something to set her apart. It never satisfied her to be... well, either Danya's younger sister, or the girl that boy's thought was some simple and easy sexual treat.

In all honesty, that was why she delighted in Dante denying her about sexual things.

"I can compel you," she stated, staring at him. He hovered over her on the bed now, watching her with interest and concern. "I could make you agree to have sex with me, you know?"

Dante grinned wide. "You could, couldn't you? Will you, then?"

"I hardly want to now," she said, acting haughty. "You've bored me."

"I've bored you? Already?"

"Why are you reading?" she asked. "What are you reading?"

"Why or what? One answer involves another."

Alena furrowed her brow, confused. Dante said things sometimes, and she didn't understand them entirely. He didn't treat her like an idiot, though. "I don't know," she said.

"I'm reading a book about dragons and princesses," he said. "I like to think that someday I might need to rescue a damsel in distress, and if I read up about it, I'll know how to go about it when the time arrives."

"I'm in distress," Alena said, hurried.

"Are you?" Dante asked.

"Yes. There's a handsome man that I know,

and even when I'm laying atop his bed in a nightgown, he won't seduce me. It's distressful."

"Distressing," Dante corrected. "I wonder why he won't? Odd."

"I think he likes me," she whispered, shifting her eyes from side to side. "Do you think that's it?"

"Hm." Dante tapped his chin in thought. "You think he likes you so he won't have sex with you?"

"Seduce, I said. He likes me so he won't seduce me, because he wants there to be more."

"More than what?"

Alena smiled and fidgeted, rubbing her legs together. This was so fun and she loved it. She just wanted to talk with Dante forever. Nothing more. Or, maybe something more, but they'd talk after, too. Maybe during? Was talking allowed during sex? But what would they talk about then? About... about things, about...

Dante sidled into bed with her, laying alongside her. Kissing her forehead, he swept her long, dark hair back across her ear, watching her.

Alena broke away from her mental babbling and gasped. "Dante! I'm sorry! Did I compel you? I didn't mean it. I don't know how it works entirely. I... no, no we don't need to have sex. I was just joking."

"You didn't compel me," he said smirking.
"Oh."

"I do want to have sex with you," he said.

"You do?" Oh, this intrigued her.

"Yes, eventually."

"How so?"

"How do I want to have sex with you or how do I plan to do it eventually?" he asked.

"Do you have plans for it? I never thought of that." Someone had plans for her? To seduce her? What did they involve? What was that about? Was that good, or...?

"First," he said, teasing a finger from the side of her hair to her cheek, then her nose. "I'd like to get to know you better. I'll ask you to dine with me privately, and perhaps I'll do it very soon."

"You will?" she asked.

"Yes. And then..." He caressed down her nose and touched her lips with his fingers. "I'll flirt with you at dinner, and hopefully make you laugh and smile. I think you have a beautiful smile."

His finger traced down her chin to her collarbone, and stopped as it reached between her breasts.

"I don't think anyone's ever flirted with me before," she said. "I wish they would."

"I will," Dante reaffirmed. "And I'll make some excuse to ask you back to my room. Perhaps to see a hunting trophy I collected a long time ago."

"You have a hunting trophy?" she asked.

Dante's lips touched against the side of her neck while his fingertip drew a faint, gentle line against the curves of the tops of her breasts. Alena's eyelashes fluttered and she let out a gasp of a sigh.

"I do," he said, kissing her neck between each word. "And then, as I show it to you, I'll creep up behind you and place my hands on your waist and breathe heavily on your neck, almost as if I'm going to kiss you, but I won't, not yet."

Alena grabbed at the sheets beneath her, digging her fingernails into them. "Dante..."

"You might chide me, and I'll apologize. Did I bring you back to my room for this? You'll ask me that, but I'll deny it. Oh, no, of course not. I'm a gentleman, Alena. I would never..."

Smoothing down the silken fabric of her nightwear, Dante's finger trailed lightly up to the peak of her breast and barely touched the tip of her nipple. Alena breathed heavily, clenching her eyes shut, practically ripping the bed covers between her fingers.

"And then," he said, but he didn't get any further.

"Dante, Dante stop," Alena said. "Please, I... Dante, please, we... we can't. Not yet. You haven't asked me to dinner yet."

He removed his hand from her body, and his lips away from her neck. Laying on his side next to her, head propped up on his hand, he smiled. "We can't what?"

"We can't have sex," she said.

"Oh?" he asked.

She blinked, confused for a moment. "You've tricked me, haven't you?"

"I did?"

"I wanted you to have sex with me and you were going to, but I just stopped you, didn't I? I can't believe I've fallen for your tricks."

"You could compel me?" he offered.

"Ha!" Alena meant to cackle, but it came out more as a girlish giggle. "I don't want to waste my magic. I'll make you seduce me properly, and then you won't be able to complain about it after. I'm not entirely positive, but I've heard that once you have sex with a succubus, you become their slave forever."

"Forever?" Dante asked. "That's quite a long time. Are you sure?"

Alena nodded, matter-of-fact. "Yes, I..." She looked away, unsure, her voice turning timid. "Dante, if we have sex like that, will you stay with me after? I know that asking you to stay forever is a lot, but I'd like you to stay at least a little while. At least a few days or maybe a week. Not along-side me for always, but if you would ask me to eat dinner with you again and... and if we could lay next to each other and cuddle and..."

"If we're going to be sleeping together like that, we should probably live in the same room, I'd say."

"Really?" she asked. "Are you sure?"

"Yes, definitely. Also, I think there's ceremonies involved."

"Like magic?" She didn't know about magical sleeping ceremonies, but she liked the idea of it.

"Somewhat. I believe the spell works in that I offer you a ring, and then we recite words in front of a divine witch, and after that we're bound together."

"Is that a spell, really?" Alena asked. Then it dawned on her, and she slapped at his side. "That's marriage, Dante! You tricked me again and I don't like..." Her eyes widened. "Wait, no! I like it. I swear, I promise. If you marry me, you can't leave ever, though. Never. Not at all, not once. Alright? Not... not now. We can't get married now. That's just silly, right? I mean... if you asked me now, I'd have to say no, because... well, you need to ask my father for permission first. He's a little strange, but I do love him. Also, do you think Danya will marry Everett, because that might be odd. We'll need to get married before they do, since if we don't you'll be my brother after that, and then we can't have sex. A marriage without sex doesn't sound altogether too entertaining."

"We could have forbidden and taboo sex," Dante said. "Sneaking away together in the night like illicit lovers. Depraved and desirous, siblings through circumstance, not blood, forever forced apart, but unable to tear themselves away from each other. Denying all logic and guilt, frantic with passionate need, tugging and pulling at each other's clothes, then coupling in some lewd and carnal display of prohibited love."

"Are you saying that if I were your sister

like that, because of Danya and Everett marrying, you'd still want to have sex with me?" she asked.

"Yes," he said.

"That's... that's so *naughty*, Dante. I'm the succubus, but you're worse. Maybe... maybe we should let them marry first. You haven't even asked me to eat dinner privately with you yet, anyways."

"Alena, will you eat dinner privately with me tonight?"

"Dante, no! Stop it! Danya and Everett need to marry first. They..." Alena paused, wrinkling her nose. "You've tricked me again, haven't you? We're never going to have sex, are we ?"

"Let's eat dinner privately tonight, but not tell anyone," Dante suggested.

She frowned. "I want you to tell someone. I don't want you to be ashamed of me. I..."

Dante shook his head and sighed. Grinning, he snuck forward and kissed her on the lips. Alena blushed and looked away from him, nervous.

"All I can say is that Everett and Danya better marry each other soon," he said. "I'm entirely certain I won't be able to keep myself away from you for very long."

"Really?" Alena asked, entirely too pleased at his words. Oh, this was so interesting and different than what she was used to.

"Yes," he said, kissing her once more.

...

DANYA AWOKE AND... WHERE WAS SHE?

The last thing she remembered was standing in some impossibly high tower room somewhere, completely separated from the rest of Everett's mansion. That witch, the one that came from the tree that Beatrix summoned, had talked to her and then... she remembered.

Some spell or other, some way to control her. That's what all of these witches wanted, wasn't it? Anyone to do with magic seemed this way, too. Everett wanted control, and to satisfy his own needs. Beatrix did, too. Perhaps now, as some conglomeration of demon and human, even her sister might. Would Alena become like that, heedless to the needs or emotions of others?

Danya knew she wasn't perfect. She knew she'd made mistakes in the past, and she understood there was nothing she could do about it now, but that didn't mean she didn't regret it. She despised what she needed to do in order to survive, and she hated how her father idly sat by, oblivious. Would he be proud of his daughter for selling her body and sexual services to keep their family afloat?

Some sudden thought struck her. Perhaps he knew already. Perhaps he knew and he did nothing because what could he do? The alternatives were possibly worse, and if he feigned innocence and denied it in his mind, then what? It might seem like paranoid thoughts, but it wasn't entirely farfetched. Michael knew, and others, too. She tried to be discrete, but one word from the wrong person could send rumors flying through town as easily as that.

And what then?

It didn't even matter anymore. Danya didn't know where she was or what she was doing here. She lay atop the dining hall table where Everett had first taken use of her body. Dishes of food and assorted plates and cutlery surrounded her, prepared for use in some grand banquet. Danya wore nothing, or so it seemed, but she felt fully clothed. What was that about? She didn't understand it, but then again ever since she'd arrived at this hidden mansion in the woods she barely understood anything.

A dinner bell chimed and people filtered into the room. And still she lay there, nude, for all to see. Ladies and gentlemen sat at their places around the table. Danya tried to move, to get up, to flee from their scrutinizing gaze, but she couldn't. When she glanced to the side and towards her feet, she saw her wrists and ankles bound to the table with ornate napkin rings intended for fancy displays.

The people sat and served themselves and ignored her as she struggled to move and free herself. Was she part of the meal or the entertainment? Would they feast on her next? Pull down their pants after clearing away their dinner and use and abuse her like some tender piece of meat? Or would they feast on her literally, slice into her body, ignoring her screams, while peeling away slivers and putting them on their plates? Would they...?

"That's really enough of that," a woman said from somewhere far off, but nearby. Immediately, the dinner setting vanished, and all of the people along with it.

Danya lay in a bed, not bound or tied or trapped. She sat up and blinked, confused.

"You have such strange thoughts," Beatrix said. "Why would anyone place you on a table to eat you?"

Danya glanced down her body; she wore her beautiful pale blue dress again. Beatrix loomed nearby, watching her. There was a door in this room, unlike before, and a quick check out the window showed that she was in the mansion proper now. Some room, a bedroom. Whose?

"I wanted to apologize," Beatrix said.

Danya narrowed her eyes at the witch, unsure. "For?"

"My anger was with Everett, not you. I pulled you into all of this through the curse, though. I don't believe it's my fault entirely, but if I hadn't done it, none of this would have happened to you. Everett wouldn't even be alive now, either, so you wouldn't know him. Perhaps the mansion would be abandoned, and you could have lived your life peacefully within the town. Is that what you would prefer?"

Danya choked back her anger and sorrow. Was that what she wanted? Not really, no. There wasn't anything for her there, except perhaps her youngest sister, Felice. Danya had no other ties binding her to the town, nor did she want any. Everyone who knew her treated her either callously or with general disregard and indifference. No one cared, but to be honest, she found it difficult to imagine anyone here that cared, either.

"I have a proposition for you," Beatrix said.

"What is it?" Danya asked.

The witch smiled and seated herself on the edge of the bed next to Danya. "It's going to sound silly, really."

"Don't say it if you don't want to," Danya said. "It doesn't make any difference to me."

"True," Beatrix said. She shrugged and glanced around the room. "I think I'll say it, though."

Danya waited, but the witch said nothing. Was this some game of hers? It bothered Danya. She didn't need to sit here and be harassed and pulled into another magically contorted version of reality. She didn't need to do any of that.

"That was magic before," Beatrix said finally. "You atop the table. I thought you might like it. I should have warned you. I apologize. None of it was real."

"Alright," Danya said.

"You see, the thing is, I know magic, of

course. Most people are frightened of it. Everett... wasn't. For a time. I'm unsure if he still feels that way. You weren't before, though. I really do appreciate that."

"It's not about fear," Danya said. "I wasn't scared, because I didn't care. If you killed me, it wouldn't have mattered. I felt so alone and trapped, and I still feel that way. None of this makes sense. Do I have a sister anymore? I was angry with her for what she did with Everett, but now I don't even know. Is she like you? Is she going to become vile and vicious and awful?"

Beatrix smiled, revealing her pure white teeth. "I *can* be rather vile and vicious and awful, but I don't like to be. Matilda thinks it's odd. She always told me there was no such thing as good or evil. There just *is*. Everything is, or it isn't, and you can make it be or not. It's lonely like that, though. Like you said, being able to do everything that you want is lonely too, and I feel somewhat trapped because of it. No one wants to be close to you if you're like that. No one wanted to be close to me, even when I tried not to be like that."

Danya crossed her hands over her chest. "I don't feel sorry for you. That might be rude, but I don't."

"Good. I'd rather you didn't."
"Yes. Good."

They sat there, watching each other, neither moving. Beatrix breathed softly, her breasts heaving up and down, perfect and mesmerizing. It angered Danya. This woman, so close and perfect and wonderful, and what was Danya then? Nothing, really. Everett kissed her, yes, and he said some things, but she paled in comparison to the witch, no matter what she did.

"This is foolish," Beatrix said. "I hardly doubt you'll agree with it. I'm not always vile and vicious and awful, though. I like to be nice and sweet. And sometimes more than that. I like... happiness of all kinds. If that makes sense? I'd like to attempt to correct some of what I did wrong. Of course I can't break the curse without the magic from the rose, and that won't return for another century, but..."

"Everett can break it if he finds a willing woman to sleep with him," Danya finished when Beatrix trailed off.

"Yes, and if you accept, I believe he'll wish to do it with you."

Danya raised one brow, confused. "Perhaps, but I don't know if I forgive him yet."

"He could find someone else," Beatrix added.

"He did," Danya said.

"You're mad at me about that. Jealous, too."

That did it. Danya swung her hands up in the air, exasperated, then fumed at the witch. "Do you think I shouldn't be? You have magic. You can be whatever you like. You've lived forever--or will, right? What am I, then? I'm just some whore from the streets. I never wanted to be one, but I am. When I came here, I thought I might be more, but I'm not. I'm easily replaceable, and no one cares or wants to bother with me. No one..."

Beatrix halted Danya's words with a kiss. The witch's lips pressed against hers, tight and demanding. Caught off guard, entirely unsure about kissing another woman, Danya blinked and stared blankly at what was happening. Beatrix's lips felt nice, though. Soft and smooth and lusciously perfect. They were perfect, Danya reminded herself. Everything about this woman was. It was magic, and it might amaze her if it didn't frustrate her beyond belief at the same time.

Danya found herself pressed against the bed, her body pinned beneath the witch's. Sensuous and soft, Beatrix rained gentle kisses upon Danya's lips. The witch's hand shifted up alongside the other woman's dress, towards her breasts, where she squeezed gently. Despite the oddity of the situation, and the sheer uncertainty of doing anything like this with a woman, Danya realized it felt nice. Apparently it didn't matter who touched what, but if they performed with careful sensuality, it appealed to a person nonetheless.

Danya didn't want that, though. She didn't want to be some whore, who even spread her legs for another woman, who gave up everything and...

"I apologize," Beatrix said, pulling away.

"Why did you kiss me?" Danya asked. "I'm not like that, you know?"

"Well, yes. I don't think I am, either," the witch said. "The problem is that, like I said... I'm sorry, but I crave it. Intimacy and love, even of a friendly kind. It's my own doing, but I recently cursed the only man who took me to bed as a lover for centuries, and I've been worrying and regretting and pondering my revenge ever since. Do I want him to suffer, or do I want him to apologize?"

"I'd like him to suffer and apologize," Danya said. "He's an ass."

"Sometimes, yes. I think we could change that, though. What do you think?"

Danya had no idea what that meant. "Excuse me?"

"Everett loves you, of course. Or he will. I know these things. The beginning signs are easy to tell. I think you like him, too, don't you? If yes, if you accept him, you'll both marry and you'll become the Lady of the Manse alongside him as the Master."

"I..." No. Why would Everett want her? It made no sense. Danya wasn't an official lady, nor anyone worthy of wedding someone like him. She wasn't anything important, and yet here was some supposedly all-knowing witch telling her she could be. "You could marry him," Danya said.

"That won't work," Beatrix said. "I frighten people. They wouldn't accept me. Everett could marry me, of course, but he won't, either. Not just because of that, but because he doesn't love me in that way. I... I want it, though. Which..."

Beatrix waved a finger in the air, and a gentle buzzing vibration tapped at Danya's core. Between her legs, somehow thriving with attention and life, she felt thick arousal spreading into her. Slow, like sweet honey, it pushed inside of her, caressing her inner depths and teasing at her clit.

"It's your decision," Beatrix said. "I won't force you. This is just a sample, to explain. It's... I should have asked you first. Whoops! But still, it's nice, right?"

Danya wanted to object and claim that it wasn't nice, that it was horrific, but none of that was true. It was soft and smooth and sweet in some way entirely unknown to her before. Invisible magical hands caressed at the core of her body, massaging her lower lips and her stomach and her pussy and clit. They teased and tempted her, arousing her. She couldn't deny that, didn't really want to deny it. She didn't want to feel it like this, but did it hurt to listen to what Beatrix had to say, did it?

"You should be Everett's wife," Beatrix explained, kissing Danya's cheek. "Regardless of what I want, that's what will happen. But if you'll let me, discretely and hidden, known only to the three of us, I'd like to share your marital bed. All of us, together," she added. "Or apart, if you wish. I won't intrude, I promise. If you'd like to do things with just you and I, if Everett won't become angry with it, I'd like to try that, too."

"I don't know," Danya said. She didn't want

to move for fear of giving away her pleasure. She shouldn't make important decisions at a time like this.

"I understand," Beatrix said. "As I mentioned, I don't wish to come between you two. I'd enjoy playing, though. In a good, proper way. I won't use you or him. I'll agree to a pact if you like. Magical and binding. I can enhance everything for us, if you'll let me, though. I can fulfill your fantasies. Have you ever wondered what it's like to be a man with a cock between your legs, pressing atop a woman and into her slick folds? I can do that for you, give you a man's tools if only for a few hours, and I could be the woman writhing beneath you. I can..."

Danya gasped, both in pleasure and surprise. "You can do that?" she asked.

"Do you want to see?"

Danya blinked, uncertain. It... it intrigued her, and yet...

"Not yet, not entirely," Beatrix said. "I'll show you a little, though."

Confused, Danya nodded. Beatrix shifted Danya's dress up, revealing her crotch, then performed more magic, waving her finger once more. Something filled the witch's hands, some illusory, as of yet unformed magic. She swept her palm across Danya's stomach and towards her clit. With carefully guided, magical motions, Beatrix molded the magic into an illusory shaft, upwards more, forming the head, and...

Danya stared down her body, morbidly fascinated. There, between her legs, lay an erect, thick and throbbing shaft. She could see through it, though not entirely, and the rest of her body remained regular, but she had some sort of translucent magical cock now attached to the end of her clit.

The odd part, or perhaps just more odd than this already was, was the fact that she still felt everything else. Those same magical and invisible hands from before teased across her slit and her wet, aroused lips, and tapped and rubbed at her clit. Beatrix smiled sweetly, then took Danya's newfound, illusory cock between her hands, stroking it.

It... oh gods, it felt so new and different and... she was feeling both, wasn't she? Danya felt double sensations; that of having a cock stroked, plus the firm caresses against her clit and the delving pressure inside of her. It was too much, too soon, and she came hard right then and there. Her orgasm pressed into her, some fierce and needy thing, and she could do nothing to stop it.

Except how did that work? Forcing herself to keep her eyes open and watch, she stared at the magical cock wrapped between Beatrix's fingers. The shaft of it throbbed like any other man's, pulsing with inherent power. Her cockhead grew larger, brimming with sexuality, and then...

She came. Twice at once, at the same time. Not seed like a real man's cock, but something akin

Cerys du Lys

to it. Sweet, thick magic splashed from the end of the magical cock that Beatrix had created for her. The witch kept stroking and teasing her, heightening her pleasure. It was so sensitive and tickled! Danya squirmed and laughed and tried to pull away, but Beatrix simply grinned and continued.

In time, the magic of the cock illusion vanished, shriveling back into a puddle of mal-formed energy. It lay on Danya's pubis, sticky and thick like a man's cum. She touched it, moving it around with her fingers, entranced with the idea of it. Her body swelled with ecstasy and ideas and she thought she might want more; right now and immediately. But, no.

"Was that alright?" Beatrix asked.

"It..." Danya didn't know how to explain it.

"Somewhat overwhelming at first, isn't it? It takes a lot of magic to do, though it seems like some simple parlor trick in a lot of ways. Or, at least it takes a lot of magic to do properly. To seamlessly combine something that doesn't exist to the necessary points in a woman's body is difficult."

"You're trying to bribe me, aren't you?" Danya asked. She wanted to sound serious and concerned, but the stupid grin on her face from the aftermath of double orgasms refused to go away.

"No," Beatrix said, then shrugged. "Perhaps? Is it working? I just wanted to show you what you could gain if you agree to my arrangement."

"Which is what exactly?" Danya asked. "Go over it once more."

"The simple gist of it is that I'd like to share a bed with you and Everett. Not always, but often. Privately. No one else would need to know. I won't interfere with your future marriage, when he inevitably proposes to you, nor will I do anything to come between you two. I'll magically enhance what you both have, and offer you wild pleasure beyond belief, but I'll also protect this mansion and its inhabitants from harms way."

"If Everett is sleeping with the both of us, the mansion attendants will return to normal faster, too. Right?"

"I suppose that's true." Beatrix nodded. "Yes."

"You need to make sure Alena is alright," Danya added. "I'm worried."

"I shall. Matilda has offered to help, too. Dante, also, of course. She's infatuated with him now."

"Alright. Good. Wait... she's what?" Dante? Everett's brother? With her sister? Was that good or bad?

Beatrix shrugged. "I don't know. I just know that after she went through her trans-formation, she begged for Dante. He acquiesced and brought her back to his room, where she's resting. It's all rather odd. They aren't even having sex. She's wearing a nightgown, last I knew. I can sense them from here, and they're discussing not having sex, and both of them are becoming aroused by it. It's possibly the most abnormal thing I've ever experienced."

Danya wrinkled her brow. "Oh."

"She's doing well, though. Very well. For a woman who just transformed into a succubus to be able to completely deny her lust and have a conversation with a man about how they won't be having sex anytime in the near future... I hope you understand that's very out of the ordinary. A succubus is practically a being created from arousal. They can control it in time, yes, but your sister's done that in... less than a few hours? Quite incredible and fascinating."

"Oh." Danya wasn't sure how she felt about her younger sister being a creature of pure arousal. It didn't quite sit well with her.

"The scene before," Beatrix added. "On the table, where you were naked. I can perform similar with you and Everett. Nothing real, but imagined. Whatever either of you likes. And..."

The witch trailed off and Danya glanced at her. Beatrix looked troubled, with her brow scrunched up, and lips pursed.

"You'll die," Beatrix said finally. "In time, though certainly not soon. I can't do anything about that. Everett will live longer, because of the curse. That won't ever truly fade. I have the rose, though. I can bring you back if you'd like, the same as I did for Matilda. I can do it for both of you. If you want, you can live forever. I'm not saying this as a way of changing your mind, I'm just explaining. It will take hundreds of years, and you both might be apart for some time because of that, but..."

"If we do that," Danya said. "If Everett and I did decide on something like that, would you stay, too? With us? If I were dead, would you keep him company until you brought me back? Would you keep me company until he was revived, too?"

Beatrix swallowed hard, choking on her words. "Yes. I know I've been awful, and I'm sorry, but if you'd let me do that, if... if I could have companions for the future... forever..."

"That might be nice," Danya said, smiling. "We might grow tired of each other, though."

Beatrix nodded. "Perhaps. It's possible. In my experience, there's so much to do in this world that it's difficult to become bored even if you try."

Danya grinned. "We might have to try, then."

...

Beatrix was soft. And dull. How could one of her proteges become like that? Matilda didn't know, nor did she especially care, she supposed. Or, she did care somewhat, but Beatrix had done as she'd asked, and so she could hardly fault her for much else.

Presumably her softness was what did it.

What other sort of witch would use one of the century rose's ultimate wishes to bring back another witch, a potential rival for the rose?

Not that Matilda ever really wanted the rose in the first place. She wanted to live forever, yes, but besides that, what more could she hope for? Looking nice was nice enough, but it barely seemed to matter. It paled in comparison to immortality, to be honest. She could revive someone, she supposed, but she didn't want to bother with that. Too much effort involved in re-adapting a previously dead person to the land of the living.

Beatrix could manage the rose for awhile longer, at least as far as Matilda was concerned. A millennium or so, perhaps two, and what more would her student need to wish for after that? The whole thing should become tiresome by then, and Matilda might have use of a few wishes afterwards, too. Mostly, none of it mattered because if she spent enough time studying and experimenting, she could probably figure out how to do anything she wanted to do on her own, without having to rely on a rose that took a hundred years to offer her its full power.

Some small, insignificant and weakly compassionate part of her thought the girl deserved some happiness, too. This wasn't a standard sorceress mindset, but oh well. When Matilda had first found Beatrix, the young thing was whoring herself out on the streets in order to pay for some tiny little closet of a room at the worst inn in town, with nothing more than a few scraps and a biscuit every night to feed herself.

Beatrix was pretty enough at the time; she *did* make money through prostitution. But she was pallid and meek and more than a tad scrawny. The young girl intrigued Matilda, though. The witch couldn't have said why, nor exactly what she found appealing in that rat's nest of sex-addled hair and the barely suitable rag of a dress clinging to the slim ruffian's body. The little thing didn't even wear shoes, nor cosmetics, nor much else.

"How old are you?" Matilda had asked her one day, while offering a scrap of her breakfast to the waifish tart.

Beatrix devoured the morsel of bacon and egg stuck between two chewy muffin cakes. "I'm sixteen, ma'am, but I ain't into servicin' women."

Matilda stared at the creature before her, blinking, pondering. "What the hell do I need your service for, anyways?"

Beatrix shrugged, unsure.

"Do you want a job?" Matilda had asked then; perhaps the best and worst thing she'd ever done. "A place to live? Doing odd errands here and there." Odd was, perhaps, an understatement. "Nothing like what you're doing now, you dirty little tramp. Something more. Something magical."

"There ain't no magic, ma'am. That's just stories."

Beatrix both delighted and confounded the

older woman. How absurd! No magic? Really now?

Matilda smiled, remembering it. It was so ludicrous and inane, but she enjoyed the memories. Beatrix was a good pupil, too. Matilda's only one, as a matter of fact. Once the witch brushed the girl's hair, taught her how to clean properly, and gave her more fitting attire, she looked far more pleasing, too. No more servicing men in back alleyways, none of that insanity. Matilda made her work and learn and practice. Beatrix was good for testing experiments and gathering reagents, and all of that. Almost like an alchemical laboratory rat, but with a slight amount more intelligence.

And Beatrix had promised to revive Matilda with the rose, of course. Matilda started growing it on a whim, knowing she'd never live long enough to use it. She never expected to take up a student, either, but she supposed things changed sometimes. The wretched plant would probably die, she remembered thinking. Who cared?

On her deathbed, Matilda bequeathed it to Beatrix and made her promise to use its wish fulfillment magic in order to bring her back. Beatrix had cried, wept like some tiny child. That was so long ago now, wasn't it? Her protege had grown a lot since their initial encounter. How old was she then? How old were they, both of them? Not that it mattered, but Matilda was curious. She wondered if Beatrix was really as naive as she used to be.

Yes and no, probably. Two different answers, but not entirely. Beatrix must know more, but she couldn't deal with one of the named fallen angels on her own, so there was that; she obviously didn't know enough. Granted, most regular witches would never have been able to deal with one either, but most would've died in the process of summoning anything like Pinem'e, too. Beatrix obviously wasn't dead, so she must be at least competently powerful.

Good, Matilda thought. Good and, yes, she would work alongside her protege again. Despite the fact that she thought Beatrix was slightly unhinged, in a manner of speaking (because what witch would offer to safeguard an entire household for paltry compensation?), Matilda liked her.

That Danya girl was similar in some ways, too. Perhaps that's why Beatrix wanted to be closer to her. That'd hardly work out, but whatever they wanted to do. What business did Matilda have butting into personal stupidity? Sharing Everett between them, though? Really? Ha! Beatrix should've just taken him for her own and cursed the other girl into the form of a frog or something similar. That was the easiest, and thus the best solution, but alas, no. Beatrix and her softness...

The other sister intrigued Matilda, though. Some sultry demoness now, was she? Somewhat, though not entirely. She seemed curious and intriguing, almost like how Beatrix initially was. Dante might spoil her and make her into some weak thing, but Matilda thought she might be able to fix that. Odd, too, she contemplated whether she could use Dante to enhance it. She'd never thought of these things before in her original life, but her revival gave her an increased perspective.

And then there was...

"Matty," someone said to her.

She didn't want to be harangued, especially by incessant nonsense. This was exactly the reason why she'd holed herself up in the library, because hardly anyone should bother coming here. But they did, and they felt confident and comfortable enough in her presence that they could call her by a nickname? She'd teach them a lesson immediately.

Glancing up, Matilda saw a man wearing butler's garb and hoisting a platter with a tea kettle, cups, and a cream and sugar cube container. He looked familiar, but she couldn't quite place it.

And then she noticed the elegant pocket-watch stuck inside his breast pocket.

"Ah, the Timekeeper. You're here, too, are you?"

"You should remember," Horatio said. "Or has death addled your pretty little head?"

"You brought me back, did you? How often?"

"As often as I could," he said with a shrug. "Tea?" The butler set the platter on a side table nearby and began pouring a cup for each of them.

"This is the first time I've fully come beyond the grave," Matilda said, indifferent. "I'm sure I'll remember in time. Feel free to indulge me with tales of your shenanigans if you so wish, though."

Horatio tipped some cream into one of the tea cups, then plunked down two cubes of sugar. He handed it to her with a smile.

"I shouldn't tell you this," he said. "But when I'd twist you into existence, I told everyone you were a maid. You played the part wonderfully, too. Mostly. No one seemed to notice when you were absent, when your time had run out, but that made it all the more wonderful. Dante knew. You'll remember that, I'm sure. He'll wish to speak with you about it later, I'm certain."

"Was I Matilda then?" she asked. "Matty? That might've been too obvious, hm?"

"Darcy to most," Horatio said. "That's the name we settled on."

Matilda considered it before scrunching up her nose. "I don't care for it overly much."

Horatio shrugged. "I didn't care for the time you grew angry at me because Beatrix hadn't revived you yet, and then you slept with Master Everett when I refused to try and persuade her. I did tell you she'd do it eventually. You should listen better."

"It was supposed to be her first wish!" Matilda said. "Her first! Well, second real wish, I suppose. She needed immortality beforehand. I never really expected her to believe me when I said I'd do the same for her if she brought me back immediately. If she did then she'd just be an idiot and no true pupil of mine. I suppose the fact that she revived me at all makes her a terrible student, but I won't quibble over minor personality flaws."

"You're a difficult woman," he said. "I can somewhat understand her reticence. I knew she'd return you to us, though. Also, to be honest, I had an enjoyable time dressing you up in servant outfits. You likely wouldn't have let me do that otherwise, correct?"

"That's a question, isn't it? You want me to dress in some costume for your arousal? Why don't you twist that pocketwatch of yours and just make yourself young again, so we can do away with that necessity? You shouldn't need some stupid costume in order for me to get you erect. Go back to your prime, old man."

"I would," Horatio said, smirking while tipping cream and placing sugar into his own teacup. "I'd like to remain here, though. Generally I don't, but I find myself interested in Master Everett's future plans."

"Just stay and tell them you can control time on a whim with that little watch of yours. You always vanish off and take up residence some-where else whenever you reset your age. It's annoying and bothersome. What if someone who didn't care about any of that wanted to find you? It's difficult, you know?"

"Who would that be?" Horatio asked with a grin.

"Shut up and sit beside me, you lecherous

coot."

Matilda scooted aside in her chair, allowing Horatio a seat. It was close, perhaps too close, but she didn't mind it. He sat there, genteel and gentlemanly. Then not.

Turning to the side, lording over her with domineering intent, Horatio licked a trail up her neck, towards her ear, where he nibbled lightly on her earlobe. Beatrix tried to restrain herself, wanted to feign indifference, but the Timekeeper knew her better than anyone. He could never give her true immortality before, but he gave her glimpses of it, and he offered her a look of nigh eternal youth, despite the fact that imminent death loomed around every the corner.

"I'll stay," he said, sending a wash of hot breath to tickle her ear. "We can be together now, and I'll stay, but I'd like to maintain my position within the mansion, Matty. Will you help me?"

Flustered, cheeks red, Matilda looked away from him. Unfortunately this revealed more of her neck, which he caressed lightly with his fingertips. "How?" she asked.

"We can explain to Everett and the sisters, but I'd prefer everyone else forget. If you do that for me, cast the spell to make them think I've always been young and dapper, I'll stay and please you whenever you wish."

"And..." Matilda started to speak, to potentially protest, but Horatio pawed at her breasts roughly with his time-worn hands. She gasped, eyes opening wide.

"Please, Matty?" he said.

"What," she said, labored, "makes you think I want your pleasure, Timekeeper?"

"You're the only one I've ever wanted, Matty. And I'm the only one who's ever pleased you."

"Not so," she said. "Beatrix is doing a good..."

"Like this," he said, throwing up the front of her dress and stuffing a greedy hand between her legs. His fingers snuck past her panties and plied at her delicate folds. "Not like that, Matty. Like this."

"Show me," she said, trying to maintain some modicum of demurity. "Show me and I'll consider it."

"I think we both already know I was planning on doing exactly that," he said.

He teased a finger inside of her, causing her to bite her bottom lip in excitement. "Why do you want to stay with them?" she asked. "They're just... mortals. Why would someone like you want to waste your time here?"

Horatio kissed the archwitch hard, forcing her body against the back of the chair while he teased and tormented her sex. "Fond attachment," he said. "It is what is, nothing more nor less. Why else do you think I'd bring you back occasionally after you died?"

"You sound like Beatrix," Matilda scoffed.

"Ridiculous."

"Shut up, you wench, and let me feel your pussy clench around my fingers while I bring you to orgasm."

What should she say to that? She did as he asked. The fate of Beatrix and Danya and Everett could be determined later. Alena and Dante weren't much more of an issue in her mind, either. Her heart pulsed fast, body tightening, as the Timekeeper pushed his fingers hard inside of her.

Perhaps he was right. Perhaps love and affection weren't a terrible thing, and everything would work out in the end. She doubted it, never really understood it either. Except she supposed she might now. Initially she'd sought the Timekeeper out as a means to immortality, but things escalated from there. When it was obvious he couldn't give her what she wished for, well... the rose was something, but it'd never work. And then Beatrix.

Beatrix's life expanded, too. Grew out-wards. She found more, wanted more. Matilda only wanted to live. More could come after she figured out how to conquer time and eternity.

And she had, hadn't she? Unfortunately she grew fond of people in the process, despite what she wanted. Fondness never turned out well. Someone always got hurt by it. She remembered an expression she'd gathered from the future: You're fucked.

The Timekeeper was fucking her right now,

wasn't he? With his fingers, but she knew there'd be more. Again. Over and over. They had an eternity, if they wanted. He'd lived forever already, and he wasn't jaded and cynical, so maybe she should let go of her apprehension, too.

She might consider it. Currently all she had on her mind was her impending climax.

...

EVERETT LEANED AGAINST THE FRONT GATES OF the mansion grounds and stared into the surrounding forest. Everything used to be more lively here so long ago. The manse lay hidden in the woods, but there were paths and passageways created just to lead to this one, solitary point. People used to visit on occasion and play in the lake, bringing their children--or simply them- selves--to swim on a hot summer's day. In the winter months, when the lake froze over, some visitors enjoyed setting up huts for fishing, while others frolicked and skated across the ice with specially-crafted shoes.

Everett used to do these things, too. He remembered it all fondly. Chasing after someone atop the ice with a predatory grin on his face, catching the woman up in his arms and swinging her around. Then they fell, together, landing on the lake's frozen surface, both of them laughing.

He'd bedded more than a few women that way. Playing, teasing, flirting. Nothing ever came of it. He never expected it to, never even wanted it to. What did they want, though?

Most of them wanted more, and he knew it. They'd sleep with him, then watch him, gazing at him with a sense of adoration and affection that he couldn't return. Am I the one, he imagined them thinking. Is this finally it? Has the Master of the Manse chosen a Lady to sit by his side.

It angered him in a way. Was that all he was to them? It only angered him for a little while, though; up until he thrust his cockhead between their willing, arousal-slick folds and plunged his cock deep inside of them.

Everett was no stranger to sex. He'd been having it for quite a long while, in fact. Dallying with some of the servants initially, then playing at seducing the daughters from families in the surrounding areas. Playing at seduction became actual seduction with barely any more effort, he learned, and it escalated from there. More, higher. Who could he seduce today? The daughter of a Lord? Her handmaiden? The Lord's wife, herself?

He remembered wanting to couple with a Queen at one point, but none lived near here. Everett's father and mother were as close as it came to being a King and Queen in this area. His only chance would be to visit surrounding regions, become accustomed to their households while on a trip, and bide his time until he could sneak into intimacy with someone as powerful as he would become.

That never happened, but Beatrix arrived sometime during all of this. He'd thought nothing of it at first, because... well, she was a witch. Except he watched her, spied on her, discovered more about her. She was a witch, yes, much more powerful than a Queen, but less than that, too. He had read and heard that witches were indifferent and crass, yet Beatrix was never like that. She apologized if she made mistakes, instead of blaming everything on someone else. She seemed genuinely interested in helping others, too.

Yes, people feared her, and Everett had to a point, but not for too long. Dante spoke with her, even. Beatrix liked his younger brother and they laughed together on occasion. There wasn't anything more there, though. Nothing that Everett could see, at least.

He'd grown obsessed soon after that. More obsessed, he supposed. Every woman he coupled with seemed beneath him all of a sudden. Or he imagined them being Beatrix, squealing and moaning as he pounded hard into them. He went harder, harder still. Beatrix was a witch and would never be so easily broken by roughness, or so he assumed. He found himself with more than a few tearful, frightened women laying under his spent body after that.

That intrigued and bothered him all at once. They climaxed, he knew. He felt their tremoring grip upon the shaft of his cock and the tensing of their bodies. Their eyes, their face. When a woman was in the clutches of orgasm, she always looked slightly in pain, or so he thought. Except now they truly were. Not only was he forcing an orgasm upon their weak and frail bodies, but he was inflicting pain on them, too.

Beatrix wouldn't be like that, he told himself then. These other women were useless, unacceptable, completely ordinary and dull.

And, in fact, Beatrix hadn't been like that. Everett never really had a chance to put his full force into fucking her, though. She'd restrained him, kept his sexuality in check with her odd perfection. It unnerved him and excited him. He'd thought to treat her like the other women he fucked, rutting hard into her plump, tight snatch and forcing her to acknowledge his cock as he dominated her completely.

He couldn't, though. He couldn't because her body controlled his. He'd first spent himself inside of her within mere seconds of entering her, and then after that it took all his will and control to hold himself back from repeating this humiliation. She controlled everything about their sexual encounter; the first and the second time. It was alarming and eye-opening.

The rest was mostly history. He grew scared of her, feared her power over him. He'd wanted to seduce a Queen, or more than a Queen, and he couldn't even control himself in the presence of a witch. Was this love, though? Was this more? Was this what he needed all along?

No, not entirely. Similar to how he toyed with other women, he sensed Beatrix was toying with him. Not in the same way, though. He came to realize the difference over his many years of beast-cursed existence. She enjoyed the game, reveled in it, and did it for the sake of doing it, which was entirely different than his initial logic. He did it to be better than someone, to prove a point to himself, to add a notch to his belt and brag about it to other men.

Now was different, though. He understood better. He had grown greedy and fallen into a similar groove upon first seeing Danya, but that had passed. It angered him so much to see her fucking other men, to know about it, but why? Well, of course he knew why; he wanted to fuck her himself. He wanted to make her his, to own and control her, to bind her to his will, and...

The only thing he knew how to do after he finished with her was to toss her aside. He never really wanted to do that, but he'd never done anything else. Perhaps unintentionally, or because of some innate fear dwelling inside him, he'd done it; left Danya after fucking her. Later, Alena served a purpose, but...

He grew fond of Danya's younger sister, too. They'd only mated once while he was the Beast, but he felt badly about it. She reminded him of Dante in a way. His younger brother was more carefree, despite being what essentially amounted to his indentured servant. Everett would never use his brother like that, and tried to set some equality between them, but Dante knew it was a lie. Their father and mother raised them both to be specific things, and no matter what Everett wanted, he couldn't change that.

He thought maybe he could, though. Later in life, once he took a wife and became the true Master of the Manse, he'd give Dante freedom to do as he liked. He never ordered Dante around anyways, but sometimes he needed to tell him to do things. A facade, he thought to himself, just a show, but maybe it wasn't really. No matter his intentions, Dante was always inherently less than Everett, through simply being born a few years later.

Alena was like that. He could tell. She craved affection in a similar way to Dante. His younger brother hid it well, as he must, but Everett knew. Alena liked Dante now, too. They should be good for one another.

He hoped, at least. The curse wasn't fully broken yet. It might all come crashing down at any moment. If Danya decided to leave, if Beatrix abandoned him once more because of his folly, then within a matter of weeks he would return to his beastly form and everyone that he'd freed from their soul-imprisonment would go back into their respective inanimate objects.

He'd almost broken the curse once, or so he thought. It involved trickery, yes, but it should've worked. He knew now that it would never have worked, but what did that matter? He'd lured a woman to his mansion during a storm and donned a heavy cloak to hide his features. While she slept away her fatigue, he teased her legs apart and played with her feminine folds beneath her skirt. She kept sleeping, and he moved slowly so as not to wake her. Using her dreams as fodder for his needs, he somehow managed to push his erection into her wet pussy while she slept.

Slow motions then, not enough to wake her. Gentle rocking back and forth. It worked! Oh, yes, it worked. Could this go on forever, he wondered? Hiding his face from her, refusing to let her know that he was cursed to look like some horrific beast? Rain pattered outside, tapping hard against the window panes, and he pushed in a little more, deeper, and lost himself within the slumbering maiden.

He came hard inside of her, his seed filling her. She shifted in her sleep then, yawning, smiling. Her eyes opened slightly and he tried to move away, to hide his horrible and forbidden depravity, but it didn't work as planned. As he moved back, the hood on his cloak fell away, revealing his yellow eyes, fur-covered face, and sharpened teeth. The girl woke slowly, or she had, but when she saw him like that and realized what he'd done, she screamed.

She screamed and ran away, fleeing the mansion. She tried to break through the gates, but they were magic and contained her. Everett stared after her, watching in the rain, feeding on her fear and arousal. He could chase her, tie her down, keep her trapped in his mansion forever until he broke through her resistance and she became mindless and willing towards his rapacious intent.

Dante revived then and saw Everett standing there. He knew. The look in his brother's eyes as he stared with disdain at Everett was something he never wanted to experience again. Dante rushed into the heavy rain, wearing nothing more than light clothes which became immediately soaked, and he opened the gates for the girl. She escaped into the darkness of the woods.

Dante stayed for a few weeks after that, revived and wandering the mansion. Everett tried to talk with him, but he couldn't do it very well. He tried to explain, to apologize, to... to what?

Was it Everett's fault? If he wanted to free everyone, was that really his fault? What else was he supposed to do? No woman would come to him, no woman would couple with him normally under her own free will while he remained like this. Dante vanished again, bound inside of the suit of armor that he'd previously inhabited. Everett was alone once more.

Danya came, though. She accepted him. She stayed. She was here now, speaking with Beatrix. Beatrix told him somewhat of her personal desires for staying, but Everett didn't know if any of that would happen. He didn't care about Beatrix's offer, couldn't even think about it right now. He just wanted... needed...

"Everett," Danya said, coming up beside him.

In his beast-cursed form he would have smelled her approaching, would have heard the soft falls of her feet along the mansion path. As he was, he noticed none of this until she was already upon him.

He turned to offer her a sad smile. "Danya," he said, nodding a greeting. "I'll open the gates for you."

Using his inherent magic given to him by Beatrix, he focused on the metal gates. They shuddered and shook, then swung open, offering her a way to escape him. Why else would she be here, he wondered? What other reason did she have?

And she left. Walking through the gates onto the open path winding around the lake and into the forest, Danya left. Everett watched her go, unsure what more he could do. Should he say goodbye, or should he remain silent? Should he close the gates and return to the mansion and beg for Matilda and Beatrix's forgiveness? Could they stop his curse with their magic and free him from this torment?

Danya didn't go far, though. She stepped right outside of the gated area, then turned to look at him, offering him a quizzical glance. He watched her, unsure.

"Will you come swimming with me?" she

asked.

"I..." All sense of words or how to use them vanished from his mind.

"Not in what you're wearing," she added, grinning. "It's interesting to see you wearing clothes."

She wore clothes, too. A pale blue dress given to her by his seamstress. Taya had mostly only crafted clothes of high quality, and then typically only for those who could afford her expensive services, which was essentially no one except his family. Only his mother had ever worn her exquisite dresses. Occasionally she gave in and created lesser quality gowns for servants or what-not, but the seamstress hated it and barely put any effort into doing so.

It somewhat surprised him that she spent so much time and patience on Danya's dress.

"I don't have swimwear," Everett said, stumbling. Before, once upon a time, he would never have said anything even close to resembling that statement.

Danya winked, then blew him a kiss. "Neither do I."

"Danya, I..."

"I think I'd like to stay," she said suddenly. Her expression changed from playful to more austere, as well. "If I do, we'll need to get to know each other again. We haven't really done a good job of that, have we?"

Everett nodded. "No. I'm sorry. That's my

fault."

"We can still have sex," she said. "I know the curse will come back if we don't, but to be honest I kind of enjoy it, too."

He gaped at her, jaw dropping. This was altogether not what he expected.

"I shouldn't tell you this, but I really liked when you buried your nose between my thighs and smelled my arousal," Danya said. "I guess there's not much of a reason for you to do it now, though. You can't smell as well, and..."

Oh, he would do it, he thought. He'd delight in her scent and her wetness and press his nose hard against her clit while plunging his tongue into her depths and savoring her lower lips with his mouth. He'd... no, no, he couldn't. He couldn't give in to those urges. He...

Danya lifted the skirt of her dress up and pulled the entire thing over her head. Tossing the garment to the ground, she stood before him, naked and smiling somewhat shyly. Not entirely demure, though, oh no.

Everett stared at her beauty. Danya wasn't perfect, but he loved her body. She was real and perfect in that way. Not fake, not throwing on a million types of cosmetics like many other women he used to know, nor using magic to enhance her appeal. He didn't mind those things, and in fact enjoyed them sometimes, but... Danya was different.

He stripped himself of his clothes as quickly

as possible and threw them into a heap near hers. She watched him struggling to remove his socks while bouncing back and forth, first on one foot and then on the other. Once he tossed the last sock away, now standing before her naked, she ran from him.

Laughing, fleeing, sprinting towards the lake, Danya ran. Everett chased her, grinning. Before she could escape into the water, he grabbed her by the waist and picked her up into the air, spinning her around. She giggled and flailed before catching hold of him. Her arms held onto the back of his neck and he pulled her close to him, embracing her.

"I don't know if this will work," she said.

"I don't know, either," he said.

"We might be terrible for each other."

He nodded.

"None of this started well."

He agreed.

"If you'll try, then I'd like to try, too," she said. "And maybe... I don't know for sure, but maybe we can take Beatrix up on her offer," she added. "Not right away. Not yet."

"I'll try," he said.

"Is this like the legends?" she asked, worry creasing her brow. "Like the stories?"

"Hm?" he asked.

"Do... do you think we'll live happily ever after?"

"We can try," he said.

She smiled and nodded. "I'd like that, if we could. If that's how it works. I'd really like that, Everett."

They kissed, soft and sweet, holding onto each other while standing at the edge of the gentle waters of the lake. They would try. They would live happily ever after.

A NOTE FROM CERYS

And they all lived happily ever after! Perhaps. It's not definitive, but I think everyone has a good chance at it, don't you?

I first started writing this on a suggestion from someone. They wanted to read a story about obsession and stalking and lust. I took those ideas and went with them, eventually letting the idea of an erotic fairy tale re-imagining of Beauty and the Beast form in my mind.

I've always been fascinated with fairy tales. I think they're some of the most interesting stories for a lot of reasons. Everyone's more familiar with the more recent sorts, where everything ends up wonderfully and everyone lives happily ever after, but fairy tales weren't always like that, you know?

The original Grimm's versions, and others, were darker and contained more grit than otherwise. To be honest, some of them were downright scary, too. I don't know if anyone actually told these stories to their children, but if they did then I imagine it was more to keep them from doing things than anything else. Don't go into the woods at night or the wolf will eat you! Right?

I kind of wanted to mix the two with this. I don't like sad or dark endings very much, but I like the idea of darker fairy tales. I like the idea of some romance and fantasy mixed in, too. The setting is otherwise relatively ordinary, except... then there's a witch. And a man cursed to look like a beast. A magical rose appears, and we learn that Everett's servants are trapped within various items in his mansion. More and more, onwards, Pinem'e the fallen angel, plus Alena becoming a succubus, another witch, and finally Horatio is revealed as the Timekeeper.

You might have noticed, but this story has a lot of sex, too. I'm going to be honest and say this is probably the most sex-filled story I've ever written. A lot of that stems from there being multiple characters, mostly in the form of Danya and Alena. I can't really just abandon one of them, you know? While the story is mostly about Danya and her situation, Alena plays an important role in that. It's kind of about both of them in a lot of ways, and their similarities and differences. They both feel trapped and stuck in life, but neither of them really realizes it, you know? Danya thinks that Alena's life is a lot more carefree and easy, while Alena wishes for the exact same things that her sister does.

I liked the parallel of Dante and Everett, too. They have a similar situation going on among them that Danya and Alena have, but in a different sort of way. It worked out well, I think. Dante just kind of shows up on the scene all of a sudden, seemingly, but I really enjoy the allusion of more, too. Dante *does* appear more through the story, and he's got to be the one who Horatio mentioned earlier (when he said that someone put a pitcher of water on the table, remember?), but he's scared of what's going to happen, and so he hides himself away in his room.

I think Alena is similar. Early on we see her hiding behind a silly facade, but that's how Danya sees her, right? When we get into Alena's mind, we see something more.

In a lot of ways, this made the story a little more difficult to tell. More detailed and intricate, at least. You sort of have to take everything into consideration there. Danya might perceive something as one way, but if we get into the mind of a different character at another point in time, we see something else entirely, you know? Which is correct? Or are they both correct in their own ways? Perhaps they're both wrong, too.

I enjoy the concept of unreliable narrators like that. I think it's a lot of fun and an interesting

Cerys du Lys

idea to explore.

Anyways! I hope you enjoyed this story.
It's got some romantic aspects to it, but it's a
different sort of romance, too. I know that some of
it isn't exactly what people think is typical, but I
hope you're willing to suspend some of your
traditional values and enjoy the fairy tale aspects
for what they are, too. It's hard to delve into the
darker side of myths and legends without adding
some taboo and forbidden types of situations along
the way, right?

If you enjoyed this story, please know that I
plan on writing some more erotic fairy tale re-
imaginings in the future. Currently I have a Red
Riding Hood retelling titled Bargain with the Wolf.
This is only available as an e-book at the moment,
and it's shorter, but it tells the story of a woman
named Scarlet who makes a deal with a man who
was cursed by a witch to look like a wolf. Conner
runs a magical sort of store where he can sell
anything, and in the context of the story, well...
Scarlet is looking for a way to cure her
grandmother's illness, and...

It's a fun story, and if you enjoyed this one, I
think you'll enjoy Bargain with the Wolf, too. I'll
have more in the future, also.

If you prefer to read paperbacks, I have a
few of those, but nothing quite like this at the
moment. I'd love if you checked them out, though.
The Billionaire's Ultimatum is a contemporary
erotic romance, while Princess Miri: An Erotic

Coming of Age Monster Romance is more of a fun and silly medieval fantasy (with a bratty, sexy princess and her forbidden, taboo romance with her hulking brute of a monster troll servant). The former is more serious, while the latter is more silly, but both of them are a lot of fun.

I'll have more paperbacks in the future, too, but a majority of my books are available mostly as e-books for the time being. If you'd like to check those out, I'd highly suggest The Monster Within series, as it's somewhat similar to this one, though more sweet and less dark. My Soulless series is more on the paranormal side, dystopian apocalypse kind of thing, and a bit darker, but also a sweet and nice erotic romance. If you're looking for something with a lot of sex, well... lots of my shorter works fit the bill more. Sex Kitten in particular might fit your tastes wonderfully.

And that's about it! I like writing these notes. They're a lot of fun and you get to see inside a little of what I'm thinking.

If you enjoyed this book, I'd love if you rated and reviewed it. It helps me out a lot and I really appreciate it. As an indie author, I do a majority of this by myself, and my readers (you!) and word of mouth. I read every review and I'll reply if you have any questions, so just know that it means a lot to me if you help me out like that. Thank you, too!

You're also more than welcome to email me anytime. You can reach me at:

CerysduLys@gmail.com and I check my email daily.

I also have a weekly newsletter that I send out with news about upcoming releases, some fun random things I like to talk about, story ideas, tips (some sexy or some sweet), freebies, and more, so definitely check that out, too:
CerysduLys.com/Newsletter

Thanks very much for taking a chance on my book! Bye for now!

~Cerys

ABOUT THE AUTHOR

ERYS HAS CHARTED ON NUMEROUS BEST sellers and hot new release lists internationally with multiple books.

She lives in the Greater Boston area in a small town in New Hampshire. She spends her days writing, reading, learning, and working. And maybe sometimes she flirts with the mailman. Some of her most favorite activities involve understanding and learning about emotions and relationships.

She adores pondering sexuality and sensualness. Most of her writing delves into this in some way, exploring reactions and relationships between different people. While she enjoys writing erotica and erotic romance, her goal is to also keep a certain literary appeal to the writing instead of something purely pornographic. Every story she writes has a delightful plot along with the more devious and delicious scenes we all want to read.

She prefers romance settings, with the occasional monster or fairytale. Her secret kinks include reluctance, interesting paranormal creatures, romance(even with monsters), and fun. She loves writing about all of these things, though very strongly acknowledges that fantasies are fiction and nothing more.

Made in the USA
Lexington, KY
03 October 2013